7

Borghild Dahl

HOMECOMING

BY BORGHILD DAHL

GLIMPSES OF NORWAY
I WANTED TO SEE
KAREN
HOMECOMING

E·P·DUTTON & CO.INC
1852   1953
CREATIVE·101 YEARS·PUBLISHING

HOMECOMING

by

BORGHILD DAHL

E. P. DUTTON & CO., INC.

New York, 1953

PRINTED IN THE UNITED STATES OF AMERICA
BY THE WILLIAM BYRD PRESS, INC.
RICHMOND, VIRGINIA

Library of Congress Catalog Card Number: 53-10339

TO

DR. WILLIAM L. BENEDICT

AND

DR. RAYMOND L. PFEIFFER

who have helped me to see.

HOMECOMING

CHAPTER ONE

THE COOL weather that had persisted in Minneapolis through May suddenly gave way to summer heat. A lot of people blamed the shooting down in Cuba. War affected everything so it wasn't strange it upset the seasons.

On the last Thursday of the month Miss Moran, the second-grade teacher in the Clay School, told her pupils it was warm enough for a picnic. Tomorrow she would take them all down to Minnehaha Falls to spend the day. Lyng Skoglund could scarcely wait to tell her grandmother about it, and ran all the way home from school.

On the back stoop she reached for the doorknob and pushed the kitchen door open with her knee.

"Grandmother Skoglund," she called, "Grandmother Skoglund, our room is going to have a picnic tomorrow and our teacher said—"

The kitchen was empty. Without stopping to throw off her hat, she ran into the next room.

"Grandmother Skoglund," she called out again, "where are you?"

Grandmother Skoglund appeared in the doorway of the parlor. She wore her old, gray calico scrub dress, and a faded blue-and-white checked gingham apron was tied around her small waist. Her head was wrapped in a white cloth.

"There's bread and syrup for you and the boys on the kitchen table," she told Lyng. "But change your clothes first. I'm cleaning Nils Johnson's room."

Lyng tossed her school dress in a heap on the bed, left half the buttons of her old dress unbuttoned, and gulped down the bread and syrup set out for her. Then she hurried into Nils Johnson's room, which had been the parlor before they started taking roomers. His wastebasket, heaping full, stood just inside the door. Lyng cast a quick glance in the direction of Grandmother Skoglund, but she was taking sheets and quilts off Nils Johnson's bed. Carefully Lyng picked up an ink bottle and discovered that it still contained a few drops of blue-black ink. She tried to remove the cork, but it stuck, so she put the bottle in her lap. Then she found a calender which had lost all its months except December. Lyng was pleased to be able to read the large black figures "1895," but the picture above the figures excited her even more. It showed red cows grazing on a yellow-green meadow under a bright blue sky and a richly golden sun. Lyng rolled up the calender and laid it in her lap. The stub of a pencil whose rubber could still erase was a valuable find. She was picking up a cracked shaving mug decorated with blue forget-me-nots when Haakon and Kristian came running into the room. They wore blue cotton shirts and gray pants with brown leather knee caps. Both boys got down on the floor beside Lyng.

"I want to see, too," Kristian said. "I want—"

"Go and change your clothes, boys, or you won't have anything to wear to school. Then you and Lyng can empty the basket out on the floor in the corner near the window and take turns choosing what you want."

"Doesn't Nils Johnson want the things any more?" Haakon asked.

"No," Grandmother Skoglund said, "he's gone back to Norway."

When Lyng's mother came home from work, Grandmother Skoglund hurried out on the porch to meet her.

"Nils Johnson has left," Grandmother Skoglund said. "He's gone back to marry an old sweetheart. I let him understand it was no way to do—leaving without giving notice. But he just kept packing things into that old, homemade Norwegian chest of his. I waited to put up the 'For Rent' sign until we had cleaned up after him."

"It won't be necessary to hang out the sign," Lyng's mother said. "We'll use the room as a parlor this summer. I want the children to have memories of dignified living in their home."

She took off her blue hat with gray feathers and started into the house. Grandmother Skoglund followed her.

"But the rent money," Grandmother Skoglund reminded her anxiously.

"We'll manage."

Lyng's mother folded her blue suit jacket carefully and hung it over the back of a kitchen chair. Grandmother Skoglund poked the fire in the stove and set the water kettle over the open flame.

"I was sorry to see Nils Johnson leave. He was steady and he always paid his rent on the day."

"That's true. But for all he was an honest Norwegian, I'm pleased to be making a change. Nils Johnson wasn't careful of his manners or his language. The children are old enough to notice both." Lyng's mother laid her suit skirt over her arm, picked up her jacket and disappeared into the next room. By the time she came back, wearing a purple moiré dress trimmed in lavender, Grandmother Skoglund was frying salt pork and potatoes.

"When we are ready to rent the room next fall," Lyng's mother said, "don't promise it to anyone until I have had an opportunity to find out whether he is a gentleman."

"But be sure he is the kind who pays his rent, Reidun,"

Grandmother Skoglund said. "Will you tell the children supper is ready? I'd like to get back to cleaning Nils Johnson's room."

"You mean the parlor," Lyng's mother said.

Grandmother Skoglund scrubbed woodwork and washed the windows after Lyng's mother had taken down the curtains. Haakon and Kristian raced from one end of the room to the other. At first Lyng played at housecleaning with the grown-ups, but Haakon and Kristian's romping soon proved to be more interesting and she joined them. After Grandmother Skoglund had taken up the worn red carpet to be cleaned, the children skated on the bare floor.

All at once Grandmother Skoglund's scrub pail was tipped over and soapy water flowed in all directions.

"That's enough of your racing," Lyng's mother said as she helped Grandmother Skoglund wipe up the mess.

"I didn't do it. Honestly, I didn't," Haakon said. "Kristian—"

"All three of you were playing," Grandmother Skoglund told him. "One was as much to blame as the other."

The children took turns rocking in the beautiful blue upholstered rocker, which Grandmother Skoglund had dragged out of the closet under the staircase and taken from its cloth wrappings. The rocker had a delightful squeak that grew louder the faster the children rocked in it. Kristian tried to find the place where the squeak came from and got his finger caught. He let out a loud howl of pain.

"Kristian, you always manage to get into trouble," his mother scolded.

Grandmother Skoglund smeared the finger generously with lard and bound it up in a clean white rag.

"You're getting tired," she said. "Try not to play so hard any more."

"Can we look at the pictures in the Bible with the shiny clasps?" Lyng begged.

Grandmother Skoglund looked inquiringly toward Lyng's mother.

"I suppose so," Lyng's mother said, "if you promise to be quiet."

Grandmother Skoglund spread newspapers over a dry spot on the floor and placed the huge brown-and-black leather Bible upon it. With Grandmother Skoglund's help, Lyng unfastened the shining clasps. Although she knew her Norwegian A B C's, she didn't try to read the heavy Norwegian print. Instead she paged through it to find the familiar pictures she and the boys loved so much: Joseph in his coat of many colors being sold into slavery by his brothers; Daniel in the den surrounded by golden-brown lions; Satan and his black-clad fallen angel companions in the midst of flaming red hell; and Jesus walking on a brilliantly blue sea surrounded by sea-green hills. When Lyng dwelt too long on the picture of Jesus on the sea, Haakon impatiently tried to turn the page.

Grandmother Skoglund, who was brushing the wall with a long-handled broom, came over to the children. "Let Lyng turn the pages," she said. "They tear so easily."

Kristian's head drooped. Then he rested it on Lyng's shoulder, while Lyng and Haakon went on looking at the pictures.

Lyng's mother stopped polishing the metal lamp that had stood on Nils Johnson's bed table. "It's time you children went to bed," she said. "Wake up, Kristian, and let Lyng help you undress."

Kristian rubbed his eyes and sat up straight. "Are we going to sleep in the parlor tonight?" he asked.

"No, it isn't ready yet. It will take hours for Grandmother Skoglund and me to finish."

"You can all say your prayers in here before you undress," Grandmother Skoglund said soothingly. She was standing on tiptoe, her head upturned, vainly trying to reach the ceiling with the long-handled broom.

"Let me do that," Lyng's mother said. "You shouldn't try it without standing on something."

"I want to be the first to say my prayers," Haakon said. "I know mine the best, don't I, Mother?"

"I think you should all say them together," Grandmother Skoglund said. She began to unbutton the buttons at the back of Lyng's dress.

Lyng's mother brushed the ceiling wth sure, hard strokes. "And after that not a peep out of any of you."

"They're so tired they'll be asleep the minute they're in bed," Grandmother Skoglund said.

Lyng went into the bedroom she shared with her mother and climbed into bed. She was almost asleep when she suddenly sat up. "Oh, the picnic," she thought. "I forgot to ask Mother if I can go to the picnic tomorrow."

She wondered if she ought to stay awake until her mother came to bed and tell her about it. Then she decided to wait until morning. Her mother would be tired after working hard all evening. She would be much more likely to give her permission to go to the picnic after she had fixed up Nils Johnson's room. As far back as Lyng could remember her mother had wanted a parlor.

The next Lyng knew, it was broad daylight. Her mother was already dressed and out of the room. At once Lyng thought of the parlor. She would go and see how it looked and then she'd hurry out to the kitchen and get her mother's permission to go to the picnic.

At the threshold of the parlor Lyng stopped and took a deep breath. She had never seen any room in any house as beautiful as this. She walked across the freshly-scrubbed, red-flowered carpeting to the blue upholstered rocker and sat down in it to look around.

The washstand on the opposite wall was gone along with the red-and-white pitcher, the wash bowl, the soap dish, and the slop jar that had stood on the open shelves. In place of the brown-figured oil cloth which had been tacked on the wall behind the wash stand, hung the painting of the Skoglund estate in Norway. It had been kept behind the bed in Lyng's and her mother's room and was taken out of its newspaper wrappings only to be dusted every spring and fall. Now, as it hung on the wall, the landscape seemed actually real. Lyng jumped down from the rocking chair and ran over to look at it more closely. There was the large white manor house where her mother grew up, and around it were cottages of rough-hewn logs with shaggy green grass growing on their roofs. Grandmother Skoglund and her father had lived in one of these cottages, but Lyng had never been able to find out exactly which one. Perhaps it was the cottage that had the white curtains behind the wide, small-paned windows. It stood by itself in a clump of evergreens down near the bend of the river. Beyond the river were the open fields that ended in foothills covered with more evergreens. Above loomed purple mountains and a blue sky dotted with fluffy white clouds.

Lyng went back to the rocker. A large red wagon drawn by four brown horses was passing by outside the triple bay window. It was wonderful to be able to live in the front part of the house where you could watch everything going on in the street while you sat in a rocking chair in the parlor. It was about as exciting as—a picnic.

Lyng almost tumbled headfirst out of the rocking chair. She had been wasting time in the parlor when she should have been out in the kitchen explaining to her mother about the picnic. Her mother would be ready to leave for the shop by now and she never allowed anything to interfere with her arriving there on time.

Lyng ran toward the kitchen, calling out at the top of her voice, "Mother, our room at school is having a picnic down at Minnehaha Falls today. Can I go, Mother? Please!"

Lyng heard the door open. "No." Then the door slammed and Lyng knew her mother had left for work. Her first impulse was to run after her and beg hard to be allowed to go, but her mother would be angry at her for running outside the bedroom in her nightgown. Besides, once her mother had said "No," nothing could move her.

Lyng stumbled back to the parlor. In the rocking chair she sat staring into space, seeing nothing. She dug her chubby fists into her smarting eyes, and tears rolled down her cheeks. Then she burst into a loud wail.

Grandmother Skoglund appeared in the doorway.

"Now, *Vesla-mi*." she said, going over to the rocker where Lyng was sitting, "you mustn't feel so bad."

Lyng answered with a fresh outburst.

"Your mother meant it for the best," Grandmother Skoglund said, stroking the top of Lyng's head. She tried to wipe Lyng's cheek with the corner of her apron, but Lyng pulled her head back.

"She didn't either. She never wants me to have any fun."

"You mustn't talk like that. She does her best for you and Haakon and Kristian."

"I want to go to Minnehaha Falls with the rest of the kids in my room. I've never been to a real picnic. They're going to have bought lemonade and ride on the ponies and—" Her words ended in a sob.

"You should have said something about it yesterday. Your mother was late this morning and had to hurry getting started for work."

"I forgot. Nils Johnson—"

"Yes, I know. I guess it wouldn't have made any difference." Grandmother Skoglund sighed. "For one thing, you haven't a dress good enough to wear to a picnic. Your mother has been wanting to lengthen those you've grown out of. But she's had to work evenings so much up at the shop that she hasn't been able to do it. It's a pity I'm no hand at sewing."

Lyng continued to sob.

"Besides," Grandmother Skoglund said, "it would have taken money to go. This spring things seem to be even harder than usual. The shoes of both the boys are completely worn out and they'll need new ones for Sunday right away. With this room empty so long, too—Your mother can't manage. She simply hasn't got the money."

Lyng swallowed hard and wiped her cheeks with both hands. "Then why doesn't she let me take a slip of paper to school? Miss Moran said she'd pay for anyone who didn't have the money. Hattie Fleming said right away that her folks were broke and Miss Moran said that she and her brother Bert should come anyway."

"You don't understand, *Vesla-mi*," Grandmother Skoglund said, a proud ring in her voice. "The Skoglunds have never accepted charity. Not even those of us who lived in the cottages on the estate. As for your mother—her father owned all of Skoglund. He was called the Timber King. Everyone looked up to him and admired him."

"I don't care what kind of a king he was," Lyng said, fresh tears filling her blue eyes. "I want to have some fun."

"When you're older, you'll know better," Grandmother Skoglund said. She took Lyng by the arm and pulled her gently but firmly out of the chair. "Now," she said, "I want you to get dressed and eat your breakfast. If you show me that you are a real Skoglund instead of a Yankee cry baby, I'll tell you about a surprise I've planned for you and Haakon and Kristian. But if I have to stand here all morning, I'll never get my work done."

By the time Lyng had finished her breakfast of *prim ost* and bread and skim milk, Grandmother Skoglund had stacked the dishes at one end of the table with a dishpan full of steaming soapsuds beside them. She handed Lyng a dish towel.

"There, *Vesla-mi*," she said.

Lyng scowled. She wished Grandmother Skoglund wouldn't talk Norwegian, and especially that she would stop calling her *Vesla-mi*. In Norwegian it meant *my little one*, and Grandmother Skoglund pronounced it with love. But if Hattie or Bert Fleming happened to hear it, they would repeat it to the other children. *Lyng* was bad enough. Out on the school grounds the children often teased her, calling out, "Lyng, Bing, Ring. Ding, Dong, Ding." Even Miss Moran had stumbled over her name the first day of school and had asked if any of her ancestors came from China. If only her parents had chosen Gwendolyn or Maybelle or some other American name!

Once Lyng had told her mother how she felt about this. There was both hurt and disapproval in her mother's eyes as she said, "Your father gave you your name. In Norwegian it means *heather*. It is a hardy little flower that grows up in the mountains of Norway, and it was your father's favorite."

Suddenly Lyng felt the plate she was holding pulled out of her hands.

"You've been standing there rubbing that plate for at least five minutes," Grandmother Skoglund said severely. "Now stop that daydreaming and show me how quickly you can finish these dishes. If you learn to work, you will soon be able to earn money enough to go to picnics and do many other things you want."

There was a flutter of the newspaper fringe that Grandmother Skoglund had tacked at the top of the screen door to shoo the flies out, and Kristian came in.

"Haakon says you've promised us a picnic!" he exclaimed breathlessly, hitching the strap of his overalls to the top of his left shoulder.

"Little pitchers have big ears," Grandmother Skoglund said smiling.

Kristian tilted his head back and fixed his deep brown eyes on Grandmother Skoglund's faded blue ones. "Aren't we going to Minnehaha Falls with Lyng?" he asked.

Grandmother Skoglund set the dishpan down on the edge of the stove and wiped her hands with her apron. Then she ran them through his tousled brown hair and over his ears and down his tanned cheeks.

"You're all full of sand," she said, "even your hair and ears. And that blue shirt you just put on is gray with dirt. Do try to be a little more careful of your clothes, Kristian."

"Please, can we go to Minnehaha Falls?" he begged.

"Such foolishness! Who ever mentioned Minnehaha Falls? Run out in the yard and play with Haakon and tell him not to send you in with any more silly questions. And tell him to keep away from the ash pile and the manure that have been dumped in the alley. The flies are swarming all over it."

Kristian was out of the house before she had finished. Lyng looked inquiringly at Grandmother Skoglund.

"Such foolishness," Grandmother Skoglund repeated. "When you have wiped the dishes, I want you to get the vegetables ready for the soup. The beef and ham bones that Butcher Sather saved for me yesterday are boiling. They can simmer on the back of the stove while I'm ironing. I'm baking bread, too, to make use of the oven."

She took the slop pail and carried it outside. Through the window Lyng watched her pour the dishwater over the tiny lilac bush that the entire family had been nursing all spring.

"Nils Johnson promised to spade up the back yard and

sow grass seed," she said briskly as she returned to the kitchen.
"But I guess he was too taken up mooning over that girl in
Norway to think about anything else."

"How could he moon across the ocean?" Lyng asked
curiously. "Mother says the sun is shining in Norway when
it's moonlight over here."

Grandmother Skoglund smiled broadly. "You can never
tell about moonlight," she said. "It has a way of working
wonders with people."

"I'm going to ask Mother about it."

"You mustn't." Grandmother Skoglund looked uneasy.
"Now, *Vesla-mi,* will you be so kind as to go down into the
cellar for the vegetables? Take ten potatoes and about half a
dozen carrots out of the vegetable bin. Oh, yes, and a turnip.
The onions are in a bushel basket and you can bring up a
couple of rather large ones. I'm making a good big kettle of
soup. It will keep sweet for several days if I set the kettle
down on the cellar floor."

She pulled up the trap door that was just inside the pantry
and held it open while Lyng went down into the small, round,
brick-lined cellar. It was pleasantly cool and she took her
time counting out the vegetables.

"You must know I haven't all day to stand here," Grandmother Skoglund called from up in the pantry.

Lyng set the pan of vegetables on the stairs and moved it
upward with each step she climbed.

"That's good, *Vesla-mi,*" Grandmother Skoglund said, taking the pan as soon as she could reach it. "Now I'm going to
show you how to scrape peelings off carrots and potatoes so
there won't be any waste. The turnip skin is tough and it's
easy to slice it too thick. The onion skins slip off without any
trouble. It's time you learned how to do these things."

Lyng sat at the table with one of Grandmother Skoglund's
aprons tied around her neck, while Grandmother Skoglund

stood nearby, ironing shirts. Finally all the vegetables had been peeled to Grandmother Skoglund's satisfaction.

"That's fine, *Vesla-mi*," she said, patting Lyng on the head and untying the apron around her neck. "Now you had better go out in the yard and play with the boys."

"But you said you had a surprise for us," Lyng reminded her.

"So I have. I haven't forgotten it either. But I also told you that I have to finish my work first."

It was noon when Grandmother Skoglund called Lyng and the boys. The kitchen was fragrant with the smell of clean clothes, freshly baked bread, and boiled meat and vegetables. The children sniffed hungrily.

"Is it time for the picnic now?" Haakon asked. In spite of having just come from out of the sunshine, his face was pale and the long overalls emphasized the slightness of his build.

"After you have washed your hands and faces, sit down at the table and say your prayers," Grandmother Skoglund told the children.

> In Jesus' name, we come to this board
> To eat and drink, blessed by Thy word.

"That's right," Grandmother Skoglund said. "And now you know, of course, that we are down at Minnehaha Falls. I have found this nice shady spot for you where you are to eat your picnic lunch."

"Where are the falls?" Kristian asked.

"Stupid. We don't go so close to the falls that we get all wet from the spray while we are eating," Grandmother Skoglund said as she set a fork and spoon and cup at the place of each child.

"Where are the trees that make the shade?" Haakon asked. "Bert Fleming said that there is grass too, down by Minnehaha Falls, and they'll let you walk on it and play all you want."

"Haven't you any imagination at all?" Grandmother Skoglund asked. "Of course, there are trees and grass. And many birds. Can't you see that robin sitting over in the elm tree? There's a big bed of geraniums just beyond it."

"I can't see the robin," Kristian complained.

Grandmother Skoglund puckered her pale lips and let out a shrill whistle. "At least you hear it singing over there."

Haakon jumped out of his chair. "I can see it, Grandmother. And I can see a bluejay and a crow and—and—"

He danced around the table, but when he tried to sit down again, his chair slipped and he sprawled full length on the floor. Lyng and Kristian burst out laughing.

Haakon glared at Kristian. "You made my chair slip," he said.

"I didn't."

"You did, too. I saw your hand—"

"I barely touched it."

"I'm going to fix—"

"Children, children. Don't quarrel just because your stomachs are empty."

Grandmother Skoglund went over to the stove and took the lid from the huge, black iron kettle. A cloud of steam rose up and she stepped back to avoid it.

"Are we going to have soup now?" Lyng said. "I thought you said—"

"Silly. They don't have soup at picnics," Haakon scoffed. "Bert Fleming said they were going to have sandwiches and—"

"Do they have soup at picnics?" Kristian looked earnestly at Grandmother Skoglund. "Do they, Grandmother?"

Without another word, Grandmother Skoglund went into the pantry and the children heard her slicing bread on the wooden board. Pretty soon she reappeared, holding the bread-board heaped high with bread in one hand and a stack of plates in the other. Then she picked up one of the plates and a thick slice of the brown-crusted bread, skimmed the bread deftly over the top of the soup kettle and laid it dripping down on the plate. When she had finished, she carried the plates to the table where the children were sitting.

"Now eat to your hearts' content," she said. "You can have as much as you want."

The children ate hungrily. Again and again Grandmother Skoglund went over to the soup kettle. "It's a good thing there's a deep bottom in this pot," she beamed.

"Miss Moran said they were going to have bought lemonade at the picnic," Lyng said wistfully.

"Bought lemonade! Pough! Wait until you see what we are going to have," Grandmother Skoglund said.

She brought out sugar and baking soda from the pantry and a large brown jug.

"What's in there?" Kristian asked.

Grandmother Skoglund pulled out the cork and Lyng put her nose to the spout.

"Ish," she said. "It's vinegar."

"Don't say *ish* until you know what I'm going to use it for," Grandmother Skoglund said.

She measured out sugar and vinegar into three cups and poured them three-quarters full of water. Then she put a pinch of baking soda at the tip of the bowl of a spoon, dipped the spoon into the first cup, and stirred the mixture. It fizzed and foamed to the top of the cup.

"Here, *Vesla-mi*," Grandmother Skoglund said, handing the cup to Lyng.

Lyng barely touched the cup to her lips.

"Let me taste it, Grandmother," Kristian begged.

He emptied the cup to the last drop, his nose and chin white with foam.

"I want some next," Haakon said eagerly.

He finished the cup, too, without once stopping for breath.

"What about you?" Grandmother Skoglund suggested. "Don't you want to try it now, *Vesla-mi?*"

Lyng held up the third cup. Grandmother Skoglund put soda into it and stirred it and gave it back to Lyng. The drink had a sour-sweet taste and a pleasantly sharp tang that made the inside of her mouth tingle. She emptied the cup as quickly as the boys had done.

"There you see!" Grandmother Skoglund exclaimed triumphantly.

"Can we have more?" Kristian begged.

"One cup more for each of you," Grandmother Skoglund said, measuring out vinegar and sugar.

Haakon and Kristian gulped down their second cups.

"I'm thirsty," Kristian said.

"Enough is enough," Grandmother Skoglund said emphatically. "Now it's time to thank God for the food."

"I'll bet they don't say their prayers down by Minnehaha Falls," Lyng said.

"We always thank God for the food, no matter where we eat it," Grandmother Skoglund said. "And it is correct to talk to Him in any language. He understands many of them, I'm sure, even though He may like Norwegian best."

"Bert Fleming told me he was going to ride the ponies down by Minnehaha Falls," Haakon said.

"That's exactly what we're going to do now," Grandmother Skoglund said.

"I don't see any ponies." Kristian frowned.

"If only you didn't take on Yankee ways so fast. In Norway children waited for their elders to explain things."

Kristian's lip trembled and Grandmother Skoglund put her arm around him. "Now you will see how we ride ponies at our picnic."

She stooped and unfastened her green-and-red knit wool

garters. With these she tied two chairs together, back to back.

"Now we're ready," she announced.

The children waited expectantly.

"Lyng, you are to be the pony's first rider. Sit on his back toward his tail and hold the reins. Haakon, you are to sit up close to the pony's head, and you must hold Kristian in your lap. The pony is strong, so he can easily carry all three of you."

Lyng sat down sideways on the chair and let the garters hang limply from her hands.

"That won't do," Grandmother Skoglund told her firmly. "Straddle the pony and hold the reins tight. How do you suppose we would have reached the mountaintops on horseback in Norway, if we had slouched like that?"

Grandmother Skoglund pulled her skirt up and tucked it in at the waist. Then she bent forward and took hold of the seat of Lyng's chair and started pushing. Both chairs moved forward.

"It's fun, Grandmother Skoglund," Haakon yelled.

"Go faster, Grandmother Skoglund, go faster," Kristian screamed.

"Don't be afraid to give the pony a slap or two with the reins, *Vesla-mi*," Grandmother Skoglund panted. "He can gallop if he wants to."

Lyng hit the two chairs in front of her with the garters. The chairs, with Grandmother Skoglund shoving from behind, whirled around the room.

"I want to be the driver now," Haakon called out "I want to hold the reins."

"Me, too," Kristian yelled.

Grandmother Skoglund stopped. "Change places with the boys, *Vesla-mi*," she said between gasps. "They can each hold one of the reins."

They had several more turns around the kitchen. Grandmother Skoglund's breathing became faster and sweat dripped down her face.

"*Vesla-mi*, maybe you could shove a little now," she said. "And then Haakon can take his turn at it. Kristian is too small."

"I am not. Anyway, I'm stronger than Haakon."

"You'll have to sit up front by yourself," Haakon said, pushing Kristian from his lap.

"Be careful no one gets hurt, children. Don't go too fast, and don't bump into anything. I'm going into the parlor to darn stockings. The light is good in there."

Lyng started shoving. Haakon spread his legs straddling the chair as he held both reins.

"Grandmother is sitting in the rocker," Kristian said. "I can hear it squeak."

Haakon was taking his turn at shoving when the kitchen door was pushed open. Hattie and Bert Fleming, back from the picnic, dashed into the house. Hattie's best green dress was wrinkled and soiled, and Bert's blue sailor suit looked as though it had had a ducking. So did his fiery-red, straight hair that hung in long strands over his big ears.

"We went on the streetcar and drank bought lemonade," he began. "Gee—"

He stopped.

"What are you playing?" Hattie asked curiously.

"Nothing," Lyng answered. There was a note of triumph in her voice. "We're driving our own ponies."

Without being invited Bert rushed up to Haakon and started to help him shove the chairs. Hattie sat down beside Lyng. All five children were shouting at the top of their voices when Grandmother Skoglund came into the kitchen.

"It's almost time for your mother to come home," she said. "I must straighten up in here before she does. If you want to play any more, you had better go out into the back yard."

Haakon moved the chairs toward the door.

"Oh, no," Grandmother Skoglund said sharply. "You'll have to think of something else for ponies and reins out there." She bent down to untie the garters on the chairs.

The children scrambled out the back door.

"Aw shucks," Haakon complained.

Lyng looked about the tiny square of bare ground that was their back yard. Only a few weeds were pushing above the hard-crushed earth! The precious lilac bush and the manure and ash piles in the alley did not seem to offer any suggestions.

"I know," Lyng said. "The wash bench."

"But how about reins?" Haakon demanded.

"Here's the strip of red cloth Grandmother Skoglund uses to tie up the clothespin bag," Lyng said. She unfastened it from the leg of the wash bench.

"It's your bench and stuff, so Bert and I will be the first shovers," Hattie offered generously.

Bert scowled, but he took his post beside Hattie.

"Wait until I get the reins tied around the pony's stomach," Lyng said. "Haakon and Kristian, you have to sit up front. I'm back near his tail."

Hattie and Bert were having their third turn at shoving when Grandmother Skoglund came out of the house, carrying a plate.

"Come, children," she called. "How would you like to have another picnic out here? With bread and real butter and sugar on it for your lunch?"

At once all five of the children left the wash bench and ran over to Grandmother Skoglund, who chuckled aloud.

"I guess the Skoglund imagination hasn't died out entirely," she said. Then she added under her breath but loud enough for Lyng to hear, "All the same, I wish that I could some time give them a ride on a real pony."

CHAPTER TWO

IT WAS LATE in the afternoon of what Grandmother Skoglund called the Third Day of Christmas, and Tante Gunara and Tante Tallette had come from St. Paul for their annual Christmas visit.

Grandmother Skoglund was serving coffee and small cakes from Bernt Moe's night table, which had been moved into the center of the parlor. Bernt Moe had been their roomer going on three years now—ever since the fall after Nils Johnson had gone back to Norway to marry his sweetheart. And, since Bernt Moe was spending the Christmas holidays with his sister in Fargo, he had offered the use of his room to the family until his return the day after New Year's. Lyng's mother, who was having the day off to make up for the long hours of night work during the pre-Christmas rush, was seated in the blue upholstered rocker. Lyng and Haakon and Kristian were being served coffee with the grown-ups.

Tante Gunara and Tante Tallette were dressed almost alike —long, full, black wool skirts and black satin blouses with stand-up collars whose white ruching came up well under their chins and ears. They both had gold watch chains that looped over their wide stiff belts, and inside the belts were large gold watches. But in the front of Tante Tallette's collar was a brooch with two mother-of-pearl hands clasped inside a gold heart. Instead of high black calfskin boots like Tante Gunara's she had patent leather shoes with high heels and pointed toes. Tante Tallette's head was one mass of gold-tinted curls, and her china-blue eyes were gentle and smiling. Tante Gunara combed her straight, graying hair severely back from her thin face, and her silver-rimmed glasses made her keen brown eyes seem even more penetrating.

The Christmas visits with Lyng's aunts from St. Paul were always an occasion in Lyng's life, and today everything had seemed especially enjoyable. For one thing, her mother had been in unusually good spirits all day. She had let Lyng and the boys take turns playing the mouth organ Tante Tallette had brought them without once complaining about the noise. And during dinner, when Kristian spilled gravy on the best white linen table cloth, she hadn't scolded him at all.

As Lyng sat sipping her afternoon coffee in the parlor, she wondered if she could get up courage enough to ask her mother the question she had been wanting to all day. Ever since the disappointment of having to stay home from the picnic at Minnehaha Falls, Lyng had never asked her mother for permission to go anywhere outside their circle of Norwegian friends. But Hattie was taking part in a Sunday School program at the Franklin Avenue Church this evening and had invited her especially to come.

"Reidun, don't you think the floor in here is cold?" Tante Gunara asked. She pulled up her feet and drew her black knitted shawl closer around her shoulders. "I feel a draft from the door leading into the hall."

"I don't feel any drafts," Lyng's mother said tartly.

"I wish you had served the coffee in the kitchen where it's warm," Tante Gunara went on. "While we were eating dinner in the dining room, I didn't notice the cold too much. But this parlor—ugh!"

"I am bringing up my children to become ladies and gentlemen," Lyng's mother said. "They will be able to look back with pride to their Christmases at home. People whose early vision has been limited to kitchens retain the outlook of servants and underlings all their lives."

Tante Tallette helped herself to several of the small cakes Grandmother Skoglund offered her. "How do you ever get your *fattigmand* so smooth and crisp, Mother?" she asked, turning the thin, diamond-shaped cake with its finely scalloped edges and regarding it admiringly. "Mine are always thick and lumpy, no matter how much pains I take with them. I've tried rolling the dough out thin, but then it either tears while I'm taking it off the board, or the *fattigmand* breaks when it's coming out of the hot lard."

"It's merely a matter of practice," Lyng's mother said shortly.

Oh, dear, Lyng thought. Now Mother's cross again. I should have asked her while we were eating dinner, but the meat balls and the mashed potatoes and creamed carrots and burnt sugar pudding were so good, I couldn't risk spoiling our enjoyment of all that. Now I'll simply have to ask her before things get worse.

Aloud she said," Mother, Hattie Fleming is going to be in a Christmas program tonight in her church. They're going to give away presents to the children afterwards. Hattie got a cute little doll buggy last year and Bert got a game of dominoes. The grown-ups in the church pay for everything, so they're not even going to take up a collection. It's all free. And I'm already dressed up in my Christmas dress and new hair-ribbons. Can I go? Please, Mother."

"Where is it you want to go?" Tante Tallette asked.

"To the Franklin Avenue Church," Lyng said, trying to keep the eagerness out of her voice. "Hattie Fleming's Sunday School is having their Christmas program."

"You have already been at your own Christmas program,"

her mother said. "You got a lovely present there, too, a New Testament. I don't want you wandering from one church to another like a gypsy."

"I've never been inside any other church but our own," Lyng protested.

"Oh, let the child go," Grandmother Skoglund said gently.

Lyng's mother took a sip from her coffee cup. "That church is American. I know what happens when children start going around to these Yankee services. It was good-bye to the Norwegian after Gerd Jacobsen had been with that Baptist crowd on Twenty-third Avenue. And it was the same with Valborg Aanerud as soon as she got a taste of those Congregationalists. Both girls became Yankeefied right away. Now the parents of both girls have had to let them prepare for confirmation from books in the English language. Imagine repeating the Ten Commandments and the Lord's Prayer in a foreign tongue! It's the first time that any parents in our church have been guilty of allowing such a thing to come to pass. And once Valborg and Gerd are confirmed, you may be sure it will be the last their own church people will ever see of them."

"There can be no harm in allowing Lyng to go there once." Grandmother Skoglund looked pleadingly toward Tante Gunara and Tante Tallette.

"How do I know Lyng will be welcome there?" Lyng's mother went on. "I certainly wouldn't blame a church for not wanting to take in strangers. And I'm not sending my children where they're not wanted. Worse yet, begging for presents."

"I wouldn't be begging," Lyng managed to say. "Hattie invited me and she goes to that Sunday School. She's to be one of the angels tonight. She said for all of us to come and—"

"Who pays attention to what children say?" Lyng's mother interrupted.

"The people in the American churches are awfully friendly," Tante Tallette said. "There's a little Methodist Church near our place in St. Paul. I sometimes go there, if it's cold or I'm late. The minister always shakes hands with me and invites me to come again. And some ladies have asked me to join one of their societies. I'd kind of like to."

Grandmother Skoglund looked frightened. Lyng's mother frowned. "I've told Lyng she can't go and that settles it." Her voice sounded cold and hard. "She has company at home, and I'm bringing up my children to have good manners, even though people in America seem to pay little or no attention to such matters."

"My goodness, don't make her stay at home on our account," Tante Tallette said. "We'll have to be leaving soon anyway."

"That's right," Tante Gunara agreed. "I'm getting anxious about the fire in the furnace. Knute Bjork promised to look after it for me. But you know how it is, leaving things to others."

There was a painful silence. Then Grandmother Skoglund picked up the tray of cakes and walked over to Lyng. "You aren't eating any cakes, *Vesla-mi*."

"She's mad because she can't go to the Sunday School program," Haakon said. He leaned over to reach the tray of cakes and helped himself to a handful. "I don't wander around to strange churches, do I, Mother?"

"No, thank God, I have one child I never have to worry about."

Grandmother Skoglund kept standing in front of Lyng. "Try a sand tart," she whispered. "A heart-shaped one. You know you like them so much."

Lyng shook her head. There was another painful silence. With a sinking heart, Lyng watched the fading daylight disappear behind the thickly frosted bay window. Grandmother Skoglund blew out the last candle on the Christmas tree. The room was left in total darkness.

"If they are giving away toys anyway," Tante Tallette said, breaking the silence, "Lyng might as well get one as anyone else."

"No," Lyng's mother snapped.

Tante Gunara cleared her throat. "You wouldn't stand in the way of your children's happiness, would you, Reidun?" she asked.

There was no sound from Lyng's mother.

"Haven't you had enough of your father's stubbornness to see where it leads to?" Tante Gunara went on. "You and Markus might have been sitting pretty on the Skoglund estate, if he had been willing to listen to reason. Instead, it went to that aristocratic brother of yours who had never learned the value of a day's work, and now the place is in the hands of strangers."

Grandmother Skoglund lighted the lamp on Bernt Moe's night table. The greenness from the shade made her face look unreal. "Gunara," she pleaded.

Tante Gunara's eyes were fixed on Lyng's mother. "I don't like to have to say this, Reidun, but it's for your own good as well as the children's. You had better face facts now before it's too late. You are not going to be able to keep Lyng bottled up inside the fence of that Norwegian pride of yours much longer. Nor the boys either. If you try, they'll climb over it, and then God help you."

"Gunara," Grandmother Skoglund repeated. "Not in front of the children."

"It can't be helped. With Markus gone, there isn't anyone else to tell her. I realize what a struggle it has been for her, and you, too, Mother, to supply the family with the barest necessities. But that is all the more reason for letting the children enjoy whatever pleasures and luxuries they can get free."

Lyng's mother stood up. "They have no sense of reverence for God over there, I tell you. Putting on a show in church. Having a sinful child like Hattie take the part of a heavenly angel. It is desecrating all that is holy."

"Hattie isn't a sinful child." Lyng was on the verge of tears.

Tante Tallette stood up, too. Her eyes met Lyng's mother's squarely, but there was no anger in them. "In the old days they acted out the life of Christ in the churches," she said calmly. "And other stories from the Bible. I've been reading all about it in a book one of our roomers let me borrow."

Lyng's mother's eyes blazed. "If you will wash the dishes now, Mother Skoglund, I'll wipe them for you." With that she swept from the room.

"Mother, you sit still. Tallette and I will clear up everything in the kitchen," Tante Gunara said, starting to follow Lyng's mother. "And then we really must be going."

But Grandmother Skoglund hurried after her and the boys tagged along. Lyng was left alone in the parlor. She walked over to the upholstered rocker and climbed into it. Her eyes rested on the picture of the Skoglund estate. The green light from the lamp shade had cast a spell of enchantment over the place. Lyng could imagine her grandfather, the Timber King, a crown on his head and a scepter in his hand, standing at the entrance of the great manor house.

I'm glad Mother married Father, even though she did have to be disobedient, Lyng thought.

She could hear the rattle of dishes out in the kitchen and the murmur of distant voices.

"If Mother thought it was all right to disobey her father, it can't be wrong for me to go to the Franklin Avenue Church tonight without Mother's permission. Mother just doesn't realize how much I want to see a Christmas program in an American church, especially with Hattie acting as a heavenly angel."

She listened. Everyone was in the kitchen.

Tante Gunara and Tante Tallette thought it was all right for her to go to the church tonight. And Grandmother Skoglund did, too, even though she didn't say so.

Lyng slipped down from the rocker and tiptoed across the room to the door leading into the front hall. As she opened the door, it squeaked. She stood breathless. No one had heard. She took a step into the hall and pulled the door behind her so slowly that only a soft click told her that the lock had caught. The hall was pitch dark, but Lyng had no trouble finding her coat and cap that she kept on a peg in the front closet during the holidays. The outside door stuck when she opened it and without stopping to close it, she dashed out on the porch. The chunks of hard snow that Haakon and Kristian had been unable to pry loose when they shoveled creaked under her feet as she tore down the steps and onto the main sidewalk.

As she ran through the snow, Lyng was seized with a feeling of guilt for not having tried to take Haakon and Kristian along. They would have been thrilled to have received a toy for their very own. But Lyng knew that it would have been impossible to smuggle them out of the house without their mother's knowledge. Oh well, if she received a toy they liked, she'd let them take turns at playing with it.

Lyng caught sight of the lighted windows of the Franklin Avenue Church when she was still a block away. It stood out against the deep blue evening sky and the paler blue snow covering the ground. The door was wide open and people were streaming in.

Inside the vestibule men, women, and children stood around talking.

You wouldn't believe they were in a church, Lyng thought.

Suddenly she felt lost. She didn't belong among these people. No one was glad to see her.

"Lyng!"

Hattie had her arms around her.

"Oh, Lyng, how wonderful that you could come! But didn't your family?" Hattie's green eyes were sparkling with excitement, and her cheeks were flushed. Her red hair hung in soft curls down her back. Over her arm she carried something long and white.

"I—I—we had company," Lyng stammered. "My aunts from St. Paul."

"I wish I'd known and I'd have invited them, too. But you could have brought them along without an invitation. I'm glad, though, that you're here." She gave Lyng another squeeze. "Mr. Morrow told us on no account to leave the Sunday School room downstairs. But I wanted to be sure that Fred Sterling kept his promise to give you a seat up front, so I sneaked out. There he is now. I'll send him over to you. I have to hurry back. Mr. Morrow said we had to be dressed and ready to go on the stage at least fifteen minutes before the program was to start."

Lyng's entire body tingled. "Be ready to go on the stage." It sounded like a real theater. A smiling young man came toward her. He must be at least sixteen or seventeen years old.

He bowed. "You are Lyng, I believe. Lyng Skoglund, Hattie Fleming's friend. I am Fred Sterling. May I have the pleasure of escorting you to a seat?" He took Lyng's arm and together they started down the aisle.

They treat you like a grown-up person here, Lyng thought. Soren Bruhjeld, our church janitor, shoos us around like chickens and scolds us if we talk. He ought to come here and take lessons in good manners.

The Franklin Avenue Church was smaller than hers and there was neither an altar nor a raised pulpit up front. The pews were painted gray without cushions, but on the back of each was a long rack full of books. After Lyng had been seated, she picked up one of the books and opened it. Across its two pages were bars of music under which were printed words. Lyng read, "Holy, holy, holy, Lord, God Almighty." In her church only the words of the hymns were given and these in very fine print and in Norwegian.

This church was well heated and brightly lighted. People soon filled the pews, and after they sat down, they greeted one another cordially. Almost everyone was smiling.

A woman with three small boys sat down in Lyng's pew.

"I believe you must be a visitor here," the woman said. "I'm glad you came. You will enjoy the program our young people have prepared for us, I'm sure."

Mother would be shocked at people who talked in church, Lyng thought.

Suddenly it became quiet and everyone looked toward the front of the church. A man in a gray suit come out of the door at the right of the platform and sat down on a small, straight-back chair. He smiled, and to Lyng it seemed he had singled her out and was giving her a silent but reassuring welcome.

"Let us sing hymn one hundred and five," he said.

Where could the minister be? Perhaps he didn't attend the Sunday School Christmas program. Did he, like Lyng's mother, disapprove of putting on a show in church? If he did, why would he allow it at all?

The singing was brisk, almost gay. Lyng caught herself tapping her foot in time with it. As soon as she realized what she was doing, she stopped. That was almost as bad as dancing. Much embarrassed, she glanced furtively at the woman standing beside her. To Lyng's great relief, the woman's head was turned the other way.

At the close of the singing, the man in gray walked over to the lectern. He read a passage from the Bible and folded his hands. "Let us pray," he said. The congregation rose from their seats once more. "Our Father Which art in heaven," he began. Lyng, alone, it seemed, was unable to repeat the words after him. She had never before heard people pray in English. Nor had she seen anyone but the minister stand up front to lead the congregation in prayer. Perhaps after all he was the minister, even though he didn't wear a black robe and a white ruff. At the close of the prayer he stepped down from the platform and sat in a pew across the aisle from Lyng.

From behind a door came soft music. At first it was barely an audible hum. Then it grew louder. "Silent night, holy night." Lyng recognized the tune which was identical with one of the Norwegian Christmas carols she had known as far back as she could remember. Two little girls, dressed alike in soft green, appeared through the side door and pulled back a curtain that had closed off a part of the platform. A woman was sitting on the floor, a huge doll in her arms. She laid the doll in the cradle close beside her and bent over it. Immediately she was surrounded by white-robed, young girls who sang, "Glory to God in the highest, peace on earth and good will toward men."

Hattie was one of the white-robed girls. She waved to Lyng. Lyng stood up and raised both arms as high as she could. Then she felt herself being drawn down into the pew.

"I'm sure you'll be able to see everything without standing up," the woman whispered.

Lyng was too much excited to mind. She gazed with all her eyes at what was taking place upon the platform. Bearded men wearing all the colors of the rainbow approached the cradle. They sank to their knees and placed packages around the cradle. "We have brought gifts to the Christ Child," one of them said.

The voices of the girls rose in a triumphant finale. "Hallelujah! Hallelujah! Hallelujah!"

Lyng sat without moving. She was roused by a gentle tap on her shoulder.

"Did you enjoy the program?" the woman beside her asked.

"It—it was wonderful," Lyng breathed.

Suddenly everyone was talking. "Santa Claus." His name was being repeated all around Lyng. She became frightened. Her mother had been careful to explain to her and Haakon and Kristian that it was sinful to identify Santa Claus with Christmas, which celebrated the birth of the Savior. She had firmly refused to allow the children to go to see him whenever he appeared at the department stores downtown, or to go with Hattie and Bert when he distributed presents to the poor on Christmas morning. Surely the people of the Franklin Avenue Church didn't believe in Santa Claus or intend to include him in this beautiful Christmas celebration.

Then Lyng almost lost her breath. There he was, dressed exactly as she had seen him in pictures. He was coming down the aisle toward her. Her first impulse was to flee. But before she could make up her mind, Santa Claus was standing at her pew.

"Here are some children who look as though they have been very good," he said in an extremely deep, yet gentle voice. "Let me see. How about you three boys over there?"

"They have been very good," the woman next to Lyng said pleasantly. The boys giggled.

"Then here is a little something for them." Santa Claus handed each boy a package. "And since all three of you have been so very good, my helpers will be around soon with some goodies." Then he turned to Lyng. "And this little girl—I'm sure she deserves a present."

For the life of her, Lyng couldn't make herself refuse the flat package he held out. Instead she grasped it with both hands and stammered, "Thank you, thank you, Santa Claus."

"Oh, you're welcome. You have fine manners, child. Not all boys and girls remember to thank Santa Claus for what he brings them." The boys in Lyng's pew regarded Santa Claus sheepishly. Santa Claus chuckled and went on down the aisle.

One of the boys opened his package. He had gotten a top. In no time he was spinning it on the seat. Lyng watched it admiringly. Haakon and Kristian would have loved a top like that. It was the one thing they had wanted for Christmas this year. But Grandmother Skoglund had knitted warm woolen stockings for them, and her mother had made Sunday suits out of remnants she had bought from customers at the shop. Tante Gunara and Tante Tallette, who usually remembered the children with some toy for Christmas, had spent all they could afford this year on a pair of shoes for each of them. The battered mouth organ that Tante Tallette had salvaged from a roomer's wastbasket was all they had to play with at home.

"Aren't you going to open your package to find out what Santa Claus brought you?" the woman beside Lyng asked.

"Oh, yes," Lyng said.

Carefully she untied the knots of the string around the package and wound it into a tiny ball. Grandmother Skoglund would be glad to get it for the bedspread she was knitting. Lyng removed the paper wrapping and folded it. That could be used either to wrap up the sandwich that her mother took to the shop for lunch each day or to kindle the fire in the cook stove at home.

The gift was a book with bright red covers. On the front cover, Lyng read the title in gold letters, *A Christmas Carol* by Charles Dickens. She opened the book and turned its pages curiously. First the pictures caught her eye. One showed a man sitting at a desk with an ugly scowl on his face. Near him was another man on a high stool, bending over a table as though he was writing. Another picture showed a man carrying a tiny boy on his shoulder.

The Lyng turned back to the first page and read, "Marley was dead; to begin with. There is no doubt whatever about that."

Lyng laid the book down in her lap and stroked it lovingly. She had never owned a book written in English before. Neither had anyone else in the family except Tante Tallette, who collected books left by roomers after they had moved away. These Tante Tallette kept locked behind glass doors in the combination folding bed, desk and bookcase, and Lyng had never been allowed to touch them. To be sure, she had studied out of books written in English at school. But the textbooks were usually old, without pictures, and bound in drab gray or brown covers, and they could only be used under the teacher's strict supervision. This brand-new, bright little book with shining gilt letters on its cover and interesting pictures inside was Lyng's very own to be read whenever and wherever she pleased. And it was in English.

In her own church, Lyng had, as her mother had reminded her that afternoon, received a copy of the New Testament. It was a tiny book with fine Norwegian print, and so far Lyng had done nothing with it since she had brought it home. Grandmother Skoglund had promised that, as soon as she could spare the time, she would sit down and read parts of it aloud.

Lyng loved to hear Grandmother Skoglund read. Her voice was so soothing that listening to her made Lyng feel good all over. Grandmother Skoglund accompanied her reading with explanations of the difficult parts, and when she reached a dramatic climax she used gestures. At such moments, Lyng felt as though the action in the story was really taking place.

I'll ask Grandmother Skoglund to read aloud to me from this book, Lyng thought. Then she remembered that Grandmother Skoglund could read nothing but Norwegian.

"Here are some presents for you from Santa Claus." Fred Sterling and another boy came by, carrying a basket between them, and gave Lyng a bag of candy, an apple and an orange.

"It's nice of you to give me all this when I don't even belong," Lyng said.

"Everybody gets presents at Christmas time whether he belongs or not," Fred Sterling said.

Someone tugged at Lyng's arm. "Come on," Hattie said. "My folks are four rows behind you."

Hattie's mother put her arms around Hattie and kissed her. "Darling, you were wonderful!" she exclaimed. "I declare, you looked so much like a real angel that for a minute you had me scared."

"Did you hear, Hattie? You fooled Ma for only a minute."

"Bert Fleming, you—"

A scuffle followed.

"Didn't your mother and your grandmother come?" Hattie's mother asked. "Hattie said she had invited all of you. I did so want to meet them."

Lyng blushed furiously. "We—we had company," she stammered. "And—and they had to stay home—to wash dishes."

It seemed colder to Lyng on the way home. In spite of the woolen scarf Hattie's mother had insisted on lending her, her teeth chattered.

"I wonder if Tante Gunara and Tante Tallette have gone back to St. Paul. I hope not."

The closer she came to the house, the colder it grew. By

the time she had reached the back stoop, Lyng was numb. But before trying the door, she stopped to pull off the scarf. She wound it around her presents and tucked the bundle inside her coat.

The door was not locked. She pushed it open and slipped into the kitchen. It was dark and there was not a sound anywhere in the house. Everyone must have gone to bed. If Lyng undressed in the kitchen and was very quiet, her mother might not hear her. By tomorrow—

"You ungrateful, disobedient child! What have I done that God visits such tribulations upon me?"

In the dark Lyng heard her mother strike a match and by its flickering flame, she lit the small night lamp she held in her hand.

Never in her mother's worst moods had she spoken like this. Speechless and horrified, Lyng gazed at her mother. Her face was outlined by a white, tight-fitting nightcap. Deep shadows streaked her cheeks from which all color was gone. Her eyes looked twice their natural size.

Lyng put her arms protectingly up to her face.

Her mother set the lamp down on the kitchen table. With slow, deliberate motion, she approached Lyng and took her arms in an iron grip. "I'll teach you to disobey me!"

Lyng screamed.

"Reidun!"

Lyng's mother, still keeping her grip on Lyng's arms, turned her head. "This is one time when I shall not tolerate any interference."

Grandmother Skoglund came over to them. "Reidun," she repeated. There was not the slightest trace of fear in her voice.

"Obedience is the first duty of a child toward its parents," Lyng's mother said. She was breathing hard.

"I know, Reidun. Only sometimes we elders forget that the

problems of our children are different from our own. And
we ask unreasonable things of them."

The pain in Lyng's arms made her tremble, but her mother
did not let go of them.

"I want my children to grow up in their own church and
to have respect for—"

"You must remember that they are Americans. You can't
expect them to have the same feeling for Norway and the
Norwegian language that we do. Nor for our Norwegian
church. They don't understand the meaning of many of the
words in the sermons."

"If they are made to, they will."

"You are too intelligent, Reidun, to believe that such an
attitude will bring about good results. Surely you haven't forgotten how bitterly you cried when Markus, your playmate,
was not allowed to join you in the schoolroom because he was
a peasant. Your father, man of iron though he was, finally
gave in. And until you were both confirmed in the village
church, you and Markus sat side by side in the schoolroom
of the manor house on the Skoglund estate and received instruction together."

"Sometimes I feel that the children are yours more than
mine. All except Haakon." Lyng's mother let go her grip on
Lyng's arms and backed away from Lyng and Grandmother
Skoglund.

"Don't talk like that. Give your children a little more love
and a little less—"

"I'm trying to bring them up as Christians."

"Of course, you are. And some day they will appreciate it.
Only don't break your heart because the children want their
own language in church. And now I think we should all go
to bed. There's a draft from the floor and you and I, Reidun,
can't afford to take cold."

For a long time after Lyng had crawled into bed, she lay shivering. She remained stiff and motionless, and even tried to control her breathing so her mother wouldn't hear her. When she thought her mother had finally fallen asleep, she dared to curl her legs up under her flannel nightgown. Soon she stopped shivering and she began to feel drowsy.

"Good morning, *Vesla-mi*."

Grandmother Skoglund was standing at her bedside. Through the heavily frosted window, Lyng could see the weak daylight. Grandmother Skoglund stroked Lyng's tousled hair with one hand, and in the other she held a steaming bowl.

"I brought you some oatmeal *velling*. I thought you might be hungry this morning."

Lyng took the bowl. It was queer how Grandmother Skoglund knew, without being told, what a person needed.

She sat down on Lyng's bed, and after Lyng had eaten the last of the oatmeal *velling*, she took the bowl.

"About—about last night, Lyng," Grandmother Skoglund began.

Lyng pushed herself up against the bed board. Grandmother Skoglund had never called her "Lyng" before. It made her feel grown-up.

"About last night," Grandmother Skoglund repeated. "It would have been better, Lyng, if you had obeyed your mother."

"But I wanted to go, Grandmother Skoglund."

"I know—But maybe—if from now on, you talk things over with me beforehand—we can find some better way out of it."

Lyng's lower lip drooped. "But she always says no."

"Promise me that you will try first anyway," Grandmother Skoglund persisted.

"All right. I promise."

"That's my own Lyng Skoglund. Markus would have been proud of you now."

Lyng pushed away the bedclothes. "You ought to see the presents they gave me last night, Grandmother Skoglund."

Suppose her mother had—no! That would be too terrible. She ran out into the kitchen. Her coat and cap were still on the chair where she had left them, and underneath the coat she found the bundle. Hastily she unwound the scarf Hattie's mother had let her borrow, and inside of it were the orange and the apple and the small bag of candy. And yes, there was the red book with the gilt letters on the front cover.

"See, Grandmother Skoglund," she called out. "It's a real American book. They gave me a real American book at the Franklin Avenue Church last night. And I don't even belong."

Grandmother Skoglund had returned to the kitchen. She took the book out of Lyng's trembling hands.

"It's a very pretty book," she said, examining it curiously. "And such good big letters on the inside, too. If only it had been in Norwegian, I could have—"

"Oh, but Grandmother Skoglund," Lyng interrupted her, speaking eagerly, "I'm going to read it to you. And after I can read English a little better, I'm going to teach you the words."

Grandmother Skoglund put her arm around Lyng's shoulders. Together she and Lyng looked at the first picture: Scrooge and Bob Cratchit in the counting-house. Then from the opposite page Lyng started to read slowly and laboriously:

A CHRISTMAS CAROL
Stave 1
Marley's Ghost

Marley was dead: to begin with. There is no doubt whatever about that.

CHAPTER THREE

"WE OUGHT TO PRINT the entire program in the paper," Russell Stone said.

Lyng handed him a sheet she had already neatly typed.

He smiled. "You think of everything, don't you? The Lincoln High School News wouldn't have been much good this year, if you hadn't been my assistant editor."

Lyng blushed. "Thanks."

"I'll have to be on my way to the printer. We've had the paper out on time every week so far and I don't want to spoil our perfect record."

Lyng tried to find a comfortable place for her arms as she stood beaming at him.

"I'll call for you at six tonight, Lyng. I've got the address so I won't have any trouble finding the place."

"All right." Lyng was too excited and happy to think of anything more to say.

Russell Stone glanced quickly over the dummy for the Lincoln High School News. Then, giving Lyng a mock salute and whistling the opening bars of *Oh You Beautiful Doll*, he dashed from the room.

Left alone, Lyng started to clean up the cubby-hole known as the Press Room. Loose bits of paper were scattered everywhere. On the table lay an open dictionary; over all were

strewn gum and candy wrappers and empty crackerjack
boxes, which still smelled of syrupy popcorn. Lyng picked up
a dried-out ink bottle and another one that had contained glue
and threw them into the wastebasket.

Lyng knew Grandmother Skoglund would have been horrified at seeing the least thing discarded if it could have been
put to any possible use, so she collected a few pieces of blank
paper, some pencil stubs, rusty pens, worn-down erasers and
the dictionary and put them on a shelf in the closet. Then she
took the battered broom and dustpan she found there and
swept up the litter from the floor. All the while, she kept
framing the words without saying them aloud, "I'm going
with Russell Stone tonight. I'm going with Russell Stone
tonight."

She emptied the rubbish she had swept up into the wastebasket.

Lyng's senior year in high school had been the happiest in
her life. By helping Russell Stone put out the high school
paper, she had become better acquainted with him than any
other boy her age. And through him and Hattie and her
friend, Clifford Best, she had become one of a small group
that ate their lunches together, talked and walked together
between classes and studied together during vacant periods.
But Russell Stone's invitation to be his partner at the senior
banquet at the Antler Hotel this evening was something special. It was the first time any boy had asked her to accompany
him to a social event and she was thrilled. Surrounded by her
friends as she would be at the banquet, she was assured of a
wonderful time. She could scarcely bear to wait for the mo-
mentous occasion.

As soon as Lyng had finished tidying up the Press Room,
she left for home. Since it was May, it would be warm enough
to carry the washtub into her own room for her bath. Her
white cotton undershirt was brand-new and, after much per-

suasion, her mother had allowed her to wear a Ferris corset waist. Then she bought her some mercerized, tan, clocked stockings and Lyng could have wept for joy.

Her mother had certainly entered heart and soul into the preparations for this high school banquet. She had insisted on embroidering in solid work and eyelets an acorn pattern on both Lyng's corset cover and the big flounce of her top petticoat. She had wanted to buy expensive linen lace for the other petticoat and the umbrella pants. But Grandmother Skoglund had argued with her, saying it would be much cheaper and fully as nice to trim these with homemade lace, which Grandmother Skoglund offered to knit herself.

Lyng was especially excited over the dress she was going to wear at the banquet. It was made of deep rose satin and trimmed with heavy, cream silk lace. Lyng had never dreamed of getting a real silk dress for the occasion. Her only silk possession was a handkerchief embroidered with pink and blue flowers, which Tante Tallette had given her as a birthday present, and she prized it so highly that it still lay in its white tissue paper wrappings without ever having been used.

Lyng's mother had been in fine spirits the evening she had brought the rose satin dress home. She had gotten it for a very reasonable price from the wife of a leading surgeon in Minneapolis, who was a customer at the shop. The woman said the dress had been worn only once, at her daughter's wedding, and there wasn't the slightest blemish on it. She had thrown in black satin slippers and a black velvet cape because they completed the costume, and Lyng would be wearing them tonight.

The minute she stepped into the house, she smelled freshly baked bread. The scrubbed kitchen floor was gleaming and there was a clean white napkin on the table where the family ate its meals. Grandmother Skoglund wore her best black-

and-white checked house dress and a shining white, starched apron with knitted lace across the bottom.

"Why, Grandmother Skoglund,—"

There was a twinkle in Grandmother Skoglund's eyes. "It isn't every day that the daughter of the house steps out into society," she said. She took Lyng by the hand and led her into the bedroom. There, spread out on the bed, were the clothes that Lyng would wear at the banquet tonight.

"I dipped the corset cover and umbrella pants and the petticoats in thick starch," Grandmother Skoglund said, "and ironed them real wet so they would stick out nice."

"Grandmother Skoglund, you're the best person in the world."

"Never mind what I am. You are the one that matters today. Come out into the kitchen for a few minutes. I've heard that there is usually plenty of style at these fine Yankee affairs, but that the food they serve is pretty skimpy. So I thought you should have something solid before you started out. I baked biscuits and melted *prim ost* in sweet milk to make *mos smor*. It's just right now, while it's still a little warm, to spread on the fresh biscuits."

When it was time for Lyng to put on the rose satin dress, she was so nervous that she got herself tangled up in it.

"Grandmother Skoglund," she called out, "can you come and help me?"

Grandmother Skoglund hurried into the bedroom. "I was just giving the boys a taste of the food I prepared for you. As they used to say in Norway, 'When it rains on the preacher, it drips on the sexton.' You should see how those boys can eat."

Her gnarled, rough fingers rasped against the smooth satin. "I hope I'm not snagging this beautiful silk," she said anxiously.

Finally Lyng was in the dress and Grandmother Skoglund

stood back and regarded her admiringly. "If only Markus could have seen his daughter now," she said wistfully. "He would have been pleased, too, at your going out with a real writer. Markus was so fond of books. I can remember how excited he was the time Jakob Bull, the great Osterdal author, was a guest in the manor house at Skoglund. Markus bribed the maids to let him polish Bull's shoes, so he could have an excuse to talk with the great man. Bull became so interested in the boy that when he left he gave Markus one of his own books. We still have it in the parlor."

Lyng looked into the mirror. She turned first to one side and then to the other, giving her dress little pulls and pats.

"I wish your mother could see you before you leave," Grandmother Skoglund said. "She has worked so hard getting things ready for you. Last night I don't know how late she sat up putting the finishing touches on the dress. The lady she bought it from must have laced herself in terribly, the waistline was so small, but the hips and the bust could have held two of you. Your mother certainly got the dress to fit you beautifully. My, how sweet you look!"

Haakon appeared in the doorway. "Whew!"

Lyng swung around. "Listen, Haakon," she said earnestly, "no foolishness from you. Nor from Kristian either. I'll answer the doorbell and let Russell into the front hall where he can wait while I get my cape on."

"How'll you get to the front door? Halvor Frostad is at home."

"Grandmother Skoglund," Lyng exclaimed, "I thought you told me that Halvor Frostad never came home until late on Fridays."

Grandmother Skoglund's forehead became lined with deep wrinkles. "Oh, I forgot to tell you, Lyng. I've been so excited all day about your party. Halvor Frostad came home at noon sick. But—"

"But what? I can't go through his room with him there, and—"

"I'm sure if we listen carefully, we can hear the doorbell in the bedroom," Grandmother Skoglund said. "Then Haakon can go around to the front and say that we aren't able to open the door today—it won't be an untruth, you know—and he won't have to explain the reason why. Then you can hurry around to him, Lyng, and meet the young man outside."

"Lyng, oh, Lyng, somebody wants you. He's waiting outside the kitchen door." Kristian, his thick brown hair rumpled and his shoes caked with mud, dashed into the room.

"Oh, Kristian, why didn't you tell him to wait for me on the front porch?" Lyng asked.

"That can't be your young man," Grandmother Skoglund insisted. "Why, you just got back from school only a short while ago. Kristian must be mistaken."

Lyng began frantically to comb her hair. "Who else could it be? Oh, why didn't I start getting ready right away?"

"It's him all right," Kristian said. "He asked if Lyng Skoglund lived here. You ought to see how he's dressed up!"

Lyng's hands shook so that after three attempts at braiding her hair, it still looked untidy. "Kristian, you should have told him—"

"How could I?" Kristian interrupted. "He was already on his way to the back door. He said that someone answered the bell in front and told him that we always came into the house through the kitchen. That was Halvor Frostad. I saw him in his underwear."

"Don't worry, Lyng," Grandmother Skoglund said quietly. "That's nothing so terrible about your young man's coming around to the back door, or having seen an older man in a clean suit of underwear. I'm sure it isn't the first time, and it probably won't be the last that he has had either experience. Let me braid your hair. There, that's better. But you've pulled it entirely too tight away from your face. Here's your mother's shell comb on the dresser. That fluffs it up more. I'll explain to your mother I insisted on your wearing it."

Lyng regarded her reflection in the mirror.

"It's much higher than I wear my hair—and the shell comb makes it look like—"

"It looks real nice," Grandmother Skoglund said. "The comb goes with the dress."

Somewhat comforted by this remark of Grandmother Skoglund's, Lyng snatched up the velvet cape from the bed and threw it over her shoulder. Grandmother Skoglund put her arm around Lyng and stood on tiptoe to kiss her cheek.

Kristian had not exaggerated when he said that Russell Stone was dressed up. He wore a very light gray spring suit, a light gray felt hat and a tie the color of young grass. To Lyng, he looked like a model for a fashionable men's clothing store.

"I'm sorry," Lyng began as the screen door slammed behind her, "that—you—"

She teetered as the high heel of her black satin slipper caught in a loose board of the stoop.

"I'm sorry to have kept you waiting," she started again, trying to pull herself together.

"I thought at first I had the wrong house number," Russell Stone said.

They went together, side by side, on the narrow walk that led to the street. At once Lyng realized that the black satin slippers were so loose that she was going to have trouble keeping them on. If she had noticed it earlier, she might have lined the slippers with paper.

It was easier going on the main sidewalk. After some experimenting, Lyng discovered that if she curved the soles of her feet and drew her toes together, the slippers would be less likely to fall off. She was much relieved.

"Did you find Joe in down at the printer's?" she asked.

"Yes," Russell Stone answered.

They boarded the streetcar on Riverside Avenue. The lace flounce at the bottom of Lyng's skirt caught in the gate and held up the line waiting to get on. The conductor set Lyng free, but there was a hole in the lace where it had been caught.

"It's a good thing the flounce is so full that it won't show," Lyng told Russell Stone as they made their way to a seat. He looked down at her dress but made no comment.

Their seat was near the front of the car. Lyng sat next to the window. Now I won't have to worry any more, she thought, breathing easier. The hotel is only a few steps from where we get off. Aloud she said to Russell Stone, "I've been having a lot of fun lately with the girls at school—especially Hattie. She's been dying to find out what I was going to wear tonight. But I didn't drop a hint. I wanted it to be a surprise," she chuckled.

Russell Stone took two nickels from his pocket and gave them to the conductor. Lyng sat up straighter and pushed her shoulders back. It was the first time she had gone on a streetcar with a young man and had him pay her carfare.

"I know all the girls will have pretty dresses," she babbled on. "Hattie's is white organdy with pink and green figures." She stopped. Still Russell Stone said nothing.

I wonder if he's nervous about the speech he's making tonight, Lyng thought, beginning to notice his silence.

Russell Stone kept his gaze fixed out the window.

"Do you like a rose color?" Lyng prompted him.

"I—yes—it's all right."

Still he looked past her and out the window.

Perhaps she ought to explain about Halvor Frostad, but that would only recall an embarrassing experience.

She began to look out the window, too. All at once she noticed how shabby Riverside Avenue was. Run-down store buildings, squatty houses standing up to the very edge of the sidewalk without a tree or a blade of grass to relieve their bareness, vacant lots overgrown with weeds and littered with refuse. The buildings on Cedar Avenue looked worse, and as the car turned at Seven Corners and started up Washington Avenue, she wanted to close her eyes. No wonder Tante Tallette had taken to calling Cedar and Washington *Sill gata aa Snoos Bullyvard* which in her mixed-up Norwegian and English meant Herring Street and Snuff Boulevard. Farther up Washington Avenue, the Milwaukee Railroad Yards extended for blocks on one side and sooty two-storied buildings lined the other. Lyng began to feel a growing sense of guilt inside of her, as though in some way she was responsible for this ugly part of Minneapolis.

In the shiningly elegant hotel lobby, there was loud talking and much laughter.

"I think I'll take off my cape," Lyng told Russell Stone.

For an instant he stood holding it, and then, to Lyng's great surprise, he blushed as though he had suddenly become embarrassed about something. Could it be that he thought that she was more dressed up than he was? She might tell him how very well he looked. But no, that wouldn't do. Her brothers, especially Kristian, hated to have people make remarks about their clothes.

"Are you sure you won't be needing your cape?" Russell Stone asked.

"Oh, no. Can't you feel how hot it is in here?"

"All right. Let me take it to the cloakroom," he said hurriedly.

Lyng decided to join two of her schoolmates standing nearby—Marion Marsh and Elsie Waters. For once Lyng would be able to hold her own with these two leaders of fashion at Lincoln High School. Marion Marsh wore a dress of sheer pink cotton material, made perfectly plain with short puffed sleeves and a square neck. Its only trimming was a pale blue taffeta sash tied in a crisp bow at the back. Elsie Waters' was much like Marion Marsh's except that it was yellow and her sash was made of the same material as the dress. It was queer they weren't wearing silk on this gala occasion. Perhaps their parents weren't as rich as the two girls had made them out to be.

Lyng waited for a compliment on her own appearance. Instead she thought she saw the girls exchange winks. Lyng began to feel uncomfortable. Even though her clothes were better than theirs, they still maintained the aloof manner they had always had toward her.

She would go in search of Hattie. Hattie was always kind and never envious of people. But first she would look around at the other dresses to see if any girl in the room had as fine a one as hers. They were all much like Marion's and Elsie's—simply made out of fluffy cotton material in light shades of green, lavender, blue and more pink and yellow. There wasn't a single silk dress among them.

Suddenly Lyng caught a glimpse of her own reflection in the mirror on the opposite wall. The long skirt, overloaded with heavy trimming and pushed out by starched petticoats, formed a circle on the floor around her, and it looked exactly like what it was—a hand-me-down costume of an elderly society woman for some elaborate function fifteen or twenty years back. Lyng felt her cheeks go hot and she turned her eyes away from the mirror.

It seemed to her that everyone in the crowded lobby was staring at her. But she couldn't leave. She couldn't go home and admit why she hadn't stayed at the banquet. Nor could she wander the streets, dressed as she was, until the time arrived when it would be over. She would just have to stay and live through the evening as best she could.

Russell Stone returned as the line was forming to go into the dining room. When Lyng passed through the narrow doorway, she felt the flounces of her petticoats brush against his legs. He drew away from her and after that Lyng did her best to avoid getting close to him again. Inside the crowded dining room, she succeeded in separating herself from him entirely. While the others were milling around, trying to find their places at the table, she stayed out of their way in a corner by herself.

"Lyng, you're to be over here next to us." It was Hattie. To avoid making herself even more conspicuous after all the others were seated, Lyng hurried across the room and took her place in the chair reserved for her between Clifford Best and Russell Stone.

It was a relief that now only the part above her waist showed. But she found that the low neckline in her dress was pulled even lower by the heavy lace flounce. In desperation, she took hold of her dress at the back and drew it down so hard that the lace flounce in front moved tight over her neck, almost up to her chin. Why hadn't she asked Hattie what girls wore on such occasions instead of being foolishly secretive and superior? In spite of the uncertain finances of the Flemings, Hattie always managed to do what was correct in any situation.

Lyng heard the rattle of dishes and the clicking of silver. Everyone had started to eat. She hoped they wouldn't be focusing their attention on her any more.

Hattie, on the other side of Clifford Best, leaned over toward Lyng and whispered, "You haven't forgotten that you and Russell Stone are coming with us for a soda after the banquet?"

Lyng shook her head. "I can't," she whispered back.

At long last the dinner and the speeches and the applause were over. People got up from the table. Hattie and Lyng did, too.

"Listen, Hattie," Lyng said, so low that no one else could

hear, "I have to run along. Tell Russell that something has come up so I can't go with you for the soda."

"Are you sure?" Hattie asked anxiously.

"Yes, but tell him to go with you anyway. Maybe he can get some other girl to take my place."

Without giving Hattie a chance to say anything more, Lyng pushed through the crowd and fled. She walked as fast as she could manage in the high-heeled slippers, hoping to get ahead of all the others who had been at the banquet. To her relief, none of them boarded the same streetcar.

It was still early when she reached home. Grandmother Skoglund was knitting and Lyng's mother sat reading her New Testament.

"I'm pleased to see what sensible hours American young people keep," Lyng's mother said, looking up. "At least the group you are with have had the correct upbringing. And now that you have a dress to fit such occasions, I shall not mind your going with them once in a while, not too often, of course."

Lyng made no comment.

"Was it a very nice banquet?" Grandmother Skoglund asked.

"Yes."

"Were there any dresses as nice as yours?" her mother asked. "I must say I'm rather proud of how it turned out. That rose satin is exquisite."

"All the girls had pretty dresses," Lyng said.

"What did Russell Stone say when he saw yours?" Grandmother Skoglund asked, a mischievous gleam in her eyes. "Didn't he keep close watch on you all evening?"

Lyng's mother caught sight of the hole in the lace flounce. "Take your dress off right away so I can mend it," she said. "Tomorrow Mother Skoglund will press it for you. I want you to go down to Dorge's photograph gallery and have your picture taken in it, so I can send some photographs to Norway. I'm going to show those people over there that the Skoglunds in America are still able to hold their heads high. I saved a couple of good-sized samples of the rose satin when I made the dress over and some ends of lace and I'll enclose them in the same envelope."

Lyng took off the dress and her mother regarded it critically.

"You certainly got the bottom of it very dirty for having worn it only once. I hope it won't show in the photograph."

"How would you like something to eat?" Grandmother Skoglund asked, finally noticing Lyng's silence.

"How can she want something to eat when she has just returned from a banquet?" Lyng's mother demanded.

"Maybe you could drink a glass of milk, *Vesla-mi?*" Grandmother Skoglund suggested timidly.

Lyng's mother scowled as she bent over the dress. "I've told you that you spoil these children most shamefully. Especially Lyng. What she needs is to go right to bed."

Grandmother Skoglund came closer to Lyng and regarded her with deep concern. "You look pale, Lyng. Did the banquet make you so tired?"

"Making an appearance for the first time, dressed like a queen as Lyng was tonight, is enough to make any girl look pale," her mother said.

Lyng said nothing. After all her mother and Grandmother Skoglund had done to make the banquet a success, she couldn't hurt them by letting them know what had happened. On the other hand, she was never again going to be a laughingstock because of her clothes.

"I'm going to get a job," she said suddenly. "I want to buy clothes like other girls."

"Why do you want to look like every girl your age?" her mother demanded brusquely. "When I was a girl back in Rendalen, I prided myself on being different from any girl for miles around."

"These American girls do have a certain style about them that is really very lovely," Grandmother Skoglund said mildly. "Back in Rendalen the girls somehow didn't have it—not even you, Reidun."

"The American girls have no individuality. If Lyng imitates them, she won't have any either. She will look like any and every girl her age. Thousands of garments are being manufactured from a single pattern. All machinery, machinery, machinery. Ditto, ditto, ditto. That is why we are losing customers up at the shop."

"Doesn't that make it all the more necessary for me to get a job?" Lyng demanded.

"Lyng, you are not going to waste your life by working as a common laborer," her mother said with finality.

"Then how can I get money to buy clothes like other people? From you? You know that's impossible."

"It wouldn't hurt her to get some sort of a job for the summer," Grandmother Skoglund said placatingly.

"I don't want her to be rubbing elbows with street girls."

"I am sure that there are lots of nice girls who go out and work for a living," Grandmother Skoglund said. "Some of those who room at Gunara's and Tallette's are as nice people as you can find anywhere. One, especially, who has been working up at the Golden Rule in St. Paul for years, is a perfect lady."

"And what kind of a job is that? Standing on her feet all day and breaking her neck to satisfy unreasonable customers? I have had enough of them at the shop, even though I have been able to sit down while I have been sewing."

"I wouldn't discourage Lyng from trying to earn some money for clothes," Grandmother Skoglund said. "After all, Reidun, every bird has a right to preen itself in its own plumage."

Lyng's mother moved to the opposite side of the kitchen. "All right. But if the bird singes its wings, you, not I, will be to blame."

After Lyng's mother and Grandmother Skoglund had gone to bed and Lyng was left alone in the kitchen, she put her arms down on the table and let her head rest on them. She wanted to cry, but no tears came. Then the dull ache from the top of her head down into her neck and the small of her back hurt her so that she sat upright again. She rubbed her forehead with the tips of her fingers. She was so weary that she wondered how she would have the strength to undress and get to bed. Yet if she intended to go out and try to find a job in the morning, she had better get some sleep.

Lyng took off the clocked stockings and folded them carefully. These could be the first items of the new wardrobe she would start to accumulate for herself. But she'd also want several pair of white ones like some of the girls wore at the banquet, and patent leather slippers—low-heeled ones with two or three straps. The new undershirt would do too, and the Ferris corset waist. So would the corset cover and the white petticoats and the umbrella pants. Only she'd ask Grandmother Skoglund not to starch her underwear too much. One of her first purchases would be material for a simple cotton dress much like the one Hattie wore. But she'd want blue forget-me-nots on hers and dainty sprigs of green leaves in a white background. Hattie would know of a dressmaker who understood styles, yet didn't charge too much for her sewing. Lyng was too tired to think of any more.

Well, come what may, she'd get a job. She'd start out the

first thing in the morning so she'd have the entire day before her. And she'd keep trying, no matter how many times she met with disappointment. In a large city like Minneapolis, there must be some place where she would be allowed to work to earn the money she needed.

CHAPTER FOUR

LYNG decided that the Thomas Department Store on Nicollet Avenue would be the place to work. It had a genteel atmosphere which would be sure to please her mother. More important, Thomas' carried a smart line of wearing apparel, so that while she was working she would also be receiving a free education on how to dress for all occasions.

But the man in the employment office told Lyng that the store didn't hire any help without experience, not even cash girls. Lyng went up and down Nicollet Avenue, but she was told the same thing at the employment offices of all the other stores.

On her way home, she decided to drop in at the Emporium. The family had traded at the Emporium as far back as Lyng could remember, and she knew the manager, Mr. Cotton, by sight. Mr. Cotton told Lyng that generally the Emporium hired only experienced help, but since her family were old customers, he would make an exception in her case. He offered her two dollars and fifty cents a week if she cared to take a job as cash girl, and she accepted at once.

Lyng reported for duty the following Saturday morning and was assigned to the toy department. Miss Tennyson, whom Lyng remembered having seen there for years, was dusting the doll and the furniture counter. As usual, she was wearing her brown dress and black sateen apron and the inevitable shears on a long ribbon around her neck. Tall and thin, she loped rather than walked around the place.

A cash girl, Miss Tennyson said, was at the beck and call of all the clerks in the department. The instant she heard one of their bells, she was to hurry over in the direction from which it came. Then she was to pick up the merchandise that had been sold, have it wrapped at the bundle desk, take the customer's money to the cashier, see that she received the correct change and rush back with the change and the bundle to the clerk who had made the sale. Any damage to the merchandise or any shortage of change would be charged against her pay.

Lyng tried her best to follow Miss Tennyson's instructions to the letter. All morning she ran in answer to the bells and returned wrapped merchandise and change to the clerks. The weather was hot and sticky, and by noon her dark blue gingham dress showed darker blue where sweat had soaked through.

"It's time for lunch," Miss Tennyson told her. "I'll have mine now too, so I can show you where to eat."

Lyng followed Miss Tennyson to the little room where she had left her lunch package behind a flimsy green curtain. From there Miss Tennyson led the way to the main floor and then farther down on into the basement. It was dark there, with light coming only from a single grimy window, but Lyng could see that the place was a catch-all for boxes, paper, excelsior and other material used in the shipping of merchandise to the Emporium. Miss Tennyson found two sturdy wooden boxes and invited Lyng to sit on one of them.

"Is there a place where I could wash my hands?" Lyng asked.

"Over in the corner. There's a basin and a toilet."

After groping about through the boxes and excelsior, Lyng

found them both. She washed her hands and wiped them on her petticoat, making a mental note to bring scouring powder and rags to clean out the wash bowl and toilet.

Miss Tennyson had already opened her lunch package and was eating her bologna sandwich. Her false teeth made a clicking sound as she chewed and Lyng wondered how she managed to keep them from falling out of her mouth.

"You had better get started eating," Miss Tennyson told her. "We're supposed to have half an hour for lunch, but on Saturdays we're expected to make it in less."

Lyng tried hard to swallow the homemade bread with real butter and meat loaf that Grandmother Skoglund had prepared with such care. But the heat and excitement and filthy surroundings in the basement had made her lose her appetite. She put most of it back into her lunch package.

"You need to eat to keep going here," Miss Tennyson told her. Then she added a little less sharply, "Maybe by supper you'll feel more hungry."

Upstairs again, Miss Tennyson told Lyng to dust the doll and furniture counter because the hot wind outside had blown in sand from the street. If any customers came in, she could direct them to one of the clerks.

Lyng picked up a large doll with blonde curls and blue eyes that opened and shut. She took off the pink bonnet lined with crisp white lace, smoothed its hair and dusted its pink cheeks. Then she laid the doll tenderly back.

In all her life Lyng had owned only one doll, a Christmas present from Tante Gunara and Tante Tallette. That doll had a china head and a kid body stuffed with sawdust, and it wore a white muslin petticoat and a red calico dress made from the scraps of one of Tante Tallette's. After frequent launderings by Grandmother Skoglund, the clothes were faded and in tatters. Sawdust leaked from the doll's body, leaving it flat and spindly, and the paint on its china head wore off almost entirely. Finally Lyng's mother disposed of the doll, saying that Lyng was too big a girl to play with it any more. Lyng could still remember how sad she felt that day.

As she dusted, it occurred to her that the dolls were not displayed very well on the counter. If she could arrange them so people stopped to look, there ought to be more sales for Miss Tennyson.

Lyng picked up a doll in a pink nightgown and found a bed just her size. Then she brought out a pink silk quilt and a pink silk pillow from the box, laid the doll on the pillow and covered her. The effect was so touching that Lyng stood admiring the sleeping beauty for a long time.

After that she looked over the assortment of doll furniture and chose a sturdy table and four chairs from the shelf. She cleared a space on the counter by putting several boxes of less attractive dolls underneath it, arranged the chairs around the table and placed a beautiful doll on each. She had just finished setting the table with blue and white dishes when Miss Tennyson returned.

"So that is how you fiddle about while I'm gone," she said in a shrill voice. "I'll report you to Mr. Cotton for this. Now put back every doll into its place this minute. And the dishes and furniture where they belong, too."

"You won't have to report her. I'm right here."

"Very well, Mr. Cotton. But you see what I have to put up with from these inexperienced and undependable girls you keep sending me."

At first Lyng had been so frightened that she stood speechless. But at this outburst from Miss Tennyson, she felt her whole body grow hot.

"I am inexperienced, but I'm not undependable," she said. "I've tried my very best to do exactly what you said. Only I thought people would buy more dolls from you if they were displayed like real people instead of lying in boxes."

Mr. Cotton laughed. "The girl may have a point there, Miss Tennyson. Why not leave the dolls as they are for a day or two and see what happens?"

Before the afternoon was over, the bed and the sleeping beauty had been sold and so had the four dolls sitting at the table. During the evening the chairs and the table and the dishes were also gone. Lyng was pleased with the success of her experiment, but she realized that she would have to move more cautiously about introducing any more innovations. She couldn't risk arousing Miss Tennyson's displeasure a second time.

At eleven o'clock that night, Lyng helped Miss Tennyson cover the toy counters for the weekend.

"My, how my feet ache," Miss Tennyson groaned. "The rush over at the doll counter this afternoon and evening has been killing."

"Don't you like to sell things?" Lyng asked.

"Yes, but the regular Saturday trade is plenty. If you get any more bright ideas, plan to spring them on a dark rainy day when things are dull. If it wasn't for the consolation of the pay envelope, I just couldn't live through Saturday."

"There won't even be a pay envelope for me."

"Oh, yes, there will," Miss Tennyson said. "Everybody gets paid up on Saturday night. Even though you've worked for only a day. That's the one bright spot about this job at the Emporium. You never have to wait for your money as you do in some places."

Although Lyng's feet had been burning all afternoon and evening, she suddenly felt no more pain in them. There was a fifty-cent piece in the brown envelope. To be sure, it wasn't much. But it was the beginning of what was going to be a steady income. She'd think up more ways to promote sales in the toy department, and in time she might work her way up to a position that paid even better than Miss Tennyson's.

Lyng liked being at the Emporium. No one inquired who your ancestors were. They weren't particular about your nationality either or the style of your clothes. Nothing counted but the sum total sales for the day. And if a cash girl was quick and expert, no one cared what she was like otherwise.

Saturday night with its brown pay envelope became the highlight of Lyng's week. She started looking forward to it on Monday morning. By noon she figured she had earned twenty cents. By night, forty. And so on until the store closed on Friday night. Saturday brought her the last fifty cents of her two-fifty, since her working day then lasted from eight in the morning until eleven at night.

One Saturday afternoon late in August, Miss Tennyson told her that Mr. Cotton wanted to see her in his office.

"What does he want?"

"Don't ask me. He just said for you to come to his office."

"Does he want me right away?"

"Yes."

Lyng's heart beat fast as she went up the narrow steps that led to the low balcony where Mr. Cotton and his assistants had their offices. She had climbed these steps only once before —on the day she applied for this job. She was much more nervous now than she had been then. Nothing worse could happen than to be told by Mr. Cotton that she was being laid off.

Mr. Cotton was seated at his desk. He looked up. "Come over here and sit down," he said.

Shaking inwardly, Lyng obeyed.

"I have been noticing you all summer," he began. "From up here, I am able to see much of what goes on down in the store."

Lyng felt actually sick. If she had realized she was being spied upon, she would have worked even harder, and her job, which demanded so much speed and accuracy, would

have been even more strenuous. In spite of the money it
brought her, she doubted that she would have been able to
stand it.

"We plan to go in for more children's wear," Mr. Cotton
went on. "Some clothing manufacturers are beginning to put
out very attractive infants' garments and coats and suits and
dresses for very small girls and boys. We feel that this market
is not at all seasonal—in other words, we should be able to
make good all-year sales."

If he is going to fire me, Lyng thought, why doesn't he get
it over with? It won't improve matters for me to know he in-
tends to make money on children's clothes instead of their
toys.

"So I'm asking you, Miss Skoglund, to take charge of the
infants' section of this department. That is, to be one of the
clerks there."

Lyng jumped. "Oh, thank you, Mr. Cotton."

Mr. Cotton smiled. "I am glad to see you are pleased. You
may report for duty on Monday. Your salary will, of course,
be the same as that of other clerks in the store—six dollars a
week."

"Oh, thank you, Mr. Cotton," Lyng repeated.

"Since it's such a hot afternoon, I don't believe there'll be
any extra business in the toy department. So, if you care to,
you may as well go home. Tell the cashier I said you could
get your pay envelope now."

Lyng's first impulse was to hurry home and break the news
to Grandmother Skoglund. Then she decided to wait until her
mother could be present. Lyng's mother had taken for
granted that she would enter the University of Minnesota in
the fall, but with this promotion at the Emporium, her
mother would, of course, realize at once how ridiculous it
would be for Lyng to give up this fine opportunity. Still
Lyng might as well be diplomatic. Her mother's reaction to

any proposition depended entirely on the mood she happened to be in at the time.

She'd take the family on a picnic and break the news then. Since none of them had ever been to Big Island at Lake Minnetonka, an outing there would be a special treat.

It was fortunate Mr. Cotton had allowed her to collect her week's pay before she left the store. She would buy whatever she needed for the picnic on her way home. The boys would like a big chocolate cake more than anything else. She had learned to bake American cakes in cooking class in school but they had never had one at home. They never got enough fruit salad either. Dutchess apples, which were home grown in Minnesota, were both plentiful and cheap. She'd use them for the base of the salad, which could easily be brought to the picnic in a two-quart mason jar. The cake would be more difficult but she'd manage somehow. About the salad—a couple of oranges and two or three bananas would add to its flavor. She would have liked to buy a small bottle of cherries, but that would be out of the question. She would have to keep out carfare for the entire family, out to Lake Minnetonka and back in to the city. There ought to be some kind of meat. A meat loaf would go far and, if she bought just the least bit of smoked ham to grind with the pork and the beef, it would be special. There would be plenty of everything so the boys would get filled up.

A pleasant young man waited on Lyng at the Williams Market. She had him wrap up each article separately as she selected it. She decided to get a box of marshmallows and a pound of extra good coffee and some loaf sugar. When she had finished shopping, there was a good-sized pile of bundles on the counter.

"Can you manage all that?" the young man asked.

"I'll have to. We need the groceries tonight."

The young man smiled. "I'll tell you what I'll do. I'll put

all your things in one of the large coffee sacks. They're stout and won't break."

Lyng could have gotten along with fewer apples, but the boys could eat all they wanted just this once. A streetcar stopped as she reached the corner and she boarded it. After all, it wasn't every day that she was celebrating an important promotion, so it should be an excuse for a streetcar ride. But she'd have to watch her pennies. She couldn't take the boys to Big Island without spending a little on them at the amusement park out there.

It would have been nice to invite Hattie Fleming to the picnic, but now that they each had different jobs and worked different hours they seldom saw each other. Hattie had already had several promotions with the telephone company. Grandmother Skoglund liked Hattie. But Lyng's mother was sharply critical of what she called her "Yankee slipshod" way of living.

Inside the streetcar Lyng jolted several of the passengers as she made her way to the front.

"We're not running a dray," the conductor growled.

Lyng was too happy to mind. She hurried to take possession of the only vacant seat and set the sack down beside her.

When she reached the house, Grandmother Skoglund was there alone.

"What is all this?" she asked curiously.

"We're going on a picnic."

"A picnic? Who's going on a picnic?"

"You and mother and Haakon and Kristian and I. We're going tomorrow. Out to Lake Minnetonka."

Grandmother Skoglund's eyes opened wide.

"It's a sort of celebration. I'm getting along so well up at the Emporium I thought we might as well celebrate a little."

Grandmother Skoglund beamed. "You're just like your father, Lyng. He worked as no one else could work. But if ever he had a chance for a good time, my, how he did enjoy it! What an American he would have made!"

On Sunday morning Lyng was the first one up. She had the coffee cooked when Grandmother Skoglund came out into the kitchen, and she brought her mother a cup in bed. It was the only cup left from her mother's Norwegian porcelain set.

"I'm not sure I'm in favor of a picnic on Sunday morning," Lyng's mother said. She sat up in bed and began to sip her coffee.

"It will do you a lot of good," Lyng said. "You know that you spend entirely too much time indoors."

"You are certainly concerned over my health of late," Lyng's mother said.

"Mother, I've always been. The only difference is that now, since I've started to work at the Emporium, I'm able to do something about it."

"We ought to go to church."

"We can take our Bible along and have services by ourselves at the lake."

Lyng's mother continued to sip coffee and to nibble at the fresh biscuit with butter and apple jelly. She made no further mention of the picnic, but Lyng knew she was willing to come.

When everyone was ready to start, Lyng brought the full picnic basket out on the back stoop. "Haakon, I think you and Kristian should carry this between you," she said.

"Everyone will be on the way to church," Haakon said, scowling. "I hate to go loaded down like an express wagon."

"Tell them it's full of Sunday School papers and hymn books," Kristian teased.

"You ought to be ashamed of yourself," his mother scolded. "Belittling the Lord's Day."

"*I'm* not going to carry it," Haakon said.

"Stay at home then," Kristian told him cheerfully, "I can carry the basket by myself."

He took hold of both handles of the basket and started down the steps of the stoop.

"Wait," Lyng said, "I'll carry the basket with you. Haakon, you take hold of Grandmother Skoglund's arm and Mother's."

Lyng's mother laughed coldly. "Since when did you get the idea that I'm so feeble I can't walk by myself?" she demanded.

"It won't hurt Haakon to get used to taking care of both of you. He's a real man now," Lyng said.

"Haakon has always been thoughtful of me," his mother said.

On Hennepin Avenue, the family got off the Minnehaha Falls Streetcar and changed to the Minnetonka Line.

"I can't believe that we are leaving Minneapolis," Grandmother Skoglund said, smiling broadly. "Except for our trips over to St. Paul, I haven't been outside the city since I came from Norway."

"It's time you started traveling," Lyng told her.

"Oh, I've traveled more than most, Lyng. It was a good big trip from Rendalen to Minnesota."

At the outskirts of the city, the streetcar passed Lake of the Isles, Lake Calhoun, and Lake Harriet. There were stretches of dense green woods, and Lakewood Cemetery was like a large, well-cared-for garden. Grandmother Skoglund took deep breaths.

"My, it smells sweet out here," she said. "I haven't had so much clean air in my lungs since I left the mountains of Norway."

"You'll be having lots of such outings from now on," Lyng told her. "There are a lot of pretty places near Minneapolis where we can go for picnics—White Bear Lake, Forest Lake,

Red Wing and other beautiful spots along the Mississippi. We might even spend a day on one of the excursion boats that go from St. Paul down the river."

"I gave in today. But I don't intend to allow my family to make a practice of pursuing such worldly pleasures on the Sabbath," Lyng's mother said.

At Excelsior the family boarded what was called the streetcar boat, which took them to Big Island.

There was a soft breeze over Upper Lake, just strong enough to stir up tiny ripples. The water was dotted with rowboats, flat-bottom fishing boats, canoes, gasoline launches, boats whose tall white sails stood out against the blue sky, and a red coal steamer that sent a streak of black smoke behind it.

The streetcar boat moved quietly through the calm water with only a slight vibration from the motor.

"Don't you love the smell of smoke coming from that steamer over there?" Kristian asked.

"It reminds me of the dirty fishing boats on the west coast of Norway," his mother told him. "I spent a summer with a cousin of mine at Bergen, and it seemed to me that the whole city smelled of fish and the smoke from the fishing boats."

"We are going to land at Big Island now," Lyng said brightly.

There was a rushing of water at the stern of the streetcar boat, and the vibration from the motor stopped as the boat glided smoothly along one side of the dock. Two men jumped out and with the help of others already there, fastened the boat with heavy rope to the thick posts.

"Haakon, you had better help Mother," Lyng said. "Kristian, you and I will put the basket up on the dock. Then stand and watch it until I've brought Grandmother Skoglund ashore. I'll be back to help you with the basket."

When everyone was safe on land, Lyng said that the first thing to do would be to find a good picnic spot. They finally chose one in the shade of a large basswood tree, near the lake but on a little hill high enough above the water to escape the smell of fish. Grandmother Skoglund and Lyng began to unpack the picnic basket.

"It's almost a shame to eat so much good food all at once," Grandmother Skoglund said. She set the large chocolate cake on the tablecloth spread over the grass and beamed admiringly at it.

Lyng laughed. "No, it isn't. We Skoglunds can afford it, so why shouldn't we enjoy ourselves?"

"You had better cover the cake so the flies won't eat it before we do," her mother said.

"I brought several of our best napkins for that very purpose," Grandmother Skoglund assured her.

"I hope the coffee is hot," Lyng's mother said, helping herself to a slice of meat loaf. "In Norway we used to call cold coffee the poor man's left-over drink."

Lyng removed layers of newspapers from a brown jug and pulled out the cork. "The coffee is still steaming," she said.

For a while everyone except Lyng was busy eating.

"I thought you said you were hungry," Grandmother Skoglund reminded her.

"I'll eat. Don't worry about me," Lyng said.

Kristian finished first.

"Can we go to the amusement park now?" he asked.

"Don't rush so," his mother told him. "Haakon hasn't nearly finished yet. Besides, where do you think you will get the money to waste on those silly machines?"

Lyng opened her purse. "Here is thirty-five cents for each of you," she said. "But you are both to sit still until we have said grace after our meal."

"We said it once before we started to eat. Whoever heard of saying grace at a picnic?" Kristian demanded.

Lyng put up a warning finger. "Just for that you're going

to carry the scraps away into the woods. We don't want our afternoon spoiled by flies swarming around us."

After the boys had left, Grandmother Skoglund and Lyng's mother and Lyng sat chatting. Lyng's mother was in excellent spirits. She told about an outing she and some other young people had had at their chalet in the mountains of Norway.

"It was the first time Markus told me he loved me," she said blushing. "What a time we did have!"

"How would you like a cup of coffee and a sugar lump?" Lyng suggested after a little. "The jug is still warm."

She rinsed out three cups and filled them with coffee and passed cream and sugar.

"You spoil all of us," Grandmother Skoglund said contentedly.

It was cool and pleasant under the big tree. Already long shadows had begun to stretch down over the green knoll.

"Now I am going to tell you about something wonderful that happened to me yesterday," Lyng said.

Her mother looked at her inquiringly. Grandmother Skoglund leaned forward.

"Yes," Lyng said. "I've been promoted at the Emporium. Mr. Cotton called me up to his office. He said that, beginning Monday, I am to be taken on permanently as a regular clerk at the store, and I'm to get the same salary as the others who have been working there for years. Isn't that wonderful?"

Lyng's mother set her cup down so hard that the coffee spilled and soaked into the cake on her plate. "No daughter of mine is going to spend her life clerking in a store," she said. "Do you suppose for a minute I would have allowed you to start working at the Emporium last spring, if I hadn't been sure you would eventually come to your senses? That you would realize you were out of your own class, working side by side with the rabble? Your father and I didn't leave everything that was dear to us back in Norway and come to this huge, unfriendly, foreign land only to have humiliation heaped on the heads of our children."

"Humiliation? Why, Mother, it's a promotion. Viola Ryan, the other cash girl, would give her right arm for the chance I'm getting. And she's worked there much longer than I have."

"Then why do you suppose this man—Mr. Cotton—why do you suppose he picked you out especially for this grand job you're telling us about? What do you suppose that other cash girl will say about the two of you behind your backs?"

"Mother, you have no right to insinuate—"

"Lyng," Grandmother Skoglund interrupted quietly. "Let's not spoil this day with an argument. We were having such a beautiful time."

"But I have to talk about this now," Lyng insisted. "Mr. Cotton expects me to start tomorrow morning."

"Last spring when you asked permission to work there," Lyng's mother said, "you made it clear that all you wanted was to earn money enough to buy clothes so that you would look like every other girl your age. Although, as I told you then, why this should give you so much satisfaction is beyond me."

"Mother, you have been saying lately how slow things are getting at the shop. Suppose some day there won't be any work for you up there? Can't you understand how important it is for me to have a steady job at a nice place like the Emporium?"

"It isn't a nice place and you know it. Lyng, you are not going to work at that store after the fifteenth of September."

"What do you want me to do then? Sit at home and eat off you?"

"No, you are going to the University of Minnesota."

Lyng set her cup down on the cloth that had served as their table. "Mother, even you ought to know that is impossible."

"Why is it impossible? Ever since your father died—it's thirteen years now—have you lacked anything? Haven't you had a roof over your head and a clean bed to sleep in and three nourishing meals a day?"

"It isn't fair to you, Mother. Nor to Grandmother Skoglund. She hasn't been at all well lately and—"

"Lyng," Grandmother Skoglund pleaded again. Then she sat up straight. "Your mother is right. You must go to the university."

Lyng stared at her unbelievingly. "Not you, too, Grandmother Skoglund. Surely you understand how hard it has been."

"Of course, I do. So does your mother, only sometimes you two don't seem to understand each other. It has made it nice for all of us, Lyng, the way you have brought home money this summer. But being a clerk isn't going to get you anywhere. That is what your mother is trying to tell you."

"If I'm a clerk, we'll at least live."

Grandmother Skoglund moved closer to Lyng. "If your father could have been with us today, he would have sided with your mother and me. Hard as he had to work as a newcomer in this country, trying to make both ends meet, he was always studying. 'Learn so you can earn,' he repeated over and over. 'In America even the poorest peasant can do both, if he has the will.'" Grandmother Skoglund had been speaking Norwegian, but this last she quoted in her halting English. Then, reverting to the Norwegian, she went on, "For years he kept going to that school for Norwegian boys that Mr. Skurdalsvold had in his barn. Your father didn't have the money to buy his own books so he rented the ones he needed from Mr. Skurdalsvold, and you should have seen how he pored over them. He took them along when he went to work so he could study on the streetcar or any spare minute he might have at noon. And no matter how late he returned from work and how tired he was, out came the books again before he went to bed. Oh, your father certainly believed in learning."

For several minutes no one said anything. From the lake came the putting of the gasoline launches and the shrill whistle of the coal steamer.

Grandmother Skoglund raised her eyes to Lyng's. "Surely," she said, "you who are born in America and have had the advantage of growing up in this wonderful country, know better than to throw away your birthright."

There was a long silence.

Grandmother Skoglund laid her hand on Lyng's arm. "Lyng," she said so softly that it was almost a whisper, "if I ask you to do it for my sake, won't you go to the university?"

Lyng stirred uneasily. In all her life, Grandmother Skoglund had never asked a favor of her.

"If I do, how are we going to manage?"

Grandmother Skoglund smiled. "We must all work together. You, Reidun, if you expect Lyng to continue at school, must do your share." Lyng's mother opened her mouth as if to speak, but Grandmother Skoglund continued. "Oh, I don't mean about yourself, Reidun. It's about the boys. I have felt for some time that they should contribute something toward the upkeep of the household."

"They worked over at their aunts' yesterday," Lyng's mother said. "Remember, they are still growing and need plenty of rest."

"Markus worked from the time he could manage the sheep and the cattle," Grandmother Skoglund said. "He couldn't have been more than nine years old at the time. It will do Haakon good to realize that he is going to have to work for a living. And being busy will help to keep Kristian out of mischief."

"Haakon works hard at school," Lyng's mother insisted. "He brings home good marks."

"So does Kristian," Grandmother Skoglund said. "At least they aren't bad. But when Lyng was much younger than the boys are now, she was expected to help with the work at home."

"What could the boys do?" Lyng's mother demanded.

"Bert Fleming always has jobs," Lyng said. "He's had a paper route for years, and now he works at the macaroni factory over on Franklin Avenue on Saturdays."

"Haakon isn't strong enough to work at a factory," Lyng's mother said.

Lyng stood up. "All right," she said. "I'll go back to school on one condition. That Haakon and Kristian get some kind of work, and that you, Mother, will promise not to coddle them and let them quit when the going gets a little hard."

"Of course, the boys will get jobs and be told they are expected to make good," Grandmother Skoglund said. "You won't have to worry about them, Lyng. They're fine boys, both of them." With difficulty she got to her feet. "I'm as stiff and bent as a corkscrew," she said laughing and brushing off the back of her dress. "I'm not used to sitting on the ground these days." She looked at the sun. "It's really getting late. We ought to start for home."

Lyng put her arm around Grandmother Skoglund's waist and drew her closer. Then she leaned down and touched Grandmother Skoglund's cheek with her own. In the whole world there was no one she loved quite as much as Grandmother Skoglund.

CHAPTER FIVE

Lyng leaned on the banister and pulled herself up the steps leading to the main reading room of the university library. When she reached the top, she stopped to rest. She might as well give up. For a month now she had been under the load of trying to attend the university and help at home, and she had done a poor job of both.

She had known from the start that it couldn't be done. She should have had more backbone than to give in. But when Grandmother Skoglund begged her, as a special favor, it hadn't been easy to refuse her. If Grandmother Skoglund were to express an earnest desire to fly to the moon, Lyng supposed she would do her best to help her to get there.

But this afternoon Lyng knew she was facing an impossible situation. Her long paper in rhetoric was due tomorrow and so far she had done nothing except select a topic. She had chosen to write on Alfred the Great because he belonged to the history of England. Miss Scherf, the rhetoric teacher, only had to mention a person or an event that had figured in American history and up went a dozen hands. Lyng wouldn't risk revealing her ignorance by venturing to write on anything American.

In the reading room of the main library she made out slips for the first two books she found listed under Alfred the

Great. When the gray-haired librarian brought them to the desk, Lyng said she'd take both. By skimming through two books, she ought to be able to find the most important facts about Alfred the Great and to fill enough pages for what Miss Scherf would consider a long paper. She took the short cut down by the river bank in order to reach home as quickly as possible and start reading.

When Lyng opened the kitchen door, she was greeted by clouds of steam and the strong smell of soap suds. Grandmother Skoglund was standing by the stove taking out the white clothes from the steaming wash boiler with a long stick and putting them into a dishpan on a nearby chair. She picked up the bottom of her apron and wiped her face.

"I had hoped to finish everything but the starching before you came home," she apologized. "But one of the customers of the shop came here this morning and asked me to launder some curtains for her right away. So I had to wring out our clothes that had been put to soak and get at the curtains. I'm only taking out the first boiler of our wash."

"You look tired, Grandmother Skoglund," Lyng said anxiously.

"Well, I am a little," Grandmother Skoglund admitted. "I'd have left the regular wash until later if it hadn't been that the boys were wearing their last suits of clean underwear and neither one has a shirt to put on tomorrow. Besides, the white clothes had been put to soak and it's messy having them around the kitchen for days."

"You go and lie down while I put on an old dress," Lyng told her. "I'll help you with the washing. But first I'll make a cup of coffee for both of us."

"Well," Grandmother Skoglund said uncertainly, "that would help a lot. But haven't you school work you need to do?"

"It can wait," Lyng said. But she thought again how foolish

she had been to allow herself to be talked into attending the university, as she cleared off one end of the table and wiped it with a damp rag.

"The coffee is ready," she called out finally to Grandmother Skoglund.

Grandmother Skoglund, looking much brighter, came into the kitchen and took the chair Lyng had drawn up for her.

"My, but this tastes good," she said, smacking her lips. "There is just nothing like hot coffee to put life back into an old tired body. But are you sure, Lyng, that you oughtn't to be studying instead of helping me?"

"The studying can wait. And now, if you don't mind, I'll get at the rest of the white clothes that need to be rubbed. If you want to, you can rinse and wring out those that are clean."

While Grandmother Skoglund worked the squeaking hand-wringer, Lyng rubbed on the washboard tubful after tubful of clothes. "Even if we have to wash Sundays, we're never going to let clothes accumulate like this again," she told Grandmother Skoglund.

"It should be getting better now that the weather is cooler. Although Kristian can't help getting his clothes soiled carrying barrels and boxes out of the dirty basement at the Williams Market."

"I suppose so," Lyng said.

"We'll hang up the colored clothes in the kitchen tonight and the white ones that will be needed right away. The rest can soak in the tubs until tomorrow. I'll hang them out the first thing in the morning."

"Couldn't we hang the colored clothes in the yard tonight?"

"My, no! Mrs. Oyan lost a blanket that way last week. With the livery stable so close by, you can never tell what kind of people are lurking around nights."

Lyng strung up lines from one end of the kitchen to the

other until there was a clear space only around the table and the stove. Lyng's mother arrived when she was hanging up the last of Grandmother Skoglund's gingham aprons.

"It's good you came home and helped Mother Skoglund with the washing," Lyng's mother said.

She went at once into the bedroom. Lyng and Grandmother cleaned up, leaving only two full tubs of water to be emptied.

"Mother might at least have offered to make supper," Lyng said as she carried the clothespin bag and the washboard into the tiny storeroom off the kitchen.

"She's probably as tired as we are," Grandmother Skoglund said. "Why don't you go and study and let me do that?"

"No. You set the table and I'll get everything else ready."

Lyng stirred up the fire that had begun to die down and made hamburgers and brown hashed potatoes and opened a mason jar of applesauce.

Haakon and Kristian came bounding in at the same time.

"Empty the tubs before you wash up for supper," Lyng told them.

"I won't," Haakon said.

"Come on. Take hold," Kristian commanded.

All the food was on the table when Lyng's mother came into the kitchen. She was wearing a new orchid silk kimono.

"How do you like it, Lyng?" she asked. "I got a remnant real cheap at the shop."

"It's pretty," Lyng said shortly.

It wasn't hard to persuade Grandmother Skoglund to go to bed right after supper. Lyng's mother insisted that the boys get at their lessons in their room without delay, so that they would be sure of having a good night's rest, and she offered to wipe the dishes for Lyng. By the time Lyng brought out her books on Alfred the Great and her writing materials, it was nine o'clock.

"I'm going to study in the parlor," she told her mother. "I'll have writing to do and the night lamp will be good to work by. It's too messy out here in the kitchen."

"The curtain stretcher is up in the parlor," her mother objected.

"I won't mind."

"Be sure not to wake the boys when you pass through their room."

By ten o'clock Lyng was having difficulty keeping her eyes open. She got up from her chair, stretched, and went out into the kitchen for a drink of water. She had closed the door between the parlor and the boys' room on her way and, returning in the dark, she stubbed the toes of her stockinged feet against the legs of the table. She heard her mother stir in bed and she hurried back to the parlor.

By midnight she had skimmed over only half of Abbott's *Alfred the Great*, counting pictures and all. "I'll have to do better than that," she thought. By two o'clock she had paged through the second half. "I'm so tired, there's no use trying to read any more. I wouldn't get anything out of the second book anyway. I had better start writing something."

By half past four, when she stopped, she was too exhausted to care what she had set down on paper. But she counted the pages. There were nineteen of them, enough for a long paper.

The following day in rhetoric class, Lyng was careful to keep her eyes away from Miss Scherf's. As Miss Scherf took up, one by one, the personages on the recommended list of the themes and discussed what had made each of them outstanding in their careers, Lyng became both uneasy and angry. Why had she let herself in for uncomfortable moments like these? Alfred the Great came last. By that time, Lyng felt as though everyone was looking at her, and she sat trembling with fearful anticipation of what was to come. The bell rang and Miss Scherf called for the themes. For a minute Lyng hesitated to hand in hers. Then she rushed up to Miss Scherf's desk, slipped her theme under the others, and fled.

She had to force herself to go to rhetoric class the next time it met. What did Miss Scherf think of her now that she had read that terrible paper? If rhetoric hadn't become her favorite subject and Miss Scherf her favorite teacher, she wouldn't have minded so much. But she had actually begun to look forward to this class, and it had seemed to her that Miss Scherf had approved of her work.

No mention was made of Lyng's theme during that class period nor in those that followed. Perhaps Miss Scherf didn't bother to correct long themes. The University of Minnesota was such a huge institution and the classes so large that the professors couldn't be expected to give attention to individual themes handed in to them. Much less to bother about the problems troubling the students who wrote them.

At the end of the week, Lyng received a note, asking her to call at Miss Scherf's office. When the hour for the appointment had arrived and Lyng stood outside Miss Scherf's office door, she was both frightened and relieved. She dreaded the tongue lashing she would get from Miss Scherf, but, on the other hand, this might provide the very excuse she had been waiting for. If she came home and told her mother and Grandmother Skoglund that she wasn't able to keep up with her work at the university, they couldn't very well urge her to continue. All right—best to have the ordeal over with. She squared her shoulders, raised her hand and knocked.

"Come in."

A gust of wind greeted Lyng as she opened the door.

"There's always a draft when I raise the window," Miss Scherf said. "But it was such a nice day, and I never seem to get enough of the sweet smell of the campus oaks."

As Lyng sat down, she saw how trim Miss Scherf looked in her neat blue suit and her crisp white shirtwaist. What pretty soft hair she had and how carefully manicured her fingernails were. Queer she hadn't noticed all these things about Miss Scherf before. But this was Lyng's first personal encounter with her and she seemed somehow different. Lyng had not imagined that a teacher, much less a college professor, ever unbent and talked naturally like this.

"I can't tell you how disappointed I was when I read your long theme," Miss Scherf said, coming to the point at once.

There it was, Lyng thought. She sat staring at Miss Scherf's cameo brooch without meeting her eyes.

"You had been doing such fine work all along. In fact, I considered you one of the best students in the class. But that long theme of yours—Miss Skoglund, it was the poorest one in the entire set."

Lyng remained silent.

"One of two things must have happened. Either you were suddenly seized with a lazy streak—which, in view of your consistently careful work up to now, I can't believe. Or something prevented you from putting enough time on the paper."

Still Lyng sat without saying anything.

"That is why I asked you to come here today. You don't seem to be the kind of a girl who would willingly shirk."

Something in Lyng's throat was making it hard for her to swallow.

"I was wondering whether there wasn't something I could do to help you."

Lyng raised her head. The outline of Miss Scherf's blue suit and white shirtwaist had become blurred. "There is nothing you can do," she said almost to low to be heard.

"Don't be too sure of that. After all, filling a student's mind with facts is only a small part of a teacher's job."

"I don't understand," Lyng said. "I thought everyone went to school to learn things."

"Anyone with your education and intelligence can cram

her head full of facts, simply by poring over books. If that is all college means to you, you might as well stay home and save your time and money and energy. But you really want more out of the four years you intend to spend here with us, I am sure."

"What?" Lyng asked.

Miss Scherf hesitated. "I am no mind reader, but don't you think a young person in college should have some definite goal in view—some career which she hopes to follow after she has completed her courses? It is a teacher's job to help her student find such a goal if the student hasn't already chosen one, and then help her reach it."

Lyng met Miss Scherf's gray-blue eyes. "No one has ever talked like that to me—not any teacher, at least," she said.

Miss Scherf smiled. "Now I know that you didn't really intend to give poor Alfred the Great that shabby treatment in your long paper. He deserves much better, you know."

Lyng laughed in spite of herself. "It wasn't my idea to go to the university in the first place," she said.

"Don't you like school?" Miss Scherf asked.

"Y-e-s. Especially rhetoric. But—"

"But what?"

"Things are so hard at home."

"In what way?"

Lyng started to tell what a strenuous day Grandmother Skoglund had had. From then on, without realizing how it came about, she was pouring out to Miss Scherf her whole story: her father's early death, her mother's working at the shop, and her two younger brothers who needed more and more as they grew older.

"I should say that you are most fortunate in having two such fine people as your mother and your grandmother who are willing to work and sacrifice so much for you. Many a girl would jump at the chance of a university education like yours."

"I know. But that's just it. It's too hard for them—especially for my grandmother. That's why I spend so much time helping at home, and then there isn't any left for my lessons."

"Is that all that is troubling you?"

Lyng hung her head. "No. My folks are Norwegian and they like Norwegian ways best. My mother doesn't understand how hard it is for a girl to be different from the rest of her friends. Even my grandmother, who is the most wonderful person in the world, doesn't realize it. Sometimes I'm ashamed of them for this. Yes, you won't believe it, but I have actually been ashamed of my grandmother, and then I'm much more ashamed of myself for being ashamed of her. That's why I got the job at the Emporium last summer—to buy clothes so I would be like the American girls. And that's why they had to coax me at home to give up my job and go to the university."

"You were born in America, weren't you?"

"Of course. Here in Minneapolis."

"Then you are a native American. But the number of years a person has lived in the United States isn't what counts. Nor how far back in American history he can trace his ancestry."

Lyng's ears and cheeks were burning.

Miss Scherf stepped to the window. "Do you see those beautiful oaks out there?" she asked. "Can you visualize them as nothing but small acorns? You Norwegians who have been here for only a generation or two have already contributed a good deal to the material welfare of Minnesota. You are also making your influence felt more and more in the political and cultural life of the state. With all the advantages offered you, Miss Skoglund, you have a great responsibility to do your share to continue the work for which your pioneers have laid such a splendid foundation." She walked back to her desk once more. "But I called you here to discuss your theme on Alfred the Great. As I told you it was the poorest theme in the class. It certainly doesn't represent your best efforts."

"But I told you—"

"I am thinking of that. And I hope I can help you."

"How?"

"Suppose that I suggest to you that you first make an outline of the time you will need to spend on each of your lessons here at school. Oh, I know that the assignments vary, but you have been at the university long enough now to have formed a fairly accurate estimate. Allowing seven hours for sleep and more if you require it, decide how many hours you can afford to help at home. If necessary, write out this plan and try to follow it as closely as you can. You will try, won't you?"

Lyng nodded. Miss Scherf rose from her chair.

"If you find that you are not going to be able to do a good job of some particular assignment because you lack time, come to me and we'll talk the matter over, even though the assignment isn't in rhetoric. It is much better to ask for extension of time than to hand in poor work."

Lyng stood up, too.

"Promise me if you find yourself up against a stone wall, you will tell me about it before you give up." Miss Scherf held out her hand.

It was with a light heart that Lyng rushed down the corridor and the three flights of stairs of Folwell Hall and out on the campus. She ran most of the way home. Grandmother Skoglund was ironing in the kitchen.

"Grandmother Skoglund," Lyng blurted out, "I've just had the most wonderful talk with my rhetoric teacher. Miss Scherf is simply beautiful. And she's—if all the teachers were like her, this world would be a paradise."

Grandmother Skoglund set down the iron. "I knew you

would get along fine over at the university as soon as those professors learned to know you," she said. She walked over to the line strung across one corner of the kitchen and hung up a blue shirt on which she had just put the finishing touches. Then she came back to the ironing board, and picked up the iron and set it on the back of the stove. "Now *Vesla-mi*," she said, "tell me all about it."

Lyng was still standing near the door with her coat and hat on. "Do you know what?" she went on excitedly, talking so fast that she jumbled her words. "She thinks—that is, she told me that Norwegians have done much for Minnesota. They are getting to be really important here in the state. And, Grandmother Skoglund, you won't believe it when I tell you —but she thinks that I can become important too. I mean that she thinks I ought to take advantage of all the pioneers have done for us young people born over here in America, and carry on. And, oh, Grandmother Skoglund, I'm almost too thrilled to say the words to you—I've decided to be a teacher. Not the ordinary kind like most of those I've had. But a teacher just like Miss Scherf. One who understands how her students feel and how hard it can be for them sometimes. And a teacher who cares about what happens to her students out-side the class-room."

Grandmother Skoglund put her arms around Lyng and kissed her. "I knew you would be something fine one day. I told that to Markus right after you were born. I came to see you as you lay in your crib and you looked up at the two of us as if to say, 'Well, here I am. I'm small. But just you wait!' My, how proud of you Markus was that day."

"I didn't tell Miss Scherf about wanting to be a teacher while I was in her office. It seemed too grand—I mean I want to show her that I'm good enough—that I'm worthy of becoming a teacher. From now on, I'm going to study hard, Grandmother Skoglund. Especially American history and

American literature. Because if you teach in America, you ought to know a great deal about such things. And do you know what Miss Scherf said? She said that if ever I have any trouble—even though it doesn't concern the work in her class —she wants me to come and tell her about it. Oh, Grandmother Skoglund, isn't it all wonderful?"

Grandmother Skoglund was close to tears. "It all seems too wonderful to be true. Little did I dream, the day Markus came home from the manor house and told me that the Timber King of Skoglund was going to let him sit in the schoolroom with the daughter of the house for daily instruction, that it would be the beginning of all this. That Markus would one day have a daughter of his own who would herself, become a teacher over in the great and big America." She wiped her eyes with the edge of her apron.

As soon as Lyng's mother returned from work that evening, Grandmother Skoglund told her the good news.

"I'm glad you have learned to appreciate the value of a good education," her mother said, speaking with more enthusiasm than usual. "And that you are planning to put it to some use. In Norway ministers and teachers occupy positions in society as high as the most important government officials. Tonight I shall sit down and write a letter to my cousin Lillemor over there. She has always been the best news spreader in all of Rendalen."

After her interview with Miss Scherf, Lyng went about her work with a new confidence and zeal. She followed the schedule she had made for herself almost to the letter. If for one reason or another she was prevented from finishing something she had planned to do, she either worked later that night or set her alarm clock to ring a little earlier the following morning. She had made her own decision of what her lifework should be and she meant to prepare herself for it intelligently and thoroughly. In fact, everything she undertook, at home or at school, had some bearing on reaching her ultimate goal of becoming a good teacher like Miss Scherf. This was especially true in preparing her assignments in rhetoric. Because of the Norwegian spoken in her home, her speech needed considerable correcting. She listened carefully to the way the professors pronounced difficult words, Miss Scherf most of all, and spent hours trying to imitate them. She also regarded Miss Scherf as a criterion of manners and dress. In fact she considered Miss Scherf as her ideal in everything.

Lyng's grades at the university improved steadily. At the close of the first semester of her senior year she brought home *Excellents* in all her subjects, and even her mother was impressed.

"Markus couldn't have done better," she said. "Those professors at the university will have at least one student for whom they will have no trouble finding a position. I hope you have impressed on them that you are Norwegian. I like to show those Yankees what we Norwegians can do over here in America."

Lyng made no comment but she was secretly pleased, since praise from her mother was so rare. And since she knew that she ranked high in scholarship at the university, Lyng felt confident that she would be a good teacher. Without the slightest trace of the old feeling of inferiority, she went to the office of the Placement Bureau at the university. She told the secretary that she was a candidate for a teaching position, and would like her name placed on file for the coming year. Her professors had said they would send in recommendations. Lyng filled out a questionnaire, and was told that notices would be put in her post-office box at school.

By the middle of April several of the girls Lyng knew had received notices, and Lyng wondered why none had been sent to her. The first of May came and the long-awaited slip had failed to appear. Lyng made no mention of her disappointment to the family because each day she felt sure that the following one would bring something exciting to take home to them. When the fifteenth of May arrived and she had still no word, she decided to report the omission. If the Placement Bureau was waiting for something extra good for her, she could be diplomatic enough about stating her errand so that she would not seem to be hurrying them. If there had been a mistake, there could be no harm in calling their attention to it.

Lyng gave her name to the secretary at the office, and she seemed to have no difficulty remembering her.

"Oh yes," the secretary said, "you are the one we have been wondering what to do about." She was a tall angular person with a general appearance of grayness from her stringy hair down to her heavy cotton stockings. "There doesn't seem any chance of our being able to do much for you."

Lyng was so stunned at this unexpected news that she could only stand staring.

"You lack any extra-curricular activities," the secretary went on. "According to the answers on your questionnaire, you don't sing or play a musical instrument. You haven't participated in athletics. You have had no instruction or experience in debate, oratory or dramatic art. You have had no training to fit you for leadership in school or community projects. And you haven't traveled." The secretary recited this information to Lyng like a lesson she had taken pains to memorize.

"I forgot to mention in my questionnaire that I had helped to put out our high school paper."

"Were you the editor?"

"No."

"Then it can't be counted. Our approved extracurricular activities list only editors."

Lyng swallowed hard. "But I only wanted to teach English," she faltered.

The secretary shrugged her shoulders. "The actual classroom teaching is of minor consideration for a position. You ought to know that. In the larger and better schools—in towns of a thousand or more—we receive inquiries about a teacher's ability to handle classroom work, because in these places she isn't expected to do anything else. But the larger schools also want an all-round person who will be a credit to the community. So it would be a waste of our time to recommend you to these."

"But my grades—"

"I have already reminded you that they are factors of minor importance. And now I'll have to ask you to excuse me. I have to prepare a report on one of our teaching candidates, and I have promised to send it at once to the superintendent of schools in St. Cloud."

Lyng walked out of Folwell Hall in a daze. What should she do? What would her mother and Grandmother Skoglund think? The bad news would shock Tante Gunara and Tante Tallette, too. Lyng started down the sidewalk by the Physics Building and crossed the street over to the School of Mines and on past the Pathology and the Dentistry Buildings. Then in the middle of the bridge over the railroad tracks, she stopped. She couldn't go home in this frame of mind. Her mother would blame her for having been neglectful in not investigating the requirements for teaching more thoroughly and Grandmother Skoglund would suffer needless worry in her sympathy for Lyng.

She turned around and walked back slowly over the university campus. There was no one near the Pillsbury monument and she went over and sat down on the stone bench below it.

Perhaps she should have talked the matter over with Miss Scherf and found out about all these extra-curricular activities required of a teacher. But she had done all she could to maintain a high standard of scholarship and help with the work at home. If she had attempted anything more, she would have failed in the two most important things. No, it was useless to have any regrets over what couldn't be helped. She must concentrate instead on what to do now.

It would be best for the present not to mention the bad news she had received to anyone. Until school closed the family wouldn't expect her to have secured a position. If she was no closer to having one by that time, she would try to take definite steps.

But although Lyng tried to remain optimistic, she worried. Her silence at meals and her lack of appetite did not escape the sharp notice of Grandmother Skoglund.

"You go at things too hard, *Vesla-mi*," she told Lyng. "Remember that there will be days after both you and I are gone."

In spite of Lyng's protests, Grandmother Skoglund did the entire housecleaning during the month of May all by herself.

"Do you think I would let you graduate from the university with the house as dirty as it is after the soot and smoke of the winter?" she demanded.

"But the graduation exercises will take place on the university campus," Lyng said.

"I've never known a fine-feathered bird to have flown from a filthy nest," Grandmother Skoglund told her. "I can always smell from the clothes of a person what kind of a home he comes from, no matter how fine he may try to make himself look. Besides, I have invited Gunara and Tallette to come over for a bit after the exercises, and I don't want the girls to think their mother is getting so old she can't keep up with them."

"Grandmother Skoglund, you are hopeless," Lyng laughed.

Lyng's mother, too, was busy preparing for the great event. She made a black taffeta suit for herself out of an evening gown she had bought from one of the customers of the shop, and the result was astounding. No lady with a fortune at her command could have looked smarter than Lyng's mother did after it was finished. Her mother also made a summer coat for Grandmother Skoglund from material she brought home from the shop, and a pretty black-and-white mercerized print dress was a present from Tante Gunara and Tante Tallette. Lyng's mother wanted to sew a dress for Lyng, but she refused this offer at once.

"You have more than enough to do as it is," Lyng said. "And I've already made plans for what I shall wear at the graduation exercises—a plain white, ready-made cotton skirt and one of my white shirtwaists. They won't show much under my gown anyway."

"I hope the university isn't making an old maid of you," Lyng's mother sighed.

At last the day of Lyng's graduation arrived, and the morning was cool but clear. Grandmother Skoglund came out of her room all ready for the celebration. Her starched petticoats rustled under her mercerized black-and-white dress and there was the slightest suggestion of a squeak from her new oxfords. Her fine white hair lay in soft ringlets around her face.

"You look positively beautiful," Lyng said, leaning down and kissing her.

Grandmother Skoglund beamed. "I do feel dressed up," she admitted.

The three of them, Lyng and her mother and Grandmother Skoglund, started out in good time for the commencement exercises. They boarded the streetcar on Riverside Avenue and changed for the Interurban on Seven Corners. Grandmother Skoglund pressed her face against the window as the streetcar crossed the Washington Avenue Bridge.

"You Tom Lowry, you Tom Lowry! What a man you were," Grandmother Skoglund exclaimed. "Crisscrossing the city with steel lines and sending cars over them without the help of horses or steam engines—way out to Lake Minnetonka and on the water itself, and now over the mighty Mississippi on this high bridge!"

On the campus, groups of cap-and-gowned men and women were already assembled in front of various buildings.

"It looks like they're going to have several graduations here today," Grandmother Skoglund remarked wonderingly. "I didn't know there were so many big schools so close together."

"All this is the campus of the University of Minnesota," Lyng explained to her. "These are students from the various departments who are assembling and will later join the main line of march."

"You mean that for four years you have been going into all these buildings?" Grandmother Skoglund asked.

"Oh, no. Not all of them. Most of my classes were in that long narrow building over there called Folwell Hall, but I worked a lot in the white building which houses the main library. And I had classes in a few of the others."

"No wonder the Americans put out great people, sending them to such gigantic institutions!" Grandmother Skoglund exclaimed. In the distance, the band was playing the *Star Spangled Banner*. Tears rolled down Grandmother Skoglund's cheeks. "It is all too beautiful," she said. "If only Markus could be with us today, how proud he would have been." Suddenly she dried her tears, and a worried expression appeared on her face. "Do you suppose we'll ever find Gunara and Tallette in this huge place?"

"Oh, yes," Lyng assured her. "They are going directly to

the Armory where the exercises are being held. We made arrangements that whoever gets there first would save seats for the others. Hattie is coming with them. She and Clifford live only two blocks from their place since he has been working in the Ramsey County Clerk's office. You remember Clifford Best, don't you, Grandmother Skoglund? He and Hattie went together all through high school and were married almost two years ago. Hattie's mother went over to St. Paul yesterday and brought the baby back with her so Hattie could come today. But we'd better get started ourselves. Seats can't be saved too long, and I'll have to join my class and be ready to march."

After Lyng had taken her place in the line formed in front of the Library, she felt happier than she had for months. She was one of these fortunate people assembled here on the campus to receive a degree from this mighty institution. She had worked faithfully for the degree and no one could take it away from her. Maybe those extra-curricular activities which the secretary had stressed as so important would make it difficult for her to secure a position at first. But she would hound that secretary so hard and so consistently that in sheer self-defense, she would have to get her something. Once she had a chance to teach, she would make good. She'd see to that.

The line started to move. On the corner, outside the School of Mines, it was joined by another line. As it advanced across the campus, it grew longer and longer. Then the faculty and distinguished guests in black academic robes and brilliantly colored hoods took their places at the head of the procession. The band was playing *Hail Minnesota* as Lyng and her partner passed through the entrance to the Armory. The immense structure was crowded, with people standing along the walls.

As Lyng sat surrounded by hundreds of students who were graduating with her, she thought how silly she had been to let her fear of failing to get a job blur her appreciation of the privilege of getting an education. How happy and proud Grandmother Skoglund was today, basking in the reflected glory of her achievement. Even her mother, who certainly did not admire most things American, had the good sense to know the value of a degree from the University of Minnesota. Well, she was through with being a baby, allowing herself to sink into a mire of self-pity.

After the ceremonies were over, Lyng found her mother and Grandmother Skoglund and her aunts and Hattie waiting for her outside the Armory.

Hattie put her arms around Lyng and kissed her. "I was so proud of being your friend, Lyng, when I saw you marching into the Armory that I could have squealed."

Grandmother Skoglund asked at once to be allowed to read what was printed on Lyng's diploma. Lyng untied the maroon and gold bow and unrolled the parchment. Grandmother Skoglund held it in both hands.

"I was right," she said, giving it back to Lyng.

"About what, Grandmother Skoglund?"

"That the president himself signed it. Your mother said she didn't think he would have time, there being so many young people graduating."

Lyng smiled. "It wouldn't have been legal otherwise."

"It must be grand to be carrying around in your head all you've learned over here," Hattie said. "But then I'd never have had the stamina to keep at the grind for four long years. Our family always does things that bring immediate results."

"Let's go home," Lyng's mother suggested. "We can talk there."

"I'll have to go now," Hattie said. "Clifford's coming home early from the office tonight and I promised him a chicken dinner. I do want to wish you lots of luck, Lyng, and I hope you get a perfectly grand teaching job. Only don't be too hard on your students. Most people aren't as smart as you."

"Thanks, Hattie," Lyng said, laughing. "I won't."

Lyng's mother had started down the walk.

Grandmother Skoglund hesitated. "If—if it wouldn't be asking too much, do you suppose anyone would mind, if I could see just one more of the buildings over here? They do look so beautiful."

"Of course not," Lyng said. "It didn't occur to me that you would care to. I've been coming here for four years and I take it for granted. I think you should be interested most in Shevlin Hall. That building is just for girls to rest in and enjoy themselves and even to eat their lunches there."

"I'd love to see that," Tante Tallette said. "Imagine having a building for just that."

The bridal wreath was in full bloom and there were luxuriant clusters of it bordering both sides of the walk. When the five of them reached the east entrance, Grandmother Skoglund turned back and gazed at the white bushes admiringly.

"The Americans are so richly blessed with everything," she said.

She was even more impressed with the large living room in the center of Shevlin Hall. "Who'd ever think of putting a balcony in a living room?" she exclaimed. "And what elegant upholstered furniture! No wonder things are turning out so fine for you, Lyng, going four years to such a wonderful school. I think I'll take this chair over by the window. Then I can enjoy all the beauty, both inside and outside, at the same time." As she sat down, a look of surprise came over her face. "Why, Lyng," she asked, "are they really so backward here that they still have fireplaces? Even in Rendalen in Norway they heat with stoves these days. I should think a place like this would have central heating, as we have in our church and Gunara and Tallette have in their rooming house over in St. Paul."

"It's only another of the inconsistencies of the Americans,"

Lyng's mother said. "They do have central heating here. But they have a fireplace for decoration."

"Think of all the wood and ashes they have to carry for such a big one," Grandmother Skoglund sighed.

"I'm sure this is the proudest day of Mother's life," Tante Tallette told Lyng in an aside.

A fresh wave of anxiety took possession of Lyng. If the family knew what the secretary of the Placement Bureau had said, would they have the same feeling of pride? The very first thing in the morning, she would go to the office and let the secretary know in no uncertain terms that she expected the Placement Bureau to help her secure a position. She had as much a right to this service as a student with a whole list of extra-curricular activities opposite her name.

As soon as the family arrived home, Grandmother Skoglund put on her Hardanger embroidered apron and, with Lyng's help, set the food she had already prepared on the table. There was fresh homemade rye bread with hard-boiled eggs and anchovies, cream pudding that only had to be re-heated, cold waffles covered with raspberry jam that had been saved from last year's canning for the occasion, tiny cakes that Grandmother Skoglund usually baked only for Christmas, and, of course, cups and cups of steaming coffee.

"I wanted to clear out the parlor for the day and give a nice party," Lyng's mother apologized to Tante Gunara and Tante Tallette, "but Lyng wouldn't hear of it. She said it would make too much work, and you two were the only ones she cared to have come anyway. I can see how she is taking on already the casual attitude toward life that is so American. Why, in Norway, if Father did nothing more than take a trip down to Kristiania, we gave a party on his arrival home that continued for several days. Everything was so festive there."

"Wait until Lyng finds herself a husband up in the town

where she is going to teach," Grandmother Skoglund said. "Then we'll celebrate for a week."

Lyng wet her dry lips with more coffee.

When the meal was almost over, Grandmother Skoglund disappeared into the pantry. She returned carrying a layer cake with four tall candles burning on top of it.

"You don't mean to say you have taken up American baking?" Tante Tallette exclaimed.

Lyng read the letters that circled the rim of the cake. They spelled the words, "Lyng Skoglund, Bachelor of Arts."

"Why, Grandmother Skoglund, how did you know?" Lyng exclaimed.

Grandmother Skoglund's eyes twinkled. "Some of the rest of us have been getting a few crumbs of this Yankee education, too, you see. I saw by your diploma that I got it all right. I had an excuse all ready so I could look at it and make sure."

One of the candles stood in the center of the letter "F," another in an "S," still another in "J," and the fourth candle in another "S." "That must stand for Freshman, Sophomore, Junior, and Senior," Lyng said. "How ever did you think of doing all this?"

"I hoped you would understand," Grandmother Skoglund beamed. "And I want you to know that the pins holding the candles on the cake are perfectly clean. I took one of your long hatpins, Reidun, down to the blacksmith shop on Ninth Street, and I had the blacksmith cut it into four pieces and file off both ends to a sharp point. Then I boiled the pins for an hour before I stuck them into the cake."

Lyng's mother gave Lyng a small package. It contained a silver teaspoon. On the end of the handle was a replica in miniature of the statue in Loring Park of Norway's great violinist, Ole Bull. In the bowl of the spoon were carved his name and the dates when he lived, 1810-1880. "Hans Englestad had many of them made for the Seventeenth of May celebration last year," Lyng's mother explained. "He had a few left, so I got this one real cheap. I thought it would be so nice for Lyng to have something Norwegian in her hope chest."

"It's pretty," Lyng said, trying to hide her indifference. Why had her mother been so insistent on her preparing herself to make a good living by attending the university, if she had her mind set on an early marriage for her? If only her mother had been practical enough to buy something she could use now. She could think of a hundred things she needed.

"Gunara, have you told Lyng about the present we bought for her?" Tante Tallette asked.

"No, you do it. You picked it out."

"We got a suitcase for you, Lyng," Tante Tallette said. "A substantial one, but not too heavy. We thought it would come in handy when you leave for your teaching job next fall."

"How thoughtful of you!" Lyng exclaimed. "I have been wondering how I would take my possessions along with me. Not that I have many. But one needs something."

"We would have brought it over today except that it would have been a nuisance lugging it all morning over at the university," Tante Gunara said.

"Tell her about the trunk," Tante Tallette said.

"Oh, that isn't really a present. One of our roomers who was going away was behind with his rent, so he left us his trunk. Later on he planned to move to Alaska, and he didn't want to be bothered with it. He came over and took the things he wanted, and we were stuck with the trunk. Tallette has scrubbed and aired it. While it isn't elegant, it is sturdy and will give you good service. And the lock is good."

"I'm sure Lyng will appreciate that," Grandmother Skoglund said. "And now I'm going to cook a fresh pot of coffee and we'll all have another cup."

"You can see now, Lyng," her mother remarked, "how nice it would have been to retire to the parlor for that."

"I like the kitchen better than any room in this house," Tante Gunara said emphatically.

After Tante Gunara and Tante Tallette were gone, Grandmother Skoglund stifled a yawn. "I don't believe I have ever been so tired," she said sheepishly. "But then I've never been so happy either. Not even the day Markus was born."

The following morning Lyng set out for the university. When she arrived at the office of the Placement Bureau, she found the secretary alone. She was wearing the same gray outfit, and her straight hair, damp from sweat, looked more stringy than ever.

"I came to find out what you are doing about securing a position for me," Lyng said.

"We have nothing for you," the secretary replied.

"I have the right to be given the opportunity to apply for one, just as much as any of the others," Lyng said.

"That may be. But it would be useless for us to have you apply for a position which we knew, beforehand, you wouldn't stand a chance of getting. We had a call for a teacher this morning, but we recommended someone else for the position."

"I'll be back tomorrow," Lyng said curtly and left.

The next morning she started out earlier from home, but this time too the secretary told her that the openings which had come in were already given out to others. Lyng received similar responses to her inquiries for two more days. On the third morning she stood outside the locked door of the office of the Placement Bureau waiting for the secretary to arrive.

"This is getting to be a little too much," the secretary said, as soon as she saw Lyng. Both her voice and her manner were angry.

"That is exactly what I am beginning to think," Lyng said. "And since it is impossible for you to have checked over the notices this morning, I am asking you to describe them to me and let me be the judge of whether I am equipped to apply for one of them."

The secretary, who went through the mail while Lyng stood close by, finally looked up and said, "Here is a position for which you might apply." She handed Lyng a letter written in long hand. It was a request for someone to teach high school subjects in a town called New Stavanger. The salary was fifty-five dollars a month for a nine-month term.

"You see that a girl of Scandinavian heritage is preferred," the secretary said. "It's the only position that's come in so far that I think you would have a chance of getting."

"I see there is no mention made of extra-curricular activities, if that is what you mean," Lyng said.

The secretary's face became a deep red. "Do you want to apply for it or not?" she asked.

"I'll apply right away," Lyng said, "although I had certainly expected something better. I have never even heard of this town before."

The secretary consulted a map. "It's in the northwestern part of the state," she said. "The population is listed as six hundred."

"Next year, after I've had experience, I'll be back here for a real position."

Lyng wrote to New Stavanger that afternoon, and, a week later, in a long white envelope, came a contract to teach there the following year. Lyng received it with mixed emotions. She did not look forward to spending nine months in such a small and obviously uninteresting town, and she had hoped to be placed in a community that did not have a predominantly Scandinavian population. But it was a position, and she would be making her living. Moreover, students in a small town needed a good teacher as much and perhaps more than those with the advantages of a large city. And she would do her best. Perhaps in another year, she might hope to secure a really good position.

To Lyng's surprise, both her mother and Grandmother Skoglund were much pleased over her contract.

"In a town that size, you will be the queen of all the social affairs of the season," her mother said. "And with twenty working days a month at the salary they are offering you, you will be earning two and a half dollars a day. That is two and a half times as much as you would have been getting at the Emporium now. Aren't you glad I insisted on your attending the university?"

"But I'll be staying away from home and will be having expenses that I wouldn't have had at the Emporium."

"A bird never learned to fly staying in the nest," Grandmother Skoglund said drily. Then she put her hand on Lyng's shoulder. "To think, *Vesla-mi*, you are the first member of our family to be holding the high position of a teacher. What a milestone this would have been in Markus' life!"

"The people in New Stavanger must be lovely," Lyng's mother went on. "The very name of New Stavanger shows that they are Norwegian. And to think they frown on dancing and cardplaying and liquor so much that they make mention of it in your contract. Lyng, if I had chosen the position for you myself, I couldn't have found one that met more completely with my approval."

CHAPTER SIX

EVERY HOUR during the night, Lyng struck matches to see what time it was. The wait from dark to dawn seemed endless. Finally the sun pushed through the heavy crocheted lace curtains and feebly struck the glass over a framed picture of the royal palace of Norway.

"This is the day," Lyng said aloud.

She heaved the piece quilt to the foot of the bed and from force of habit, went over to shut the window. Then she stopped. Only a narrow slit in the lower frame of the storm window was letting in air. The landlady, Mrs. Swenson, must already have sealed up the house for the winter, just like the people in Rendalen that Grandmother Skoglund told about. she said that after they had taken out the fireplaces and replaced them with modern stoves, they plugged up the chimneys that had been their only means of ventilation during the cold winter. Grandmother Skoglund said that people in those parts were never so robust after that, and there was a lot of tuberculosis among them.

Lyng poured water out of the gray granite-ware pitcher, into the gray granite-ware washbowl and shuddered. At home she always took the chill out of her bath water with a dipperful that had been heated in the reservoir built into the back of the kitchen stove. She wished now she had done the same for the roomers. It must have been uncomfortable for them washing in cold water those bitter winter mornings in Minneapolis. After a good rubdown, Lyng hurried to put on her clothes.

The kid curlers left her hair one mass of tight curls. She combed and brushed it hard and pulled it back tight to make her look like a schoolteacher. The Dean of Women at the university stressed the importance of first impression to the girls. "Remember," she told them, "once you let the bars down, you might as well pack up and leave."

Lyng pinned a stray lock severely above her left ear. She wasn't leaving. Not until she had made good at this job of hers. If she had had her own way, she wouldn't have chosen New Stavanger with its solid Norwegian population. But now that she was here, she'd do her best to be a good teacher.

She pulled her bed out to get at her clothes hanging on the wall behind it. At home she at least had a closet. Impatiently she pushed aside the heavy, crocheted covering that matched the curtains and the bedspread. Three rows of nails driven into the wainscoting held her clothes hangers. She noticed that her two best dresses, the black crepe and the royal blue woolen one, touched the floor. She took them down and hung them on the curtain rod above the window. No wonder she had felt as though she were smothering last night. She'd like to give the ceiling a good punch that would send it up a foot or two.

But what was the use of grumbling over things which couldn't be changed? She had better get on with her dressing. She had made up her mind and changed it a dozen times about what to wear at school today. She was tempted to put on her frilly pink batiste. Winter would be coming on soon up in this country. Mrs. Swenson had already had tar paper tacked around the foundation of her house and manure packed tight up against that in order, she said, to prevent the strong wind from blowing up under the floors. There probably wouldn't be many days this fall warm enough to come out in a cotton dress. Still she had better stick to her first choice. The Dean of Women recommended tailored clothes for teaching, and no one could look nicer than Miss Scherf did in hers. She would splurge with the silver cuff links that her mother had given her father during their courting days over in Norway.

Sitting on the slippery leather seat of the straight-back chair, the only one in the room, Lyng tried to button her black leather boots. The chair was high and her feet didn't touch the floor. She moved the chair over to the bed and braced her feet against its side board.

To save time she decided to wear her suit jacket to breakfast. Then she could go straight on to school without returning to her room. A fresh white handkerchief in the breast pocket and she'd be all set. When she tried to pull out the little top drawer of the bureau where she kept her handkerchiefs, it stuck, and an extra hard jerk sent the whole bureau lurching toward her. After she had recovered from her sudden fright, she managed to get it back on its four legs without further mishap. Nevertheless, she gave up the idea of the clean handkerchief. The least soiled one in her purse would have to do.

She wished there was a mirror long enough for her to see whether her gray, embroidered, featherbloom petticoat showed. If it didn't, people hearing it rustle would take it for taffeta. The mirror above the bureau was so high that she could see only her head and shoulders in it. When she stood upon the chair, it helped, but not enough. She tried tilting the mirror forward. Still the lower part of her skirt didn't show up in it. Then she lifted the chair onto the bed and climbed up. Not only could she see that her petticoat didn't show but she also found out that the seams in the backs of her gray lisle stockings were straight. She pivoted on the chair to get an all-around view of herself. Suddenly she felt the chair wobble. The next she knew, she was sprawling on the floor with the chair, upside down, on top of her.

"What in the world are you doing?" Mrs. Swenson stood in the doorway, scowling.

"I—I slipped," Lyng stammered, trying her best to disentangle herself.

"I should think you did. It sounded like the whole house was coming down. I hope you didn't break anything. I forgot to tell you last night, when we talked about the board and room money, that I always collect any damages that my roomers do to the house and furniture."

She walked across the room and examined the chair and the spot on the floor where Lyng had fallen.

"Well, Miss Skoglund, I guess you got out of it easy this time," she said reluctantly. "That scratch on the leather seat of the chair was there when you came. Miss McCrea did it last year and she paid for it. But you had better be careful after this."

Lyng began to make her bed.

"When I told you about making your bed, I should have mentioned that I want it to be left open to air until noon," Mrs. Swenson said.

Lyng bit her lip, but she dropped the sheet and went over to the bureau to rearrange the things that had been jolted out of place when it lurched forward.

"Breakfast is almost ready. When you've finished in here, go into the parlor and wait for me to call you. My corns have been hurting me lately and I don't want to have to do any more walking than is absolutely necessary."

It was cool and clammy in the parlor. In front of the single side window stood a massive library table with huge, claw-like legs. On top of this was arranged a collection of large photographs, some of them in frames. Over these a bouquet of dried hydrangeas in a tall vase spread like an umbrella. An organ, extending from floor to ceiling, completely filled one corner of the room between the side window and the double front one. On the organ there were more photographs and hydrangeas. Wherever Lyng looked on the walls, she saw photographs in highly polished wooden frames. Mrs. Swenson must have a lot of relatives and friends.

Mrs. Swenson was taking a long time, considering she had said breakfast was almost ready. Lyng moved into the easy chair near the kitchen door. She could hear Mrs. Swenson moving about. She looked down at the carpet and started to work out the puzzle of the pattern. Two full-brown pink roses and three sprays of bright green leaves, repeated over a maroon background.

A whiff of coffee filtered into the parlor. "I wish she'd hurry," Lyng said under her breath.

She traced the pattern of the crocheted doilies on the arm of the easy chair—a cat chasing a mouse. She figured out the clover design of the hit-or-miss wool afghan on the black leather couch. If Mrs. Swenson didn't call soon, she'd leave without any breakfast. She had started on the small doilies on the organ when the kitchen door opened and Mrs. Swenson came into the parlor. Lyng felt embarrassed again.

"I see you're one of those early birds," Mrs. Swenson said. There was no trace of sharpness left in her voice. "But I might have known, you being Norwegian. I told Professor Lokensgaard last summer not to send me any more of those Yankee or Irish schoolteachers. I've kept that kind for years now, and every last one of them has been a sleepy head. Miss McCrea—that's the girl I had last year—had all she could do to get to school in time for the first bell. But then, she had a fellow right from the start and she stayed up until all hours of the night. I never saw anyone so foolish. The minute she had swallowed her supper, she went into the bedroom and started primping up for him. She'd stand in front of the mirror for hours. At last I got so sick of it that I hung the mirror high so she couldn't see herself in it. Then she bought one of her own and kept it standing on the floor. I told her what I thought about such goings-on. That once a week was plenty for a girl to primp up and go out with fellows. But she was stubborn as a mule and kept right on. Well, she's married to him now, so I guess she sees plenty of him. And I wouldn't be a bit surprised either but that her primping days are over."

Lyng stood up. She was in no mood for an argument with Mrs. Swenson. Her one concern was to get to school as soon as possible.

"It seems to me a teacher ought to have enough to do," Mrs. Swenson went on, "without wasting her time with fellows."

Lyng wondered how she got to be Mrs. Swenson, but she probably hadn't ever been a schoolteacher. That seemed to make a difference.

"Well, come into the kitchen. Breakfast is ready."

It was a relief to be in the kitchen. Nothing shut out the light from the two windows and Lyng was able to look out on a green and not unattractive back yard.

"Sit down," Mrs. Swenson said. "I'll dish up the oatmeal and pour the coffee. I hope you like oatmeal. I always have it for breakfast—the old-fashioned, rolled-oat kind. That and a sliver of Norwegian goat cheese on homemade rye bread starts the day right for me winter and summer."

Lyng did her best with the oatmeal, but it stuck in her throat and she had a hard time getting it down. She was grateful for the piping hot coffee. The rye bread and goat cheese she decided not to try.

"I see you wear white, starched shirtwaists," Mrs. Swenson observed tartly. "As I told you, your laundry is included in your board and room money. But if you have many such fancy things to wash and iron, I'll have to ask you to do them yourself and charge you for the soap."

"That's all right," Lyng said, feeling uncomfortable again.

"I usually get up at four o'clock on Monday morning to wash clothes. I put them to soak right after dinner Sunday noon, so be sure to have your dirty things picked together by that time. In the thirty years we've been neighbors, I've had my clothes on the line ahead of Mrs. Fjoslien every Monday morning so far. Besides, I like to take them down from the line early enough so I can fold the flat pieces and run them over with the iron and sprinkle and cold-starch the rest that same afternoon. Or at least, before I go to bed that night, if it has been a bad drying day. And every Tuesday morning I iron."

"I'll have my clothes ready for you," Lyng said.

"By the way, I noticed you had some of those newfangled hobble skirts hanging on your wall. I wouldn't wear them here, if I was you. The school board wouldn't like it."

"But—they're in style," Lyng faltered.

"I know. In big cities you can expect most anything. And I wouldn't say but that there are girls here in New Stavanger —I wouldn't exactly call them fast, but girls who don't care what people think about them—they are wearing them, I've noticed. But with the teachers, it's different. They have to be more careful."

Lyng gulped down the rest of her coffee and asked to be excused.

Out on the street she passed four houses almost exactly like Mrs. Swenson's. They had glassed-in porches across the front and the storm windows were already up. Like Mrs. Swenson's, they had tar paper tacked around their foundations and manure packed up high against the tar paper. Faded hydrangea bushes and scraggly evergreens drooped down on the browning lawns. On the narrow strip of shaggy grass between

the main sidewalk and the dry ditch into which the street
sloped, elms and box elders had dropped little piles of yellow
leaves. A gust of wind sent these over the walk and into the
ditch, and a few were caught up in the cloud of dust that
rose above the sandy street.

Down toward the railroad tracks the houses grew smaller
and shabbier. Behind the houses, Lyng caught glimpses of
what must be the parched remains of summer vegetable gardens.

Main Street started just on the other side of the tracks.
Lyng was amazed at the squatty buildings, almost devoid of
paint, that lined both sides of it. Only three looked like anything at all. These were two-story brick structures with plate
glass windows on which she read: FIRST NATIONAL BANK, FIRST
STATE BANK, PEOPLE'S STATE BANK. The town must be pros-
perous in spite of its shabbiness to be able to support three
banks.

In the distance, Lyng caught a glimpse of the wooden
cupola of the school building and the huge iron bell hanging
up there. Because of the high wooden fence, she couldn't see
the rest of the building until she came up to the front gate.
In her eagerness to get inside, she started on a run down the
walk leading to the main entrance. She tripped on a loose
board and after that she picked her way more carefully.

The front door was locked. She rapped, but there was no
answer. Then she shook the door and rattled the door knob.
Still no one came to open the door for her. She pounded on
it with both fists, but she got no better result. Then she
banged on it as hard as she could. Suddenly it was pushed out
by someone in the building, sending her backwards. After
she had regained her balance, she saw a man standing in the
doorway, blocking it completely. He was short and thin and
wore blue overalls and a black sateen shirt that was open at
the neck. His head was almost entirely bald, and a heavy

growth of gray stubble covered his shrunken cheeks and his receding chin.

"I am Miss Skoglund," Lyng told him. "I am going to teach here in the high school this year."

"Miss Skoglund." The man's face brightened. "So you are the Norwegian girl that we've heard so much about. It was time they got someone but stuck-up Yankees and happy-go-lucky Irish teachers for our boys and girls."

He stood aside for her to come in.

"I'm sure that I'm going to enjoy my work here in New Stavanger," Lyng said, moving toward a stairway that seemed to lead to the first floor.

"I tell my wife that I'd go crazy penned up with thirty-five or forty of the kind of kids there are in this town, all in one room, day in and day out. We've got two at home, and that's plenty, though I will say they're better than most. My boy Bennie lost his wife last winter and he was left with two little ones—a girl of eight and a boy of six. He works on the section here in town and he's often out all hours, so it was up to Kirsti and me to take the children. Don't think we weren't glad to do it because we wouldn't trust them to anyone else. Only we aren't as young as we were when we had our own ten around us, and then it was different bringing up children over in Norway."

He picked up a broom and, holding it with both gnarled hands, rested his chin on them.

"I'm afraid I must go. Would you tell me where to find my room?" she asked. "The high school and the grades are in the same building, aren't they?"

The man chuckled. "Oh, yes, we haven't gotten so Yankee-fied yet that we need two separate buildings. People kick about the high taxes as it is."

"I ought to get started and—"

"Sure, sure. Your room is the one to your right upstairs.

But wait—I'll lock the door and come up with you. We always keep this door locked until the first bell rings so the kids won't get in and break things. The teachers go around to the back."

"Thank you, Mr.—"

"My name is Bakken," he said as he came up beside her. "Ole Bakken. I'm the janitor here. But just call me Ole. Everyone in town does."

"Thank you, Ole," Lyng said smiling.

As she walked up the creaking stairs, she was greeted by the familiar smell of chalk and sweeping compound. But now there was something new and exciting about them both. It was queer how even smells could seem entirely different when you were a teacher instead of a student.

"Is this my room?" Lyng asked, turning toward an open door on her right.

"Yes. And if there's anything you need, just let me know. I'm usually down in the basement. If I'm not, tell Marius. He's my youngest son who works with me."

Lyng went into the room and closed the door hastily. It was too bad to have to be so short with Ole, but if she let him in, it was hard telling how long she would be held up. Before she met Mr. Lokensgaard, the superintendent, she wanted to look about a little. She had learned how important it was to know as much about her job as possible when she dealt with Mr. Cotton at the Emporium.

Lyng was surprised to find that her desk was nothing but an ordinary kitchen table with a kitchen chair drawn up to it. Neither showed the slightest trace of either the paint or varnish that must at some time have covered it. At the back of the room, the morning sun filtered in through grimy windows, showing up the dark, oil-stained floor and the greenish-brown, black-streaked walls and ceiling. From the center of the ceiling hung a massive brass chain to which a kerosene lamp was attached. The brass base was tarnished, the glass was missing, and there was a wide crack in the white china shade, which was decorated with blue lilies and long green leaves. At the back of the room a clumsy pedestal, holding a huge chipped globe of the world, filled one corner between the windows and the students' seats. Her first impression of her high school room was not inspiring, but, after all, it was the quality of the teacher and the students which counted.

She went over to the side blackboard to examine what was fastened to the woodwork above it. She pulled the cord that was hanging from it and a map of Africa came down. It was badly discolored and even the black lines were dim and not easy to follow. She tried another cord and this one brought down a map of the United States. Arizona and New Mexico were designated as Territories although they had just been admitted as states. She'd certainly have to order a new set of maps. She rolled the maps up again and as she did, she noticed the clock hanging on the wall above them. The clock had an octagonal frame and circling its face in metal letters were the words, "Compliments of the Amundsen Lumber Company." The clock had stopped at twenty-three minutes after four. Even time stood still in New Stavanger.

The teacher's closet was empty except for a green felt hat trimmed with faded purple pansies, and a limp, shapeless, coverall, pink apron. These must have been left there by her predecessor, Miss McCrea. If they were at all indicative of the rest of her wardrobe, Lyng felt she could easily compete with Miss McCrea in appearance.

Lyng went back to the kitchen table, which she would think of as her desk until something better could be provided. If by accident she let slip a slighting remark about it, she might offend someone. Both Miss Scherf and the Dean had emphasized the importance of friendly relationships with the people of the community whenever possible.

A box of chalk had been left standing on her desk. Lyng picked up a long, smooth, white piece with an inviting point and wrote on the front of the board, "Miss Lyng Skoglund, high school teacher, New Stavanger, Minnesota."

But she had better return to the business of inspection or she wouldn't be ready for Mr. Lokensgaard. He should be along any minute now. She sat down in her chair and counted the seats of the students. There were five rows with eight seats to a row. That made forty in all—too many for an ideal class, according to Miss Scherf.

But in spite of the drawbacks, it was going to be fun. She could scarcely wait to put into practice everything she had learned at the university. She got up from her chair and walked to the front row of students' seats. Folding her arms as she had often seen her teachers do and looking straight ahead, she began, "Today, boys and girls—no—Today, class —maybe just students would be better. Today, students, we shall discuss the Brook Farm Experiment. As you all know, many of the greatest literary lights of American history participated in it."

Lyng dropped her arms. She, herself, had never heard of the Brooks Farm Experiment while she was in high school. No use putting on airs. Miss Scherf had warned her students against that.

Perhaps the people in New Stavanger believed in supplying the high school students with books, even though they did not seem to have been generous with the rest of the equipment. The cupboard over by the windows—she hadn't examined it yet. She opened its doors. The cupboard was full of books, arranged in neat rows on the shelves from top to bottom. This was a real find.

The first book she pulled out was a text in American history. It was torn and badly marked up with pencil scribblings. Still holding it, she leaned forward and eagerly scanned the backs of the other books on the shelves. But either the titles had been so rubbed out so she couldn't tell what they were, or there were no titles on the books at all. She took out another book. This was an English grammar and its pages were even more tattered than the American history. She had always loved grammar and had looked forward to teaching it. But as she went over the pages of this text, she realized it was unlike any she had ever seen. There seemed to be no plan to the treatment of the subject. Discussions on words, phrases, clauses, parts of speech and punctuation, sentences and paragraphs, were all jumbled together. And there were pages upon pages of intricate, spider-web figures to illustrate diagraming. It had always seemed a waste of time to try to solve the puzzle of meaningless figures instead of going directly at the business of studying the relationship of one word to another. She looked at the front of the book to see who had put out such a stupid text. The flyleaf was gone.

Lyng drew up her chair and started to go over the collection, book by book. Soon she was rewarded by coming across a copy of Scott's *Ivanhoe*. It was in fairly good condition, and the print, though fine, was clear. Beside it on the shelf, there were nine more. Lyng carried them over to a front seat and stacked them neatly on it. She'd enjoy using these books. In one of her high school literature classes, a boy had drawn a colored picture of Cedric the Saxon's castle on the blackboard, and several girls had dressed up dolls to represent Rebecca and Rowena and Ivanhoe. She'd try such projects with her students here and figure out other means of stimulating their interest. Perhaps she could have them dramatize the most exciting scenes.

After Lyng had discarded most of the other books as unusable, she found eight copies of Emerson's *Essays* and six of Thoreau's *Walden*. The book situation, though far from ideal, might have been worse. With a few additions, she'd manage.

She had just come across a whole shelf of English grammars like the first one she had examined, when there was a knock at the door leading into the hall. That was probably Mr. Lokensgaard, the superintendent.

Lyng jumped up from the chair, spilling the books on the floor. As she turned toward the door, she caught sight of what she had written on the blackboard. She dashed around the room, looking for an eraser. There was none on the ledge under the blackboard nor inside the desk drawer, and none in the teacher's closet. She pulled out more books from the cupboard, throwing them on the floor and running her hand behind those on the shelf. It was only after she had reached the very bottom of the cupboard and had pulled out several books there that she discovered a pile of erasers behind the books still on the shelf. She seized one of the erasers and rushed over to the blackboard, and with one long stroke she wiped out the writing. Then she hurried to open the door.

A middle-aged man stood outside. His gray eyes were slightly above the level of Lyng's and she looked up to meet them. A sparse, graying brown fringe marked his receding hairline and his face was sunburned. His blue shirt, tie, and suit, though not new, were neat and carefully pressed. His worn shoes shone.

"You are Miss Skoglund, I believe," he said. "I am Mr. Lokensgaard. Professor Lokensgaard, they all call me, but you need not use the title unless you care to."

"How do you do." Prepared as Lyng thought she was for this interview, she suddenly felt as though she'd like to run away.

"I see you have found the students' textbooks," Professor Lokensgaard said, glancing at those on the floor.

Lyng blushed. "I was looking and—and—"

"I am afraid you will find them a little worn."

"Yes, I noticed that. Especially the English grammars. But

they're so out of date anyway that we'll probably order new ones right away. And I'm quite sure there won't be enough copies of Scott's *Ivanhoe*. And we ought to change—"

"We do not make changes here in New Stavanger without careful consideration," Professor Lokensgaard said. "So I am afraid, Miss Skoglund, your suggestions will have to wait. Moreover, I promised the school board we would get along with the books we have this year at least."

"But Professor Lokensgaard, those grammars are absolutely outdated. In fact, I don't believe they have ever been much good."

"Miss Skoglund, I ordered those grammars myself, when we first started to have one or two high school subjects a year in our school. They have been used in both the eighth grade and in the high school ever since. I was fortunate enough to buy them from a company that was selling out, so I got a great many of them very reasonably."

"But the high school students will have to take state examinations, Professor Lokensgaard. And those going to college will have to pass entrance examinations, since they come from a small, unaccredited high school like this. With such old-fashioned texts, they won't be able to do either."

"The laws of grammar do not change, Miss Skoglund. Besides, I am afraid you do not understand the situation here in New Stavanger. We aren't worrying about college. The idea of a four-year high school is very new with us."

"You mean you have never had a high school here before? I thought you said—"

Professor Lokensgaard made an impatient gesture. "Of course, we have had a high school. I have been teaching high school subjects for years and I'm still doing it. Miss McCrea had this room last year and there have been others before her. But this is the first year that we hope to have a graduating class."

"I don't understand. Hasn't anyone in New Stavanger graduated from high school?"

"Some of our students went on to our church academies. One or two have gone to nearby towns to get their diplomas. Our taxpayers hesitated to assume the burden of running a full-fledged high school. You have grown up in Minneapolis where conditions are different. With its accumulation of wealth, its schools naturally enjoy many advantages—I might even say luxuries—which would be out of the question for a small community like ours. Some members of the board here were a little doubtful—they were afraid, coming from a large city, you might have advanced ideas. Up to this year, we've always taken our teachers from the neighboring towns. But others of the board, one in particular, thought that since you were Norwegian, it would more than offset this disadvantage. I hope you are not going to disappoint us."

"I came here with the idea of doing my best," Lyng said quietly.

"I am glad to hear you say that," Professor Lokensgaard told her smilingly. "And now that we are on the subject of books, Miss Skoglund, perhaps I should mention another matter. What you said a little while ago brought it to my mind. I have been registering high school students all summer. Oh, like you teachers, I am hired for only the nine months. But I stay here the year around anyway, so I told the board I might as well do it. My wife and I have talked about taking the family on a trip West to visit her folks. But—well—it takes a lot to keep the five of us going. And then," here he lowered his voice, "if we should start traveling around, it might cause talk. People might say they were paying for our trips."

Lyng's eyes opened wide. "How could they, Professor Lokensgaard? You work for your salary, don't you?"

"Of course. But they pay taxes for the upkeep of the school."

"The people in New Stavanger aren't poor, are they?" Lyng asked. "They can't be with three banks in town."

Professor Lokensgaard looked stern. "Miss Skoglund, I am afraid I shall have to ask you not to make any such remarks. I feel they are very generous in hiring an extra high school teacher."

Lyng swallowed what she would have liked to say. Instead, trying hard to look pleasant, she asked, "Wasn't there something else about books you wanted to tell me?"

The smile returned to Professor Lokensgaard's lips. "I was going to say that since the board has to account to the taxpayers for an extra teacher, I have tried to keep other expenses down to a minimum. It has helped a lot to see that only as many students register for a subject as there are textbooks available. So, if it should happen that any of your classes run a little large, I can depend upon you to—well, to adjust matters."

"You mean that if a student wants to take a subject and there aren't enough textbooks to go around, that I am to tell him so and get him to register for something else?" Lyng's voice was trembling by the time she finished, and her cheeks burned.

"There is no reason for you to become indignant. You will simply select another subject for him for which there are plenty of books. Of course, you will have to be on the lookout for the juniors and seniors and give them preference. The state inspector is fussy about requirements for graduation. But, as I have told you, I have been registering students all summer, so there should be only a few cases which you will be called upon to settle."

He turned to go. Then he came back and handed her a

sheaf of papers. "I meant to give you these. They contain everything you will need to know, at least for the present."

Lyng started to read aloud, "Independent School District Number 57—"

"The instructions are on the other side," Professor Lokensgaard interrupted her impatiently. "I made use of some old printed forms I had in my office."

Lyng turned the paper over. It was covered with fine Spencerian handwriting. She started to read aloud once more. "Freshmen: Gudrun Ballerud, Ragnhild Slettebak, Nicoline Fundingsland,—"

Professor Lokensgaard was all smiles. "That is excellent. Several teachers have aroused considerable ill will in the community because of the way they have stumbled over the student's names—sometimes intentionally, I am afraid."

"I have heard them all my life."

"I thought so. That is why we were so pleased when you signed up last spring. I told the board I was sure that you were the kind of a teacher we were looking for."

"I hope I won't disappoint you," Lyng said somewhat doubtfully.

"Oh, you won't," Professor Lokensgaard said confidently. "Once you understand our point of view, you will fit in perfectly." He looked up at the clock.

"It's stopped," Lyng said. "Do you suppose you could— that someone would climb up and start it?"

Professor Lokensgaard didn't seem pleased. "Get Ole to come up or ask one of the older boys in high school to do it for you. I always leave such matters to the teachers. Now I must really be going."

He started toward the door. Then he turned around. "There is another little matter that I ought to bring up. You will remember it was stated in your contract that cardplaying and dancing and drinking are prohibited to teachers in our

system. So it will not be necessary for me to say anything
further about such matters. But as far as possible, I am asking
you to avoid being seen out late on school nights. Especially
in the company of men."

"Why? Are there very bad ones here in New Stavanger?"

Professor Lokensgaard's face grew a deep red. "You don't
seem to understand. What I was trying to tell you was that
our people here have—I might almost call a prejudice—or
rather they have a strong feeling about the morals of our
teachers. Some of them haven't been so careful and—"

"Who? The people?"

"Of course not. The teachers."

Lyng took a step forward. "Now I am afraid it is you who
do not seem to understand. I am of age, and I feel that I can
trust my own judgment as to what is seemly in the conduct
of a teacher in her community."

Professor Lokensgaard began backing toward the door.
"I am sure that I shall not have to say anything more on the
subject," he said. "Nor about leaving town without giving
a proper explanation for your absence. Especially on too
many weekends. I told the board that coming from as far
away as Minneapolis, we wouldn't have to worry about your
being a suitcase teacher."

"Professor Lokensgaard, there are some things that not
even a teacher has to take." Lyng felt dizzy, but she kept following him toward the door. "Either you—"

"Would you mind writing the word 'SAVE' in each corner of the blackboard space where you want the material
left over night?" he asked. "Otherwise, the janitor's son, who
works with him, might not understand."

He made a hasty exit and closed the door. Lyng rushed
over to the other side of the room and started picking up
books from the floor and throwing them pell-mell into the
cupboard. She had never been so angry in her life. Worry

along with textbooks that were nothing but rags and had never been any good in the first place! Keep students from taking subjects they wanted and needed because the school board was too stingy to supply them with texts! Stay in town because the taxpayers might get the idea you were stealing their money! And, worse yet, never look at a man for fear you might be accused of being immoral!

Some of the books fell back on the floor. Blindly, Lyng kept picking them up and throwing them again. They could keep their old books. And their men. And their precious money, too, for all she cared. She'd show them that there was one Norwegian in America who didn't believe in sealing herself up in a little airtight town for the rest of her life, pinching and scrimping and gossiping. She'd write out her resignation here and now and mail it at the postoffice on her way to Mrs. Swenson's. She'd pack her things and take the first train for Minneapolis.

Suddenly she sat down. Where was she going to get the money to buy her railroad ticket to Minneapolis? There was scarcely enough change in her purse to buy postage stamps. Besides, she knew it would be hopeless to try to get another job from the Placement Bureau at the university. And she couldn't go home and expect her mother to support her.

She got up from her chair and went over to the cupboard. She took out the books she had thrown into it, arranged them in orderly rows and picked up the ones on the floor. The English grammars she brought over to a front seat and piled in two neat stacks.

She had been acting like an unreasonable and undisciplined child rather than a sensible and carefully trained teacher. What would Miss Scherf have thought if she had witnessed this silly outburst of anger? Or Grandmother Skoglund? Suppose Grandmother Skoglund had given up and refused to cook good food for the family at home every time she had to plug a hole in their leaking potato kettle? When the wood was too wet to burn, she piled it into the oven to dry out and afterwards swept the oven so it was fit to bake in. After their regular egg beater was past using, she fashioned one out of smoothly whittled and carefully scrubbed sticks tied together with a string.

"Many a mansion has been built with makeshift tools," Grandmother Skoglund would say as she struggled cheerfully with whatever situation confronted her.

CHAPTER SEVEN

Lyng heard footsteps in the students' cloakroom, and three girls came in. They looked at Lyng as though they expected her to say something, but she sat self-conscious and tongue-tied. So they walked toward the back of the room and took seats close together. Lyng picked up the sheaf of papers Professor Lokensgaard had given her, but the fine Spencerian writing had become blurred and she was unable to read it.

Several boys came in. Tall and big-boned, they completely filled the seats, and their long legs and clumsy work shoes spilled over into the aisles. They seemed older than her classmates at the university had been, and yet she was to be their high school teacher. The responsibility was overwhelming. As she looked into their earnest sunburned faces, it seemed to her that they must know exactly what she was thinking. She got up and walked over to the hall door, and then, keeping close to the wall, she made her way toward the back of the room. For a while it was a relief standing where the students couldn't see her without turning around in their seats. But soon she grew fidgety again. Hiding away from them wasn't going to get her anywhere.

Lyng took a deep breath and walked resolutely back to her desk. There she picked up once more the papers Professor Lokensgaard had given her, and this time she was able to read what was written on the top sheet. It contained the complete high school roll—freshmen, sophomores, juniors, and seniors. She passed over these quickly and found the paper with the caption *Teaching Schedule of Miss Skoglund.* According to this, German would be her first class.

She wished now that she had taken her work in German at the university more seriously. She had concentrated only on the written exercises in order to get good marks in the subject. To be a good German teacher it would be necessary to know more than how to write the language. Well, she had better stop worrying about this now and start seating the German class alphabetically. Miss Scherf advocated that. You would learn to know your students more quickly, she said, and it simplified taking the roll.

The last bell rang. Every seat was filled, and Lyng walked up to the front row. "The German class will please come to order," she said.

A red-haired, freckle-faced boy in blue overalls called out, "I take algebra this period."

"Professor Lokensgaard teaches that," someone else volunteered.

"I imagine you will find him in the high school assembly," Lyng told the red-haired boy.

"This is the only high school room," a boy who seemed older than the others said. Lyng had noticed him especially. He wore a green sweater and gray trousers and he had a mop of dark curly hair. "That is, except the small one above the stairs where Professor Lokensgaard has his classes. He is our superintendent and he is in his office the rest of the time."

Why hadn't she found out these details from Professor Lokensgaard before the students arrived? "I took it for granted that all of you had registered for German," she apologized. "But since you haven't, I might as well give you your room seats first. I'll start with the seniors. Bergliot Aasen, will you please take the front seat in the row nearest the hall?"

A wave of disapproval swept through the room. A tall, thin girl with a brown, pin-stripe cotton dress rose from her seat at the back of the room. "Miss Skoglund," she said, "that's wrong. The seniors' seats are nearest the window. We sat there last year because there wasn't any senior class. Miss McCrea told us to take the same seats this year. I was going to take mine when I came in, but Peter Brandvold was in it and he's new." Her voice had gradually risen until it ended in a high falsetto.

Lyng hesitated. The possibility of such a situation hadn't occurred to her. She was sorry to disappoint Bergliot and the other seniors who had been looking forward to occupying a place of honor in the high school room. On the other hand, she and not Miss McCrea was in charge of the room now. It might save considerable trouble later if the students were to realize this.

"I think we will go on with the seating as I planned it," she said gently, yet firmly. "Bergliot, will you please take the seat I have assigned to you?"

Bergliot, carrying a black patent leather purse and a stiff paper folder, moved down the aisle at a snail's pace. She looked angry and hurt, and when she reached the seat she slumped hard down into it.

"Thank you, Bergliot," Lyng told her.

There was one other girl and two boys in the senior class. One of the boys was the student who had volunteered the information about Professor Lokensgaard's classroom above the stairs. These three seniors took their seats without further protest. The freshmen filled the two rows nearest the windows. The seats in the room tallied exactly with the number of students listed on Professor Lokensgaard's roll, and for a minute Lyng had a sick feeling, wondering how many boys and girls in and around Stavanger had been told they couldn't enter high school because there weren't any seats for them. But she forced herself to stop thinking of that. Her business now was to do her best for those who were here.

"We'll get at the assignment of seats for the German class next," Lyng said.

Here Lyng met with further difficulties. It seemed that Professor Lokensgaard did not meet with his classes during the first week because he would be busy getting the grade children organized, so his classes would have to remain in Lyng's room. And some students who had a study period would have to sit there. After much shuffling of feet and confusion, everyone was settled. Lyng looked at the clock. It still showed twenty-three minutes past four.

The older boy in the senior class—Halvard Moen—raised his hand. "Would you like to have me wind the clock? I always did it for Miss McCrea."

"Thank you," Lyng said. Before she could add that it would be best to wait until recess, he was out of the room and back again, carrying a ladder. He climbed up, wound the clock and set it from his own watch.

"Thank you," Lyng told him again.

"You're welcome, Miss Skoglund," he said.

Halvard spoke with the strong Norwegian accent that seemed to be characteristic of all the people in New Stavanger. The Irish and Yankee teachers who had preceded her should have done something about it. After all, most of the students must be native-born Americans, and the public school was the place where they should have been taught to speak their own language correctly. It wasn't going to be easy to correct them without hurting their feelings, but she would do her best to help them to learn to speak like the real Americans they were.

"We haven't got any books yet," Thorbjorn Skriverud said.

Lyng caught her breath. She hadn't counted the German books she had seen in the cupboard. She hoped there were enough to go around.

"Halvard," she said, trying hard not to show her concern, "I wonder if you would please take out the German books for me."

He brought down the red books with the black backs, bearing in gold letters the title *German Grammar*, from the shelf, and as he handed them to her she counted them. Sixteen, seventeen, eighteen. There were twenty students in the class.

"Is that all?"

"Yes."

Perhaps Lyng could wait until tomorrow to give out the books.

"Do you want me to take down the gray ones, too?" she heard Halvard ask. "At least I think they're German books. The titles are in Norwegian type, only they aren't Norwegian words."

"You might as well take them down while you are about it," Lyng said.

Halvard handed her one of the books. It was the familiar little reader *Gluck Auf*. By good luck, there were exactly twenty of these.

"Would you like for me to pass the books?" Halvard asked.

"First let me dust them." She tore a strip from the pink apron in the coat closet for a dust rag. There was an accumulation of at least three-years' dust on the books. When Lyng opened her desk copy of the German Grammar, she found that the first four lessons had had hard usage, but the rest of the book showed almost no wear. The *Gluck Auf's* had clearly not been used at all. Some predecessor must have tried to teach German and then given up the attempt as a hopeless job. No matter how hard Lyng had to work, she'd keep at it all year and get through both books.

"Did you want me to record the number of the book loaned to each student?" Halvard asked. "I've always done it for my other teachers."

Lyng blushed. Would she ever learn all the things that were expected of her? "If you please, Halvard," she murmured.

She looked at the clock. It was past the time for the next class.

"I'm sorry we shall not have time to go over the German alphabet together," she told the students. "Do what you can about committing it to memory for tomorrow. There is a key to pronunciation in the introduction of the book."

Lyng had scarcely finished speaking before bedlam broke out again. She picked up the long pointer from the ledge under the front blackboard and pounded with it to make herself heard. "Return to your seats."

At once everything was quiet.

"Return to your room seats at the end of each period. The American history class will come up front now."

The seating this time, though not as confusing, took most of the following period. Lyng was able to assign only the first chapter of the American history text for the next day before the recess bell rang.

Left alone in the high school room, Lyng went back to her desk and sank down on her chair. The American history textbook was still open at the beginning of the first chapter. She put her elbows on the book and let her chin rest on the palms of her hands. She was dead tired and, worse yet, thoroughly disgusted with herself. So far the morning had been a failure, and the fault—at least a good share of it—was hers. Why hadn't she sought out Professor Lokensgaard at once instead of waiting for him to come to her? After all, as Halvard Moen had reminded her, he was the superintendent of the school and he had more than her room to think about.

Instead of getting ready for the day, she had played around, writing on the blackboard like a silly child and pretending to teach school in front of empty seats.

The shrill ringing of the bell reminded Lyng that recess was over. There was an onrush of children into the lower hall, and the creaking of the stairs told her that her students were on their way up. Both doors burst open and the boys and girls, flushed and panting, swept past her and on to their seats. Lyng felt weak and helpless. Even with their feet firmly planted under their desks, she could feel their pent-up energy. The thought of letting it loose again made her shudder. She simply couldn't subject herself to that. Not, at least, until the breathing spell of the noon lunch hour.

"Since Professor Lokensgaard will not be meeting with his classes today," she said, "I am asking you all to join our recitation in ancient history. That is, the members of the class will do the reciting and the rest will listen. It will, therefore, not be necessary for any of you to change your seats."

She checked the class roll. There were twenty students. She'd have the textbooks distributed to them and have them read aloud for the benefit of the others. If she went around the class twice, with each member reading a paragraph when his turn came, both periods before noon would easily be taken up. And she wouldn't feel that the entire morning had been wasted for any of the students.

"Halvard," she went on speaking aloud once more, "perhaps you will be kind enough to take the ancient-history texts out of the cupboard."

Halvard Moen walked across the room and gave the cupboard shelves a fleeting glance. "There aren't any ancient histories."

"There must be," Lyng exclaimed.

"We've never had ancient history in the high school in New Stavanger."

But Professor Lokensgaard had promised the school board to get along with the books on hand for this year at least. Surely he wouldn't have made that promise if a new subject were being introduced into the curriculum for which there were no books.

"There must be some mistake," she told Halvard.

A picture of her professor in ancient history came back to her—scholarly Dr. Davis, sitting at his desk on the raised platform in his classroom in the Library Building. She could hear him in his deep, rich voice, saying to the rows of students in front of him, "Everyone should have a thorough knowledge of ancient history. It is the only means of evaluating our problems of today and preparing us to meet them intelligently." At the time Lyng had regarded him rather impatiently. Instead of doing the collateral reading which he suggested on special subjects, she had hurried over the required reading in the textbook and concentrated on subjects she considered more useful and important.

"Oh, God," she breathed, "please let just a little of what I did learn come back to me."

Greece, Rome, Macedonia, Syria. Yes, those were some of the chapter headings. What could she tell her students about those countries and about their people? Her mind remained a blank. She had studied about Babylonia—at least there had been a chapter in the textbook about it. Babylonia. Babylonia. "By the rivers of Babylon, there we sat. Yea, we wept when we remembered Zion." She had committed that to memory in Dr. Burton's class on the Bible as Literature, but quoting a scriptural passage wouldn't fill the whole class period for her now.

Lyng remembered from her Sunday School lesson the story of the Tower of Babel. She told that fairly accurately because her mother had demanded perfection when Lyng had recited it to her. But her knowledge of what she had learned at the university was much more sketchy. There were the Hanging Gardens of Babylon, but what could she say of them? No self-respecting teacher ought to try to present a subject to her students with such utter lack of preparation. Moreover, if, as Dr. Davis had said, an understanding of ancient history was essential because it taught people to evaluate the problems of the present, what sort of preparation was she giving these students of hers in New Stavanger to cope with the problems they would have to face in their lives?

Yet, she had to keep on talking. Forty pairs of eager eyes were watching her and as many ears listening to what she was saying. The hands of the clock told her that time was actually passing. The farther she knew she was deviating from the truth, the faster she talked. She hoped that out of this jumble, nothing would be retained by her listeners. Her throat ached. Her voice grew husky. Then the noon bell rang.

"God, forgive me for telling my students all those things that weren't so. I'll make it up to them, honest, I will."

After Lyng had dismissed the students and was alone, she let the tears come. She sat at her desk, crying softly into her handkerchief. Then she wiped her face. The thing for her to do was to see to it that such a thing never happened again. And the first step in the right direction would be to supply the class—and herself—with a good textbook. She'd talk to Professor Lokensgaard about it right away. If she hurried, she might catch him before he went home to lunch. She rushed to the door and stepped out into the hall. Then she came back. A teacher with a tear-stained face wouldn't be able to convince a superintendent of anything. At the Emporium she had learned better than to tackle Mr. Cotton when he was hungry. She'd wait until this afternoon. Then she'd ask Professor Lokensgaard to send for textbooks in ancient history at once, and she wouldn't leave his office before she had his promise to do it. In the meantime, she had better get started home to

Mrs. Swenson's, who would be expecting her for lunch.

While she was taking her suit jacket out of the coat closet, she heard footsteps and whispering in the cloakroom. Several boys and girls, carrying pails, filed into the room. At first Lyng wondered what it meant. Then she understood. They were country children about to eat their lunch at school.

Out on Main Street, the wind blew clouds of dust that circled above the sidewalk. Grit got between her teeth and she could smell the hot wool from the suit jacket she was carrying. The heat had made her feet swell, so they felt pinched inside her high, stiff, calfskin boots. When she reached her room, it would be a relief to kick them off and slip out of her starched shirtwaist and have a good wash in cold water. She'd stretch out on the bed for a minute before going out into the kitchen to eat. She hoped Mrs. Swenson would serve a nice crisp salad and perhaps iced tea.

Long before Lyng reached the house, she smelled boiled cabbage and onions. And when she stepped on the porch, Mrs. Swenson, flushed and perspiring, met her at the door.

"Miss Skoglund," she exclaimed, "you're late! I've been watching your students pass by for the last ten minutes. Dinner is all ready. Come out into the kitchen right away before it gets cold."

She picked up her blue-checked gingham apron and shooed away the flies that had settled outside the screen door.

"I'll be there in just a minute," Lyng said, brushing past her.

She poured water from the pitcher over her hot, sticky hands and dashed more over her face. With Mrs. Swenson waiting, she couldn't take time for anything more.

The smell of cabbage and onions was even stronger out in the steaming, hot kitchen. Mrs. Swenson was already at the table. As soon as Lyng sat down opposite her, she murmured a hurried prayer in Norwegian.

After she had raised her head, she said to Lyng, "I always

have my hot dinner at noon. When I've finished with the dishes, I like to take a nap and dress up. Then I either drink afternoon coffee at home, or I'm invited out. It's nice not to have to run home and cook a big dinner with my best clothes on. Miss McCrea used to go out of her way to tell me how they served their dinners at home in the evening. But I didn't pay any attention to all her hinting."

The wood range sent waves of heat in Lyng's direction. Mrs. Swenson passed an oblong, brown-and-white platter piled high with potatoes, onions, cabbage, yellow turnips, and carrots. In the center of the vegetables was a steaming mound of sliced corned beef. Lyng helped herself sparingly.

"I always fill the pot whenever I make a boiled dinner," Mrs. Swenson said. "It saves me the trouble of thinking up what to cook for meals for a couple of days at least." She glanced at Lyng's plate and continued, "You'll have to do better than that. Otherwise, we'll be having repeats for the next week or two."

It was too much of an effort for Lyng to talk, but Mrs. Swenson didn't seem to mind or notice her silence.

"I raise a good garden," she went on. "It saves on the grocery bill. Especially since I started to room and board the teachers. I seldom have to buy a single vegetable until along in February, and even then I have the potato bin and the things I've canned to fall back on."

Lyng finished the food on her plate and asked to be excused.

"Take your time, take your time," Mrs. Swenson protested. "The schoolhouse was here before you came, and, if I'm not much mistaken, it'll be here for years after you're gone. Wait until I've finished. And there's dessert."

Lyng fumed inwardly as she watched Mrs. Swenson finish a second and then a third helping.

"Keep your fork," she told Lyng, piling her plate on top of Lyng's and carrying them both away.

But when Mrs. Swenson brought out a generous slab of apple pie, completely covered with yellow cheese, Lyng had to tell her that she was too full to eat it.

Back at school Lyng walked through the students' cloakroom. A row of tin pails was lined up along the inside wall. The lid of one of them had slipped off, showing a quarter of a waffle at the bottom of the pail. Lyng stooped down and put the lid back. At the university she used to detest the cold lunches she carried from home, even though she usually added one hot dish or hot drink at the cafeteria in Shevlin Hall. These country children must have gotten up very early in order to get to school on time. Before they left home, they probably had to help with the chores. And it would be late this afternoon when they trudged over dusty roads back to their homes. It would be still later, after they had finished with the evening chores, before they could sit down to a good warm meal. This wouldn't leave them much of a chance for homework. They'd be dead tired by then.

Inside the high school room, remnants of the children's lunches were strewn over the desks and down on the floor: apple cores, plum pits and crumbs. Lyng used the pink dust rag to brush up the litter onto a paper and then dumped it all into the wastebasket. There ought to be a place for the country children to eat their lunches, one more pleasant and more comfortable than this high school room. In the meantime, she'd have to do something about getting them to leave the room neater. Ole couldn't be expected to clean up after them. Besides, the remnants of food might attract mice.

Lyng decided to broach the subject to the students as soon as they were in their seats for the afternoon. "Before we start with our classes," she said, "there is a small matter about which I should like to say a few words—especially to you who live out of town. I know that it isn't easy to keep from spilling crumbs and other particles of food when you have to eat at a desk in this room. That is all the more reason for trying to be unusually careful. I am wondering if it wouldn't be a good idea for you to bring newspapers and cover the desks with them before you started eating your lunches. What do you think?"

Solveig Myrland, the girl with the tight blond braids wound around her head, raised her hand. "The only newspaper we take is *Decorah Posten*," she said. "My mother cuts out the continued stories for our neighbors to read. The rest we use to build fires with."

Thorbjorn Skriverud waved his hand. "We send our *New Stavanger News* to our aunt in Canada. She used to live here before she moved up there to prove up her claim. She likes to read about the people she used to know."

"How about the rest of you?" Lyng asked. "Don't any of your people take newspapers?"

A girl in a dress of large plaids, whose name Lyng hadn't learned yet, blushed furiously. "We—we use all ours in the toilet," she stammered.

"We do, too," came from somewhere in the back of the room.

"Can any of you, even though you don't eat your lunches here, bring some newspapers?" Lyng asked.

Four students responded, among them Halvard Moen.

"Thank you," Lyng said. Then she had another idea. "In case we should run out of papers, how would it be for you to bring a piece of oilcloth to school? About the size of your desks? It needn't be new. It could be washed off after you had used it and rolled up and kept inside your desks."

"Where would we get the water to wash them with?" It was Thorbjorn Skriverud's brother Conrad who asked this. He was a smaller edition of Thorbjorn—red hair, freckles, blue overalls.

"That's what I'd like to know," a junior boy, whom Lyng

couldn't identify, asked. "Ole gets mad even when he thinks we empty the drinking water tank too fast. He says he can't keep lugging up pails to fill it all the time."

"Where does he carry the water from?" Lyng asked.

"From the basement," Halvard Moen told her. "He used to have to carry it from Norstad's pump across the street. That was before we got the addition to the school house and the city water was piped in."

"Shucks, he won't even let us touch the faucets in the basement," the same junior said. From her roll, Lyng figured it must be Christoffer Lovseth. "He thinks it's so grand."

"It is, too," Solveig Myrland spoke up. "Pa says the city water is the best thing they've got in New Stavanger. Once in the old days, when he was in town with the cream, fire started from the sparks in the blacksmith shop, and it spread to the restaurant and the shoe repair and harness shop. The whole town would have burned up if Pa and some other men at the creamery hadn't put out the fire by squirting butter milk on it."

"Ya. That's the year they got the city water in town," Thorbjorn Skriverud said.

Lyng decided that after school had been dismissed, she would go down into the basement and hunt out Ole. If she made him understand how much work she would be saving him by having the students cover their desks with oil cloth, during their lunch hour and washing it after each meal, she was sure she could get him to furnish the necessary water.

All afternoon Lyng worried over the argument she was going to have with Professor Lokensgaard as soon as she asked him for an immediate supply of textbooks in ancient history. If he came into the room while classes were in session and she pretended before the students that everything was going all right, it would be harder to have to let him know after school that they weren't. On the other hand, if he came in during recess, she'd have to plunge into the subject at once. When, therefore, he came in at the beginning of recess, she was both relieved and frightened.

"How are things going?" he asked.

"Professor Lokensgaard," she said, "there are no ancient history texts. Halvard Moen said the subject had never been taught before in New Stavanger. Is that so?"

Professor Lokensgaard sat down in one of the front seats, and he let his arm rest on the desk behind him. Lyng sat down at her desk and faced him.

"As a matter of fact, it is," he said pleasantly. "Come to think of it, we didn't get around to that this morning. We'll probably have to do something about it soon. Why don't you write around to a few bookshops in Minneapolis and St. Paul and find out what they have to offer? We ought to be able to pick up the books real cheap that way."

"Professor Lokensgaard," Lyng said, "we can't wait for that. It might take weeks, maybe a month. Any books we might get at such places would be out-of-date. These books will have to be sent for this afternoon. Wired for."

Professor Lokensgaard stared at Lyng. "I'm not sure I understand what you mean. You weren't trying to tell me that we should send a telegram to some bookstore, were you?"

"Yes, it's not fair to make the students wait for the books. The ones from the country have to trudge miles to get here. Anyway, both they and the students living in New Stavanger have the right to expect to learn something while they are at school. I haven't had time to check on the high school library yet, but even with a fair supply of good reference books, we couldn't—"

"Miss Skoglund," Professor Lokensgaard interrupted her, "we have no high school library. How could you expect to find one in a high school which, only this year, is having its first graduating class? It takes years to build up a high school library."

"That's all the more reason why we ought to supply our students with good textbooks. We don't have to wait for years to do that. Professor Lokensgaard, those books simply must be sent for today. Until they arrive, I refuse to conduct a single class in ancient history."

As soon as the words were out, Lyng felt cold shivers up and down her spine. Professor Lokensgaard stood up. "Miss Skoglund, I am the superintendent of this school. It is for me to decide what the teachers are to do and for them to follow my suggestions. Even though this is your first year out of college, you ought to know that."

Lyng's scalp felt prickly and her hands were clammy. What if Professor Lokensgaard should become so angry with her that he fired her? Well, he'd just have to, then. Anything would be preferable to having to live through another experience like her shameful performance in ancient history class this morning.

"Maybe you'd rather wait a year or two before offering ancient history," Lyng said, trying to keep her voice steady. "Until the board feels it can afford to buy good texts."

"No," Professor Lokensgaard snapped.

"All right. Then perhaps you'd like to have me go before the board and explain the situation."

Lyng thought Professor Lokensgaard looked alarmed at this suggestion. "No," he repeated. "It is for me, not for the teachers, to deal with the board."

Time was passing and they were getting nowhere. In a few minutes recess would be over. Lyng would have to try a different approach. She should have remembered that Grandmother Skoglund always said you caught flies with sugar, not vinegar.

"Then why don't you go down to the school board now and explain to them individually that I can't start teaching ancient history unless the students are supplied with up-to-date textbooks? Think how proud the seniors are going to be on commencement night, and how the rest of the town will thank you, now that the boys and girls growing up in New Stavanger are getting a high school education right here at home."

"Where would you order the books from?"

"I wouldn't want to take the responsibility of selecting a text. With your years of teaching experience, you are more familiar with reliable publishing houses than I am."

"That is true," Professor Lokensgaard admitted. "I keep catalogues from year to year. Before we installed the coal furnace, they provided quite an item in our fuel supply by starting wood fires."

"Then there is nothing more for me to worry about. Perhaps you would go over some of your latest catalogues and select a few texts. As soon as school has been dismissed, you and I could get together and decide from this list which one we considered most suitable for our students here in New Stavanger. If we have the books sent C. O. D., we'll get quick service."

"Perhaps you are right," Porfessor Lokensgaard conceded. "But I'm still uneasy about the telegram. Why, I doubt that there have been half a dozen of them sent from here that haven't been announcements of deaths or very grave illnesses."

"On further thought, it seems a pity for you, with all you have on your mind, to spend time going over the catalogues. Why can't I do that? Then, from the list of four of five, the final choice would be left to you."

"It's a daring thing to do," Professor Lokensgaard said. "But as I was saying, it ought to please the taxpayers to find out how much they are getting for their money. The school board, one member especially, has been most insistent on our teaching ancient history up here this year."

"When you explain to him all the trouble you have gone to in order that there will be no delay in getting the class started, he'll certainly be pleased," Lyng said.

Only after Lyng had returned to the high school room with the catalogues, did she remember that she had planned to go down to the basement and hunt out Ole to see what could be done about having water brought up for washing the oil cloth covers. She hoped this might be the beginning of a general clean-up in the high school room and that some day it might become a much more pleasant place to work in.

But all that could wait. The chief thing now was to make sure that the students were supplied with good books.

CHAPTER EIGHT

Lyng pulled the sheet up to her chin. It was Sunday morning and there wasn't a thing she had to do all day. She closed her eyes and settled down for an hour or two of more sleep.

Yesterday she had washed out her white shirtwaists and hung them up to dry, after Mrs. Swenson had inspected them to make sure they were clean enough to be seen on the line out in her back yard. In the midst of Mrs. Swenson's Saturday baking and cooking in the kitchen, Lyng had ironed the shirtwaists and pressed her suit and her summer coat. She had struggled with the cistern pump in the cellar to get soft water to wash her hair. And she had waited for ages for it to heat, because the kettle had to be shoved to the back of the stove in order to make room for Mrs. Swenson's pots and pans. Then Mrs. Swenson had cautioned her about being careful not to spill anything or otherwise disturb the Sunday perfection of the parlor when she had to carry the hair-washing paraphernalia—soap, water and towels—through there and into her own room. It was noon by the time she had gotten at the stack of papers that had accumulated during the week. Finally, after supper, she had sat down to plan the lessons for the following week and to prepare the work she intended to present to her students on Monday. Long before she had finished, she was so tired that she had thrown herself, fully dressed, on top of the bed. She must have fallen asleep, for the next she knew, Mrs. Swenson was standing beside her.

"I saw your light," Mrs. Swenson said. "And I knocked at your door, but there was no answer. Since I couldn't hear anything, I thought I ought to come in and see. It's late—past ten. You had better undress and get into bed."

Well, the hectic week was over and it was Sunday morning. In spite of its drawbacks, being a teacher away from home had its compensations.

When Lyng felt like it, she would get up and put on her robe, go into the kitchen and dawdle over her breakfast. Then she would finish preparing her Monday's lessons and be ready to start on her second week of teaching. Now that she had become acquainted with Mr. Lokensgaard and her students, and she understood the situation in the high school in New Stavanger, things ought to run much more smoothly.

"Miss Skoglund, breakfast is ready." Lyng heard the door open.

"I'd rather not eat yet," she called, turning her head away from the wall.

Mrs. Swenson stepped into the room. "I have to get the breakfast cleared away," she said firmly. "I am the assistant superintendent of the Sunday School and I have to be there by nine."

"That's all right," Lyng told her. "I'll take a bite when I get up."

"But you'll have to get up now, if you're going to be ready for church."

"I don't think I'll go to church this morning," Lyng said. "I'm going to rest for a while."

Mrs. Swenson took a step forward. "Not going to church?" she exclaimed in unbelief. "Miss Skoglund, there is a limit to everything. You just can't do it!"

"If there are services tonight, I may go then," Lyng said.

"Miss Skoglund, you just don't understand. Reverend Klemstad and his wife have been counting all summer on your being at church this morning. So have the rest of the congregation and so have I. Mrs. Fretland and Mrs. Grocery Peterson have always taken the Norwegian Lutheran teachers to board and room and brought them over to their own churches. Their husbands are on the school board, so they've had first choice. It was Reverend Klemstad who helped me to get you."

Lyng pushed back the sheet. "Oh, all right," she said, trying to keep the irritation out of her voice. "I hope you won't mind if I come out in the kitchen in my robe to eat."

Mrs. Swenson hesitated. "I guess no one will come this early. But I had to put a stop to some of the girls' walking around half the morning in their robes and bedroom slippers, without even stockings on. I make it a rule never to step out of my bedroom before I am fully dressed. It—it just isn't nice."

Lyng dressed in a rebellious mood. If she was to be on exhibition this morning, she'd give the congregation something worth looking at. She drew aside the curtain covering her clothes and took down from the wall her pale green wool dress. She'd wear her white felt hat with the green bow and white gloves and shoes. It was warm, so one wouldn't need a coat. She had picked up her purse and had gotten as far as the parlor when she was startled to hear Mrs. Swenson call to her from the kitchen.

"Why, Miss Skoglund!" Mrs. Swenson exclaimed, eying her from head to foot. She, herself, was all in black.

Lyng pretended not to notice. "Shall we start for church now?" she asked.

"Well, you are young," Mrs. Swenson conceded, "so I suppose you can't be blamed for wanting to look nice. But after this, if I were you, I'd wear something darker and less stylish to church. Reverend Klemstad—"

Her voice was lost by the loud ringing of a church bell.

Almost immediately two other bells, each with entirely different tones, chimed in. Mrs. Swenson frowned with irritation. When she could be heard, she said, "That is the way it is every Sunday morning. The two other Norwegian Lutheran churches always wait to ring their bells until ours starts. It's a shame because ours is the finest one in town. Severin Sunde left money for it when he died."

Lyng and Mrs. Swenson started out, taking the same route Lyng had to school. But at the end of the business block on Main Street, they turned to the left. Here they passed rather pretentious houses, set far back from the sidewalk and partly hidden by tall trees, whose luxuriant foliage was already tinted with autumn colors. Smooth, green lawns surrounded the houses and in some yards bright summer flowers still bloomed in carefully tended flower beds. In the distance, Lyng caught sight of a white church steeple.

"That's ours," Mrs. Swenson said, pointing to it.

The well-kept grounds surrounding the church and the parsonage covered half a block. They were enclosed by a shining black iron fence with a gate in front of each building. Both gates were flanked by gigantic evergreens, one on each side of the walk.

"We've got the finest church and parsonage in town," Mrs. Swenson told Lyng. "And this is the best residence section of New Stavanger."

Well-dressed people stood in little groups on the sidewalk and on the church steps. As Lyng and Mrs. Swenson turned in at the gate, the murmur of voices suddenly stopped. Lyng felt many eyes fixed on her.

"Good morning, Mrs. Slettevold. Good morning, Saemund." Mrs. Swenson greeted them all by name. But she kept a firm hold on Lyng's arm, and she didn't stop to introduce her to anyone.

A small group had assembled inside the church door. These

were more expensively dressed than those outside, and Mrs. Swenson became all smiles. "Miss Skoglund, this is Banker and Mrs. Knudson. They're of the First National, you know. 'My bank,' I call it. This is Mrs. Doctor Thoreid. Doctor isn't here, I see. Is he at Klingen's? I heard she was expecting almost any day. That's a doctor's life. Never knows when he can be anywhere. Mrs. Tronder, I'm glad to see you are able to be out again. I've missed you at the Toggery. It just isn't the same store when the wife of the owner is gone. Miss Skoglund, you pass the Toggery—our biggest and best store —on your way to school. Yes, Mrs. Saxe, I was about to make you acquainted with our new high school teacher. Miss Skoglund, Mrs. Hardware Saxe."

Mrs. Swenson shook hands with all of them. Lyng tried to pull her glove back on her right hand, but it stuck and would go only part way. So she gave up and shook hands with her glove half on. Mrs. Swenson, who was holding her own black kid glove conspicuously, looked her disapproval. It was hot and stuffy in the vestibule and this, together with the strong smell of new straw fiber matting, made Lyng feel nauseated. A young man to whom Lyng hadn't been introduced whispered something in Mrs. Swenson's ear. At once she resumed her firm hold on Lyng's arm and moved forward. The young man opened one of the double doors leading into the main church and they walked in.

Except that the church was much longer and narrower, it resembled Lyng's own in Minneapolis. There was the familiar deep tan carpeting on the floor, and almost the same shade of tan paint on the walls. There were the crystal chandeliers hanging from the high ceiling, the altar, baptismal font, and raised pulpit—all white with shining gold bands—and the railing around the altar with red plush cushions for people to kneel on while taking communion. As in her own church, massive pews extended along its full length. But here the altar painting showed the Virgin Mary holding the Christ Child in her arms, and there were beautifully colored stained-glass windows.

The church was perfect in every detail. How could people who worshiped here every Sunday have the heart to send their children to spend five whole days each week in the filthy, run-down, public school building?

As far as Lyng could see, she and Mrs. Swenson were the first arrivals. Yet she felt conspicuous as Mrs. Swenson piloted her down the aisle. She kept her eyes fixed on the floor, and even after they had reached Mrs. Swenson's pew, she didn't look up.

A sudden stir told Lyng that people were pouring into the church. The pew in front of them was filled with women and children. Lyng looked up just as a tall woman in a lavender and white polka-dot dress was taking a yellow straw hat from a child's head. The woman smoothed the straight, sun-bleached, blond hair with both hands and retied the pink bow at the end of a short thick braid hanging close to the little girl's left ear. The little girl climbed upon the pew, turned around and stared at Lyng. The woman pulled the child back, but not before she had stolen a glance at Lyng herself. Across the aisle there were only boys and grown men. Their hands and faces were weather-beaten, and they looked uncomfortable in their stiff white collars and heavy black suits.

The service which followed was almost identical with the one Lyng had been used to all her life. Only here everything was conducted at a much slower tempo: the organ music, the congregational singing and the sermon by the austere, white-haired minister in the familiar black robe and white ruff. There was neither a choir nor a soloist, and only Norwegian was used during the service.

After the closing prayer, the minister rose from his knees at the altar, walked slowly inside the altar rail and disappeared into the sacristy. There was another slow hymn on the organ, and then the congregation rose from their seats. Mrs. Swenson seized Lyng's arm and was the first one to start down the aisle toward the rear of the church. People stood aside to let them pass and then closed in after them. Mrs. Swenson greeted everyone pleasantly, but she stopped to introduce Lyng to only a few. Lyng noticed that these, with one or two exceptions, were older people and all of them very well dressed. Out on the church steps, groups of young men and women seemed to be waiting for them, but Mrs. Swenson tightened her hold on Lyng's arm and swept past them with only a slight nod of recognition. Finally the two reached the gate.

"Let's cut across the back lots on our way home," Mrs. Swenson suggested. "I'm worried about the meat."

When they arrived at the house, they could smell roast pork. Mrs. Swenson dropped Lyng's arm abruptly.

"I hope it isn't burned," she said, and she rushed toward the kitchen. In a moment she returned, pulling the long, jet-beaded pins from her hat as she walked. "It's perfect," she beamed. She took off her hat, stuck the pins into it and put it on a shelf in the organ. Lyng opened the door of her room and stepped inside.

Mrs. Swenson followed her. "I have invited Reverend and Mrs. Klemstad to eat with us today," she said. "It's only the two of them since their daughter Margit was married last spring." With that, she disappeared.

Lyng closed the door. So this was how her precious day of rest was to be spent! Since morning, it had steadily grown hotter, and she was uncomfortable in the wool dress. But with the minister and his wife coming to dinner, Mrs. Swenson would expect her to remain dressed for the occasion.

The Klemstads arrived an hour later. Reverend Klemstad seemed more human in his black suit and white shirt than he had in the robe and ruff at church.

"We are very glad to claim you as one of our own," Reverend Klemstad said in Norwegian, giving Lyng a hearty handshake. "Now perhaps we shall get rid of some of the queer and senseless notions that are being tried out in the high school."

Lyng smiled, but she felt uncomfortable.

"You understand Norwegian, don't you?" Mrs. Klemstad asked in English.

"Oh, yes," Lyng answered, also in English.

"Our daughter Margit finished the eighth grade just in time to escape all this modern folderol," Reverend Klemstad said, speaking in Norwegian. "After that, we had her attend the academy, which is located on the campus of Tordenskjold College. Even down there, they are not as careful of what they put into the minds of the young people as they used to be in the old days."

"But Margit has turned out to be a wonderful minister's wife," Mrs. Klemstad hastened to add.

Mrs. Swenson, who had disappeared soon after the arrival of the Klemstads, now returned, wearing a starched, blue-and-white figured percale apron that almost covered her black dress. "Please be so kind as to come and have a bite to eat," she said.

Lyng was amazed to find that the kitchen table on which she and Mrs. Swenson usually ate was entirely filled with cooking utensils. A door, which had remained closed, was wide open, and Lyng could see that it led into a large room. In the the center of this room stood a long table, covered with a shining white linen tablecloth and loaded with steaming food.

"I didn't know you had a dining room!" Lyng exclaimed. The minute the words were out, she regretted them. Mrs. Swenson's face had turned a deep red.

"Reverend, will you take your usual place?" she said hurriedly as she stepped aside to let her guests pass. "Mrs. Klemstad, I'm going to put you in my place today, so you and Reverend can share Miss Skoglund between you for dinner. With her living here. I can always have her for meals."

A large brown leather Bible lay beside Reverend Klemstad's plate. He opened it and read the passage about the loaves and the fishes. Closing the book, he folded his wrinkled hands and prayed, asking God that He would bless this home and the people seated around this board. He asked that God would grant vision to this His child who had been sent to work among them, and that she might lead their young people to the service of their fellowmen and the glorification of their Heavenly Father.

The prayer aroused the uncomfortable feeling inside Lyng once more. It was as though she was somehow being pushed back into what she had been trying for years to escape.

Both Reverend Klemstad and his wife ate heartily of the food which Mrs. Swenson pressed upon them: large, thick slices of pork browned to a sweet tenderness; mashed potatoes with pools of melted butter; rich brown gravy; baked macaroni and cheese; mashed yellow turnips with more pools of melted butter; creamed cabbage strewn with powdered, dried bread crumbs; sweet beet pickles, onions and cauliflower pickles, and pickled crab apples; hot wheat rolls, homemade rye bread, *lefse* and flat bread. And for dessert Mrs. Swenson brought in dinner plates heaped high with two-tiered squares of juicy strawberry shortcake, topped with mounds of whipped cream.

"Where in the world did you get fresh strawberries at this time of year?" Mrs. Klemstad asked, wide-eyed.

Mrs. Swenson beamed. "My son Anton has been raising the October-bearing variety out on his farm for several years, but this is the first time that I've picked them out of my own garden."

"You are an excellent cook," Reverend Klemstad remarked gravely.

Mrs. Swenson poured steaming coffee and hot cream into generous cups and passed them. "It is only plain fare," she said modestly.

As soon as everyone had risen from the table, Mrs. Klemstad said, "Mrs. Swenson and I are going to do the dishes. You two go into the parlor and visit. I know you'll have lots of things you'll want to talk about."

Lyng cast a wistful glance at the kitchen table as she followed Reverend Klemstad into the parlor. He took the large, brown leather easy chair and pulled out a pipe and a sack of tobacco from his pocket. Lyng sat on the edge of one of the straight chairs near the organ.

"How do you like our town?" Reverend Klemstad asked, continuing to speak in Norwegian as he had done ever since his arrival.

"I haven't seen much of it yet," Lyng said, speaking in English. "Until Mrs. Swenson took me to church this morning, I had only walked to and from school twice a day."

"I suppose there is plenty of work to keep you busy," Reverend Klemstad remarked. "Yet it seems to me that much of what is taught up there is unnecessary."

Lyng wanted to ask him to name the subjects of which he disapproved, but she thought better of it. After all, he was Mrs. Swenson's minister and also her special guest today.

"Professor Lokensgaard is really a good man," Reverend Klemstad went on. "But I don't agree with his opinions in some matters. For instance, in his own church, he has been one of the staunchest advocates of introducing English into the various activities of the congregation. So far, he and those who think like him have succeeded in initiating only one regular English church service a month and that to be held in the evening. But even that one service works a hardship on poor old Reverend Tobiasen. He hasn't had time to study English and to prepare fancy sermons that will suit modern church-goers."

"But aren't there young people here in New Stavanger for whom Norwegian is difficult?" Lyng asked mildly.

"Yes, there are. But there is no excuse for it. The parents ought to see to it that the children speak the language which they brought with them from their homeland. It has grieved me very much to see the growing tendency among those I prepare for confirmation to become more and more slipshod in the use of the Norwegian. When I first came here, the young people spoke the mother tongue of their parents in its purest form. Now they take pride in becoming Yankeefied and are actually ashamed of speaking Norwegian. Even in Norway this deplorable state of affairs—of wanting to speak English—is true. When Mrs. Klemstad and I went back there several years ago, we were amazed at the change which had taken place since we left. To be sure, they offer religious instruction in the schools, but we found English being taught everywhere as far down as the grades. Several of the clergy whom we met actually started to converse in English, and fluently. It was only after I stopped them and insisted on speaking Norwegian myself that they followed my example. We are certainly living in strange times."

Lyng moved uneasily in her chair. She was tempted to voice her own opinions on the subject, but Reverend Klemstad was so positive about what he believed that she hesitated to enter into a debate with him.

"Mrs. Klemstad and I were much relieved to return to our home in New Stavanger," Reverend Klemstad went on. "In most respects conditions here, though far from perfect, are more like they were in the old days in Norway."

"Is it long since you first came to New Stavanger?" Lyng asked. She couldn't very well continue to sit dumb.

"Oh, yes, Mrs. Klemstad and I set up housekeeping here before the railroad came through. I have served my town church and my two country congregations ever since. But I should like to go back to Professor Lokensgaard for a minute, Miss Skoglund, if you don't mind. He should be given credit for one outstanding improvement this year—the introduction of ancient history into the curriculum. I can't tell you how pleased I am for ancient history is, in my estimation, the most important subject taught up there. It ties right up with the Bible history the children have been getting all along in the Sunday School. And that brings to my mind another matter which I would like to discuss with you. I am thinking how fine it would be for the young people in our congregation to have a really good Sunday School teacher now that you are here."

"Oh, no!" Lyng exclaimed. "I couldn't. Really I couldn't teach in Norwegian and everything in your church is in Norwegian, isn't it?"

"Of course. But you are too modest, Miss Skoglund. Having grown up in a cultured, Christian home such as I understand you did, I'm sure that your Norwegian is excellent."

Lyng would have to make Reverend Klemstad understand that she couldn't and wouldn't teach in Norwegian in his Sunday School. Yet it would be too bad if, in refusing, she should lose all the good will that had been built up for her in his congregation in anticipation of her coming.

"Reverend Klemstad," she said, "I have been very much impressed with the fine church you have built here in New Stavanger. I only hope that I shall be able to do half as well with my school work. That is why I feel that I must refuse to take on any additional activities which might in any way interfere with this."

"But surely, Miss Skoglund, on Sunday—no one expects you to devote the Sabbath to your school work. In fact, we should be greatly disturbed to know that anyone placed in charge of our young people was not in sympathy with the third commandment."

Evidently Reverend Klemstad wasn't a person with whom you could avoid the issue. If she remained silent about her real reason for refusing to teach the Bible class in his Sunday School, he would consider her unfit to teach the young people of his congregation in the high school the other days of the week.

"Reverend Klemstad," she said, "when I told you I couldn't teach the Norwegian Bible class in your Sunday School, it was the truth."

"But didn't your parents speak Norwegian in your home?"

"Yes, they did. And we children learned to speak it before we knew English. We also observed customs which had been brought over from Norway. We attended a Norwegian church and we received all our religious instruction in Norwegian. The result has been that all my life I have felt like a foreigner in my own country. At least this was true until I went to the university. There one of my instructors helped me to overcome this handicap, and I shall be eternally grateful to her for it. Reverend Klemstad, the condition which made things so difficult for me as a child exists, I believe, among most people here in New Stavanger."

Reverend Klemstad sat regarding Lyng in cold silence. Surprise and anger and disappointment were in his steely, gray-blue eyes.

"I hadn't intended speaking frankly to you like this," Lyng told him breathlessly. "But it seems the fairest to both of us. I feel that I would be undoing all that I struggled for at the university if I went back to Norwegian myself and pulled the young people of New Stavanger with me."

Reverend Klemstad's jaw set firmly. "So, in order to ease your own conscience," he said, finally breaking his silence, "you are throwing away your beautiful, Norwegian, Christian heritage. And worse yet, proclaiming to the town that you prefer to be regarded as a heathen."

This time it was Lyng who was surprised and angry. She sat meeting Reverend Klemstad's eyes squarely.

"I needn't tell you," Reverend Klemstad went on, "that I have never been so disappointed in anyone during all the years that I have worked as a minister of the Gospel." The tone of his voice, even more than his words, brought real fear into Lyng's heart.

"I won't cry," she thought, forcing the tears back. "I won't let him frighten me."

At that moment, Mrs. Klemstad came into the parlor, followed by Mrs. Swenson. Mrs. Swenson carried a large tray on which were cups and saucers, a plate of small cakes and a yellow satin coffee-cozy.

"What were you two talking so earnestly about?" Mrs. Klemstad asked.

"Miss Skoglund has just informed me that she cannot teach a Bible class for us in our Sunday School," Reverend Klemstad said.

"But why?" Mrs. Klemstad seemed greatly disappointed.

"She tells me that her duties at the public school will not permit her to take on any extra activities," Reverend Klemstad said shortly.

"Margit's husband said the same thing while he was teaching before he went into the ministry," Mrs. Klemstad said. "He told me that the teachers were overworked and that too much was expected of them by the community."

Deep furrows appeared in Reverend Klemstad's forehead. "I hope he has changed his mind," he said. "Otherwise, I wouldn't give much for his chances of success in his church. Especially, if his real reason for not wanting to take on extra work was what Miss Skoglund has just confessed hers to be.

She is ashamed of being a Norwegian. She feels that through her education at the university she has been able to overcome the handicap of being one, and she hopes to help our young people do the same." He spoke with real bitterness.

Lyng smarted with hot resentment at being misrepresented. But she realized that any attempt at further explanation at this point would only make matters worse.

"I am sure Miss Skoglund doesn't mean that." Mrs. Klemstad's eyes became suddenly pleading.

A stiff silence followed. Mrs. Swenson appeared in the porch doorway. "Won't you please come out for a cup of coffee now?" she asked. "I don't want to serve it cold."

The four of them sat down at a small square table covered with a white Hardanger embroidered cloth. Mrs. Swenson removed the coffee-cozy and poured steaming coffee from the shining copper kettle.

"These cups and saucers are real Porsgrund china, Miss Skoglund," she said. "The Klemstads brought them for me when they came back from their trip to Norway."

"They are a small return for all the hospitality we have enjoyed in this house," Mrs. Klemstad said.

Mrs. Swenson passed the cakes. "Mrs. Klemstad and I have been talking about the Willing Workers," she said. "It's time to get started working for our annual sale. The Willing Workers are the young girls' organization in our church, Miss Skoglund. At least, they are allowed to join when they have been confirmed, and they usually belong until they are married. Mrs. Klemstad and I sort of help out. It will be more work for us than ever with Margit gone. She has been our president for years."

Mrs. Klemstad looked at Lyng hopefully. Lyng turned her head. She wasn't going to get involved in any more discussions of church affairs.

"They use the money they raise from their sale for some

worthy cause," Mrs. Klemstad said. "For years we have been giving nice big presents to Tordenskjold College. But I'm in favor of keeping the money for some worthwhile project at home this year." She spoke fast and every now and then cast anxious glances at Reverend Klemstad.

"Yes," Mrs. Swenson said, "they bought electric lamps for the girls' dormitory last year. I went along when Reverend and Mrs. Klemstad and Margit presented them to the school in the name of the Willing Workers. It was impressive, I can tell you, and the girls were all so appreciative."

Lyng wanted to ask Mrs. Swenson if it hadn't occurred to anyone that it would be nice to have electric lights in the school building in New Stavanger. But, as it was, she had probably said too much to Reverend Klemstad. She had made an enemy of him and there were many ways in which he could make her work at school difficult. She would be foolish to aggravate Mrs. Swenson, too.

Reverend Klemstad sat in stony silence.

"That is certainly a pretty dress you have there," Mrs. Klemstad said. "I noticed it the minute you came into church this morning." Then she blushed and again looked anxiously at Reverend Klemstad.

"Thank you," Lyng said, fixing her eyes on her plate.

Mrs. Klemstad went on, "I couldn't help but notice, too, how you sang all the verses of the hymns with us. And you scarcely glanced at the hymn book at all."

Lyng waited for some word of approval from Reverend Klemstad, but there was none. Instead he pulled out his large silver watch at the end of a heavy silver chain.

"Mrs. Swenson," he said gravely, "much as I dislike breaking away, I am afraid that we shall have to leave. It is already four o'clock."

"How about another cup of coffee with a sugar lump to

finish with?" Mrs. Swenson suggested. She removed the yellow satin coffee-cozy from the copper kettle once more.

"No, thank you, we have already had more than enough," he said.

"Must you really leave so early?" Mrs. Swenson asked regretfully. "Couldn't you possibly stop for supper? I made *rullepolse* and *jule kake* on purpose and—"

"I'm afraid not," Reverend Klemstad said with finality. "Today I have a baptism on the way out to the Emanuel Church. It is at Bjelde's and I suppose they will have supper out there. They always do."

"How many does that make?" Mrs. Swenson asked.

"Fourteen," Mrs. Klemstad answered promptly. "I know because I carried the last one to baptism, and she was number thirteen. They called her Turina."

"Gjertru and Elias must have plenty of help on the farm these days," Mrs. Swenson said.

"We really must be leaving," Reverend Klemstad said. He looked at Lyng coldly. "I hope you will not regret the course you have chosen."

CHAPTER NINE

IT WAS A RELIEF for Lyng to go back to school on Monday morning. A whole weekend under the constant watchful eye of Mrs. Swenson had been wearing. Lyng enjoyed the fresh cool morning air after last night's shower and she took deep breaths as she walked through Main Street toward the school house. The closer she came, the more cheerful she felt, and she went straight to Professor Lokensgaard's office to inquire about the ancient histories.

Professor Lokensgaard was talking on the telephone and she stood waiting until he had finished.

"Good morning," Lyng said brightly. "Is there any news about the ancient histories?"

Professor Lokensgaard frowned. "That is what I was discussing just now. Reverend Klemstad has phoned saying that he doesn't think that you should be the one to decide. The main idea of introducing ancient history into the high school was to tie it up with the Bible history the children have studied in Sunday School, and he feels the text should be written from a distinctly religious point of view. He suggested that the school board send for a number of books which he will recommend. After the board has read these books and discussed them carefully, they will vote on the one they consider the most suitable."

Lyng was dumbfounded. She had not meant to give Reverend Klemstad the impression she was irreligious. Nor had she realized that her refusal to teach the Norwegian Bible class in his Sunday School would be any concern of the school board. Aloud she said, "Why should Reverend Klemstad concern himself with the choice of textbooks in the public high school?"

"He is president of the board," Professor Lokensgaard answered.

Without another word, Lyng left the office, walked slowly through the hall and into the high school room. She sat down at her desk and tried to think what to do next. The path of least resistance would be to refuse to conduct the ancient history class until texts were supplied. But this would only aggravate matters between herself and Reverend Klemstad. In all fairness to him, she had to admit that he wouldn't have taken the selection of an ancient history text out of her hands if he hadn't honestly been convinced that he was right in doing it. That only made her position more uncomfortable. A man who had braved the rigors of frontier life out on the prairies in his zeal to save souls would certainly not hesitate to get rid of a teacher who threatened the spiritual welfare of the young people.

It would not improve Professor Lokensgaard's opinion of her either if she dodged the issue. There was no alternative left to her—she must think of something to present to the ancient history class until relief came. But what?

The first bell rang and Lyng roused herself with an effort. The students mustn't find her staring vacantly into space. She resolved that, before her ancient history class met, she would be prepared to present some material relating to the subject that would occupy the entire period. Fortunately for her, German and freshman and sophomore English came before ancient history. During these classes, she turned over several

plans in her mind but discarded them almost immediately.
By the close of recess, nothing workable had occurred to her.
Better not to meet with the class this once than to give them
any more false information. So, as soon as everyone had returned to the high school room, she announced that there
would be no ancient history class today. Since she was still
waiting for the arrival of their textbooks, they might have
the period for study on other subjects. They should remain in
their regular room seats.

But all day Lyng worried for having omitted the ancient
history class this once. She worried still more about what to
do tomorrow. And the day after that, and for weeks more.

After school was over for the day and Lyng had eaten
supper and gone into her room, she unfastened her boots,
shook them off her feet and threw herself on the bed. As
she lay still in the dark, her mind cleared. Actually the situation was of her own making. If she had been a good student
in history, she could have taught her class in ancient history all
year without a textbook. It was time to stop feeling sorry for
herself and to stop blaming others.

She got up, lit the lamp and took her purse out of the top
drawer. It contained only a handful of small change. She
sat down at the table and stacked the coins into piles. There
were five dimes, nine nickels, and twenty-eight pennies. All
together a dollar and twenty-three cents. That was all she
had and all she would have until two weeks from the coming
Friday, when she received her first pay check.

She tried to remember what textbook she had used for
ancient history at school. She couldn't even do that. Well,
she'd write to Tante Tallette and ask her to go to a second-
hand bookstore in St. Paul and buy the best ancient history
book she could for the money. If with postage the book
came to more, she would reimburse Tante Tallette as soon
as she was able to.

She was stupid not to have had the idea at once of buying an ancient history textbook for herself. With this, she could get along without a class text all year, if necessary.

Lyng wrote a brief letter to Tante Tallette in which she explained exactly what kind of a book she needed. In the morning on her way to school, she would stop at the post-office and mail it. But in the meantime, there were the school periods to be taken care of before Tante Tallette's book arrived, and the problem had to be solved right away.

The ticking of Mrs. Swenson's old clock on the wall bothered her and she went over to it and took hold of its pendulum and stopped it. But she couldn't do that because she'd have to know what time it was. So she gave the pendulum a push and the clock started once more.

"Don't act like a baby. You're a grown woman now."

The dictionary Miss Scherf had given her as a graduation present lay on the table. What would the dictionary have to say about people and events in ancient history? The Greeks were important, she knew, in that era, and Professor Davis had lectured a great deal about the Battle of Thermopylae. She opened the dictionary to Thermopylae and read, "A pass between Thessaly and Greece where Leonidas died resisting the Persians in 480 B. C."

Lyng began to feel better. If she concentrated, she could think of many events in Greek history and names of people. Each day she would put a list of words on the board relating to an ancient country in ancient times. Opposite the names she would write what she had found about them in the dictionary. If the students mastered all these facts she wouldn't be wasting their time, no matter how long it took for her book to arrive or for the school board to decide on a text.

The following morning, Lyng could hardly wait for ancient history class to begin. Before she had gone to bed the preceding evening, she had made a list of twenty-five Greek names and she had written them and the information she had found about them on the board as soon as she had reached school. Plato, Aristotle, Aristophanes, Themistocles, Delphi, Ulysses, Penelope. When the class was called, she told the students they were to study these facts and be ready to recite them the following day.

Professor Lokensgaard came in while the students were copying their lesson.

"What are you doing about ancient history until the texts arrive?" he asked.

Lyng pointed to the black board.

"Where did you get this material?" he asked. "The board will want to know."

"Out of the dictionary," Lyng told him. "We shall cover one country after another until the texts arrive."

She didn't mention the book she had asked Tante Tallette to buy. She would still continue with this plan after it came. The book would help her to outline the work and provide additional data.

A week after she had sent off her letter, a reply came from Tante Tallette and Lyng tore open the envelope.

My dear niece, Lyng,

Many thanks for your letter which arrived Thursday. At the time your aunt Gunara and I were much occupied with our late fall housecleaning. So I had to wait until Saturday to do your errand. I went to the bookstore in our neighborhood, which our roomer, Mr. Gulberg, finds most satisfactory. I told the gentleman at the shop what you needed, and at once he said he had exactly the right book for high school scholars. I warned him that a dollar and fifteen cents would be my top price. Imagine my delight when he said that the book he had in mind was priced sixty-two cents. He said he was giving it to me cheap because this particular copy happened to be somewhat worn, though in perfectly usable condition. He brought it out and I found that he spoke the truth. Then he showed me several other books. These, he assured me, you would find most useful since the village was small and many books were probably not available. And he offered to throw them in with the textbook he had already recommended so highly for the dollar and fifteen cents I had mentioned I might spend. I know but little about American books. Yet, since this shopkeeper was thought of so highly by our studious roomer, Mr. Gulberg, I felt I could depend upon his word. Besides, I know how much your late father valued good books. So I told the shopkeeper that I would take advantage of his offer. I am sending the books at the same time as this letter. Do not worry about the postage. That can be counted as an advance birthday gift from your Tante Gunara and me.

With most cordial greetings,
Your father's sister,
TALLETTE.

Kind and reassuring as Tante Tallette's letter was meant to be, it worried Lyng considerably. What kind of an ancient history text had this second-hand book dealer wished on poor, unsuspecting Tante Tallette? Had he unloaded on her some out-of-date book? And thrown in a few others which would prove useless? Lyng had sent to Tante Tallette all the money she had at the time. She would have to wait until after she had received her pay check, if it turned out that she would have to buy another.

Every day after receiving Tante Tallette's letter, Lyng haunted the post office. Finally after a week of anxiety, she received the long-awaited package. To avoid giving an explanation of its contents to Mrs. Swenson, she decided to take it to school. Fortunately it was already almost dark, and she hurried through Main Street hoping not to meet anyone. People would be curious about her returning to the schoolhouse carrying a package at that late hour.

When she reached the high school room, there was just

enough daylight to enable her to pick out the ancient history text. The rest she left in the package which she put inside her coat closet. Then, slipping the ancient history text under her coat, she hurried home.

To her immense relief, she found that the book, although far from up-to-date, was, as the second-hand dealer had assured Tante Tallette, "in usable condition." With the concentrated but accurate information she found in the dictionary, she knew she could manage until the school board decided on texts for the entire class.

All the students had gone home the following afternoon when Lyng dared to take out the package again and examine it. It contained five other books. She picked up the little red one first. The front side of the binding was elaborately decorated with raised gilt scrolls. She opened the little book curiously and was pleased to find that it was a copy of the complete short stories of Edgar Allan Poe. Lyng had read *The Gold Bug* in high school and the *Fall of the House of Usher* as an assignment in Miss Scherf's class. But both had been drawn from the library and now she actually owned all of Poe's stories. Two large brown books—evidently two volumes out of a set—each contained three novels of Charles Dickens. In the one were *David Copperfield*, *Bleak House* and *Great Expectations*. In the other were *Nicholas Nickleby*, *Old Curiosity Shop*, and *Martin Chuzzlewit*. What a find! The paper of these two volumes of Dickens was yellow with age and the pages were blotched with thumb marks; the print was fine; there were two columns to a page, and the books were so large that they wouldn't be easy to handle. But they could be read and that was all that mattered. Then there was a green book by George Sheldon with the title *In His Steps*, and one with the binding gone called *Ten Nights in a Bar Room* by Arthur. The last one Lyng stuck hurriedly into the drawer of her desk. She'd read it and if it proved to be as bad as the title suggested, she'd manage somehow to burn it either in the furnace at school or in Mrs. Swenson's kitchen stove. But she'd read it first. The Sheldon book sounded safe.

Without knocking, Halvard Moen came in. "Oh," he apologized, "I though you were gone. I lost my ancient history assignment and I came back to recopy it. But I can get it from Ingrid Landstad."

"Why should you? I was only looking over some books which my aunt sent me from St. Paul. Wouldn't you like to see them?"

Halvard picked up the copy of Poe's *Short Stories*. Lyng thought she had never seen anyone handle a book with so much affection. He stroked the outside covers and his hands rested caressingly on the pages as he turned them.

"Would you like to borrow one of the books?" Lyng asked.

Halvard looked up. "Could I? I'd love to read them all."

"Well, there is no reason why you shouldn't." Lyng hadn't realized that anyone but herself would get any pleasure from the books Tante Tallette had sent.

"Do you think the other students—any of them—would like to read them?"

"There have been so few English books around New Stavanger that I guess most of the students haven't thought about it much, one way or the other." He continued to examine the books with eagerness, stopping to read bits here and there.

If these books meant so much to him, Lyng thought, there must be others in the high school to whom they would give pleasure. Aloud she told Halvard, "I think I'll offer the use of them to all the students." Then she stopped to consider. "But it would take a long time for the books to go around. Cutting up the books so that each novel of Dickens and each story of Poe could be loaned out separately would help. But it seems terrible to do that. I have never mutilated a book in any way in all my life."

"It would be the only way to give all of us a chance to read them."

"Would you like to help me?" Lyng asked.

Halvard looked pleased. "Sure," he said.

"They ought to be bound—those that are cut—so the pages won't fall apart."

"That's easy. I helped Miss McCrea bind old books last year. We still have some of the tape we ordered. I stuck it behind the books on the top shelf of the book cupboard." He pulled out some books and brought down a box and opened it. "Yes, it's here. So is the paste and it hasn't dried out. We'll need cardboard. I can get plenty at either the hardware store or the bank. It won't take more than a minute for me to run uptown."

"That's wonderful."

"I'll stop at Ingrid Landstad's. Maybe she can come and help."

Lyng was dusting the last of the books when Halvard returned with Ingrid Landstad. Halvard shoved Lyng's desk close up to one of the students'.

"Ingrid and I will sit in one of the front seats and you can hand us the books, as soon as you have separated them. Then we'll go at the binding," he said.

It was interesting for Lyng to watch these two young people. Ingrid was so quiet and retiring that, during the first months of school, Lyng hadn't noticed her particularly. Now in her red wool dress, plain but becoming with her dark wavy hair and brown eyes, she was attractive. As she worked with Halvard, cutting cardboard, binding the parts of the books and marking them on the outside with the name of the authors and the titles, Lyng saw that she was also very efficient.

Once a book was finished, Lyng noticed again how lovingly Halvard handled it.

"I wish we had these all through high school," Ingrid said.

"I'm going to read all I can while I'm still here," Halvard said.

"I think we should paste some plates into these books," Lyng suggested. "I wonder if there are any."

Halvard looked surprised. "You aren't giving all these to the school, are you?" he asked.

"Yes," Lyng said.

"I'll go and ask Professor Lokensgaard," Halvard offered. He returned immediately. "I told Professor Lokensgaard about the wonderful books you are giving to the school. He wouldn't believe me at first. Then he said that no books have been bought for such a long time that he couldn't remember anything about book plates. He had an idea that some might have been ordered from Mr. Gorman at the *New Stavanger News*. He said for me to go down there and find out."

The small, oblong, brown box Halvard brought back from the printing office was faded and squashed. A row of figures partially covered by two large blots of ink, had been written on the cover.

"Mr. Gorman found the order for the book plates, but he wasn't sure whether or not they had been called for. Finally he located them at the bottom of a drawer under a lot of other stuff. I hope you didn't mind my being gone so long."

Lyng had a sudden inspiration. "We'll add HIGH SCHOOL LIBRARY on the plates," she said, "and begin numbering them from one on."

"You mean that you're starting a high school library for New Stavanger?" Ingrid asked.

Lyng blushed. "That sounds like an ambitious undertaking. But I suppose it is really that."

"Shall I clear out the lowest shelf in the cupboard for them?" Ingrid asked.

"If you wish," Lyng said.

Ingrid went down into the basement and brought up a pail of water. Lyng gave her a part of Miss McCrea's coverall pink apron and soon the shelf was ready for the books.

"I have a notebook in my desk. Why don't we use that for recording the numbers of the books and the names of the borrowers?" Halvard asked.

It was almost dark when the last book had been placed on the high school library shelf. But Halvard insisted on staying after that long enough to make a sign HIGH SCHOOL LIBRARY.

"I'm going to get after Ole to put the lamp in working order," Halvard said as the three made their way down the dark stairs. "Goodness knows when it was used last. But you should have it ready, Miss Skoglund, when you work late up here."

"It's certainly going to get people started talking and wondering," Ingrid said, "if they see lights in the high school room."

CHAPTER TEN

POE'S STORIES were read first, because they were short and could be passed around quickly from one student to the other. Soon *The Black Cat, The Gold Bug*, and *The Fall of the House of Usher* became topics of general discussion in the high school room. The novels of Dickens were longer and for a while they remained untouched on the shelf except for the copy of *David Copperfield* which Halvard Moen had borrowed. At the end of the week he had finished it, and his enthusiastic praise of the book encouraged Ingrid Landstad to read it. Before long all of Dickens' works in Tante Tallette's collection were in circulation. But it was *The Old Curiosity Shop* that was the favorite. The demand for it was so great that Ingrid Landstad, who had volunteered to take charge of the books, set a time limit of a week for each borrower.

One afternoon when the weather was so warm that Lyng had opened several windows in the high school room, she stood looking down on the school grounds at recess. In the farthest corner by the fence, she saw a semicircle of children sitting quietly and paying strict attention to something Ingrid Landstad was doing. Since Ingrid had her back turned, Lyng couldn't make out what it was.

After recess was over and the students were coming into

the high school room, Lyng asked Ingrid what she had been doing.

"I was reading aloud to them," Ingrid said. "Everyone has been talking so much about the story of the waxworks in *The Old Curiosity Shop* that we couldn't wait for our turn to get the book. Bergliot Aasen has it now but she let us take it during recess. I sure hope I can visit a place where they have waxworks some day."

Lyng felt guilty when she thought of the stacks of books in the Franklin Branch of the Public Library in Minneapolis, which she had ignored, and the wonderful University of Minnesota Library at her disposal. She would be willing to do almost anything now to secure books for these eager young people who were starved for reading material.

For days Lyng tried to think of how she could raise money. Nothing whatever occurred to her. Then suddenly she remembered a discussion which had taken place at the university in one of her education classes. It was about the importance of good reading, and the professor had mentioned a provision of the state which allowed each community fifty dollars a year for library books. But this sum had to be matched with another fifty dollars by the community receiving the money.

Lyng thought of the auction sale which the Willing Workers of Reverend Klemstad's church had held the preceding Saturday. There had been a good crowd and sales were brisk, so the total receipts must have been considerable. It wouldn't hurt to ask what the girls intended to do with the money. Mrs. Klemstad had said that the money the Willing Workers raised this year should be spent on some local project, and Lyng could think of nothing the town needed more than a school library.

At noon Lyng brought up the subject with Mrs. Swenson. "A school library!" Mrs. Swenson exclaimed. "Why, Miss

Skoglund, that money belongs to our church!" She looked as though Lyng had suggested robbery.

"The library would be used by the young people of all the churches," Lyng argued.

"Oh, no. The money of the Willing Workers must be spent for our church only," Mrs. Swenson said emphatically. "Mrs. Klemstad and I have already decided we're going to buy wax lilies. They're so nice to lay on the coffin of those who die without relatives at the Old Folks Home west of town, and for other funerals during the winter, too. They make the wax lilies so fine these days that you can't hardly tell the difference between them and the real ones. And then, I told Mrs. Klemstad I had set my heart on a few palms. They're nice for weddings and funerals and for big church holidays. And for confirmations and baptisms of important babies and district church meetings. I saw some real nice palms in a hotel in Fargo. I had to touch them to find out whether they were really growing in the pots. The minute I got home I told Mrs. Klemstad it was time our church got some suitable decorations." Mrs. Swenson was beaming.

So that was it, Lyng thought. If she didn't receive any co-operation from Reverend Klemstad's church, which she herself attended, she couldn't expect help from the other two. Yet she wouldn't give up the idea of a school library. Maybe she could induce some other organization in town to advance the necessary fifty dollars.

If Grandmother Skoglund had been here, what would she have suggested? Lyng smiled. Grandmother Skoglund wouldn't have advised her to go to anyone for the money. She would have told her, as she so often had said to Haakon and Kristian when they tried to shift responsibility to others, "My errand boy had also an errand boy, and his name was *Go Thyself*."

During the days which followed, Lyng tried to think of

the way people she knew had raised money for projects in which they were interested. A dance like the one sponsored by the Sons of Norway in Minneapolis couldn't be considered at all. Hattie's mother had once given a card party for the benefit of an orphanage she wanted to help, but that idea too Lyng at once discarded. She wished she could put on a carnival or a circus because the young people would have a lot of fun at either one, but the grown-ups would be sure to object to anything so frivolous.

One evening Lyng sat leafing through a book catalogue. Her eyes went over the titles quickly and then suddenly they stopped. There was *A Christmas Carol* by Charles Dickens. She read the explanatory note. It said this was the dramatic version of the original story suitable for presentation by high school students.

Lyng knew *A Christmas Carol* almost by heart. Scrooge and the Cratchits and the three ghosts were more familiar to her than many people in real life. She still had the book that had been given to her when she was a little girl and which she had brought along with her to New Stavanger.

Grandmother Skoglund had used it as a sort of textbook while she was learning English. Lyng could still hear her, after she had mastered the language fairly well, read dramatically her favorite passage. " 'A merry Christmas, Bob,' said Scrooge, with an earnestness that could not be mistaken, as he clapped him on the back. 'A merrier Christmas, Bob, my good fellow, than I have given you for many a year! I'll raise your salary and assist your struggling family, and we will discuss your affairs this very afternoon.' " Other scenes which she and Grandmother Skoglund had enjoyed together came back to her. She was sure *A Christmas Carol* would make a good play.

But Lyng had no money for the script.

Well, what of it? Grandmother Skoglund would certainly be disappointed in her if she gave up so easily.

"You can always find a way if you really want it." That was also a frequent reminder of Grandmother Skoglund's. Why couldn't she write a dramatic version of *A Christmas Carol* herself, using the scenes that had impressed her the most? She could try, at least.

The scene with Scrooge in his counting house could open the play. There was plenty of dialogue and it would be easy to fill in the rest. Thanks to the training Miss Scherf had given Lyng, she knew how to go about this job. Unlike ancient history, she hadn't shirked here.

She could put on the play in the high school room and charge admission. The audience could sit in the students' seats and on benches along the walls made from planks borrowed from the lumber yard. A good-sized crowd could be accommodated that way. The audience would be sure to enjoy seeing *A Christmas Carol* and the play ought to bring in a considerable sum of money.

There might, of course, be people in town who would object to her putting on a play. She could think of several— Reverend Klemstad, in particular. It would be best, therefore, to go about it as quietly as possible. After all, *A Christmas Carol* was a classic and was being read in schools everywhere, and while she was writing the play, she could be on the lookout for any passages which might cause trouble and omit them.

As Lyng worked on the play, she was surprised at the number of omissions she felt she ought to make. When she and Grandmother Skoglund had read the story together, neither of them noticed any objectionable passages, but now they kept popping up everywhere.

The passage where the servant was sent to offer the post boy something might provoke criticism. Could she make it cake? No, because the post boy answered that he thanked the gentleman, but if it was the same tap as he tasted before, he'd rather not. Lyng decided she had better omit the whole incident.

She'd have to take the terrible misshapen creatures representing Ignorance and Want out of the play entirely. Parents would object strenuously to having their children take such parts.

Someone would be sure to consider "God knows" profanity, and the account of the death and funeral of Scrooge would have to be toned down. "Old Scratch has got his at last, hey?" really sounded pretty bad.

But the scenes about the Cratchits would make up for everything. Lyng could leave them in exactly as they were. Grandmother Skoglund and Lyng had laughed and cried many a time over the Cratchits. Anyone with a heart ought to be moved by them.

Lyng was putting the finishing touches on the play late one evening when the door opened and Mrs. Swenson stepped in. Lyng slipped *A Christmas Carol* under the pillow in her bed and opened her textbook in American history.

"I brought you a piece of spice cake," Mrs. Swenson said. "You rushed away from the supper table so fast I didn't think you had enough to eat." She looked around the room suspiciously.

"Thank you," Lyng told her. "I guess I had my mind on something I wanted to finish before going to bed tonight."

Mrs. Swenson took the hint and left, and Lyng pulled out the manuscript from under the pillow. When the last scene was finished, she felt satisfied. It ended with Scrooge making up for all the years of happiness lost to himself and others because of his miserliness. The play should send the audience home in a happy frame of mind.

Lyng gave much thought to the casting. There were three

Norwegian Lutheran churches in town, and she had students from all of them. If she wasn't careful to select an equal number of actors from each, she would probably be accused of showing favoritism. She had already heard murmurs to that effect because she attended Reverend Klemstad's church.

Halvard Moen, the only boy in high school at all capable of playing the part of Scrooge, belonged to Reverend Tobiasen's church. So did the Skriveruds. Thorbjorn Skriverud might do for Bob Cratchit, although his voice was a monotone and he stumbled over words when he read aloud. Yet she had better assign him the part. His brother Conrad could in a pinch be used as the ghost of Christmas Past. So much for Reverend Tobiasen's church.

Luckily Bergliot Aasen was a member of Reverend Johnsrud's congregation. Bergliot had developed surprisingly these last months, and she would be the best possible choice for Mrs. Cratchit. Peter Brandvold, although he was rather fat, was the smallest boy in high school and would have to be Tiny Tim. He, too, belonged to Reverend Johnsrud's church as did Solveig Myrland and Einar Ilstrup. Solveig wouldn't make a bad Martha Cratchit. As for Einar Ilstrup, Lyng could let him be the butcher boy since he wouldn't have to say any lines.

There were more students from Reverend Klemstad's congregation than from any other, yet there didn't seem to be any important parts left for them. There was Scrooge's nephew and the other two ghosts and the little squealing Cratchit children. And the people who talked about Scrooge after he was dead. In Lyng's version of the play, none of these had much to say, but the greater number of actors from this church ought to even up matters. Both Ingrid Landstad and Elvera Bjelde belonged to Reverend Klemstad's congregation, and they would have done well in any woman's part. But Lyng would have to save out Ingrid for the mistress of costumes and make-up because she knew more about clothes than anyone else in high school. Lyng could delegate almost any task to Elvera and know it would be well carried out—collector of stage properties, prompter and general promoter of the production. She was willing and capable, and she seemed to know everyone both in town and in the country surrounding New Stavanger.

The next afternoon Lyng read a list of names of students who were to remain after school, and when the last bell rang, several students whose names had not been called stayed in their seats on one pretext or another. Lyng wished she could have given them parts, too. She'd keep them in mind if she put on another play. After the last of these had finally left, she called the cast and her helpers to the front of the room.

"How would you people like to take part in a play?" she asked.

"What kind?" Thorbjorn Skriverud demanded.

"*A Christmas Carol,*" Lyng said, "adapted from the story by Charles Dickens."

"If that's the man who wrote *Old Curiosity Shop,* I'd like it," Bergliot Aasen said.

"I would, too," several others chimed in.

"My ma might not like for me to be in it," Thorbjorn said. "But I don't care. I'm going to, anyway."

"It's the story of Scrooge, a miser," Lyng began, "whose one interest in life was to pile up money. On Christmas Eve he did not have a good wish for Bob Cratchit, his helper in the counting house, and he scoffed at his nephew's invitation to Christmas dinner. That night Scrooge was visited by the Ghost of Christmas Past, the Ghost of Christmas Present and the Ghost of Christmas Yet to Come. They made him realize how meaningless his life had been, and on Christmas morning he was a changed man. He sent the butcher boy with a huge turkey for the Christmas dinner of the Cratchits and he sought out his nephew in his home. For the first time in years, Scrooge again felt the joy in his heart that could only come from a realization of the true Christmas spirit."

The little group sat listening to Lyng spellbound.

"One of the reasons for putting on this play," Lyng went on, "is to raise money to buy books for the high school library here in New Stavanger. We shall charge a small admission for the performance, which will take place in the high school room. There is a state provision in Minnesota which allows each community fifty dollars a year for the purchase of library books, provided that the community matches this allowance with a similar sum. With almost no expense in the production of *A Christmas Carol*, we should easily be able to raise this amount."

"A hundred dollars for books!" Halvard Moen said wonderingly.

"Gee, I can hardly wait!" Thorbjorn said.

After the rest of the cast had gone home, Lyng explained to Ingrid and Elvera what she wanted them to do. Ingrid assured Lyng that she would not have to worry about old clothes for the Cratchits since there were plenty around town. As for the ghosts, Lyng had only to suggest what their costumes should be like, and she would do her best to supply them. Elvera bubbled with enthusiasm, saying she knew she could get her brother Frithjof to haul in his Ford any furniture that might be needed, even if he had to go to the surrounding towns for the right kind. She was also very helpful about make-up.

"We have some baby talcum powder that we didn't use for my little brother," Ingrid said. "I know my mother will let us have that for graying the hair of Scrooge and the others that need it, and my aunt that visited us from Chicago last summer left her rouge. It wasn't enough to bother about sending it to her, and it will be plenty for coloring the actors' cheeks."

"We won't need any of that," Lyng hastened to say.

Elvera was waiting with more good suggestions. When Lyng mentioned stage curtains, Elvera thought at once of some old counter covers she had seen at the Toggery when she helped out there. They could be strung up on the kind of twine the men used on their farm. There were plenty of pieces of cracked china around town, and when Lyng suggested that the Cratchits would have a Christmas tree, small and scraggly though it might be, Elvera offered at once to bring in one from their farm.

"My grandfather brought tiny ones from Norway," she told Lyng, "and he planted them on our place when it was still a claim. He kept transplanting and setting out baby trees as long as he lived. There must be hundreds of them on our land now."

It was dark when the three finished discussing their plans. Fresh snow had fallen. Lyng and the girls walked arm in arm through Main Street to keep from slipping.

"How will you get home?" Lyng asked Elvera when they parted at the railroad tracks.

"I saw Milstuen's sleigh outside the butcher shop," Elvera said, turning back. "I'll catch a ride with Verner. Their place is only a quarter of a mile from ours."

The following morning Professor Lokensgaard was in the upper hall waiting for Lyng when she arrived at school. "What is this I have heard about turning the high school room into a theater?" he demanded.

"You have heard about the play," Lyng said quietly.

"Heard about it! I should say so. I started hearing about it at supper time last night and it's kept on ever since."

"And what are the objections?" Lyng asked.

"You ought to know. A town like New Stavanger doesn't tolerate such things."

"What things?"

"Theaters. Shows, some people call them."

"Professor Lokensgaard, is it any worse to present a story in dramatic form than to read it silently or to tell it orally? That is what the students have been doing with the classics for some time now."

"I refuse to argue the matter with you."

"I am only following the recommendations of the State Board of Education. You will remember I showed you the questions in the state examinations which called for a knowledge of the classics."

"I haven't forbidden you to have the students read them."

"But where are we to get the money to buy books? I bought some second-hand ones and a few have been picked up among the students. But these are not at all adequate."

"Putting on a play—a show—is no way to go about raising the money. Reverend Klemstad is up in arms about the matter. He feels that you are having a very bad influence on our young people."

"I tried to get the Willing Workers in his church to donate some money toward the library, since they are working for a local project this year. But I was turned down."

"Each church here is an independent unit. We never mix its affairs with anything relating to the town as a whole."

"Not even if it would benefit everyone?"

"No."

"All right. So it is clear that no help can be expected from any of the churches. You have told me that the school board cannot be counted on to appropriate the money. My students are willing to do all they can. Have you any suggestions as to where else I could turn for help?"

"I still say that putting on a play is wrong."

Lyng felt herself growing more angry by the minute. "What do you want me to do then? Perhaps I should write to the State Board in St. Paul and ask them to send a special set of questions to our high school here in New Stavanger. Shall I tell them that we can't afford to buy the books which would prepare our students to pass the state examinations?"

"You know better than that, Miss Skoglund. The board would fire you immediately."

A wave of sudden fear swept over Lyng, but she was too angry to let it stop her. "Do you want me to submit the question first to the school board?" she demanded.

"Miss Skoglund, I believe I made it clear to you in the fall that any matter relating to the running of this school—and that included the high school department—must be submitted to the school board by me. The present situation is no exception."

Lyng realized that she had gone too far, and that if she hoped to get anywhere at all with Professor Lokensgaard, she would have to stop letting her temper overrule her good judgment. "Professor Lokensgaard," she said in a voice that she tried to make mild and pleasing, "a good library would open up a whole new world to the boys and girls in New Stavanger. A few dollars spent for books now would mean everything to them."

Professor Lokensgaard's manner, though still stern, seemed slightly less forbidding, as he said, "Up to now, Miss Skoglund, I have protected you from the school board and especially from its president, Reverend Klemstad. In this latest venture of yours, I will have no part. But if you care to take the risk, I shall not interfere."

Lyng tried to feel hopeful after her interview with Professor Lokensgaard. *A Christmas Carol* was such a beautiful story that no one could help but be touched by it. And with her students so eager to do their best, she should be able to please her severest critics, even Reverend Klemstad.

Just before dismissal time the following afternoon, Halvard Moen came up to Lyng's desk. "I noticed that you were watching the clouds," he said in a low voice. "I suppose you wondered how the children in the play from the country will get home. Last night my folks told me that I could take the big sleigh, which has room for all of them, until we give the play. I drove into town in it this morning."

"Thank you," Lyng whispered. With such cooperation, surely she had nothing to worry about.

As soon as the high school room was cleared, the first rehearsal of *A Christmas Carol* got under way. Lyng sat in one of the students' front seats and the actors stood facing her, ready to read their lines.

"We have only one complete copy of the play," Lyng explained. "Each of you has received his own part and his cues. Watch these carefully, so we won't waste any time."

"What are cues?" Thorbjorn demanded.

"A cue is what someone else says just before your part comes in," Lyng said.

"Does that mean that we have to learn everyone else's part?" Peter Brandvold asked. He seemed frightened.

"Oh, no," Lyng assured him. "Only the words of the one just preceding you. For instance, when Scrooge's nephew comes into the counting house, he says, '*A Merry Christmas to you, Uncle. God save you.*' Finn Eggebraaten is the nephew, you know. Then Halvard, who is Scrooge will say, '*Bah! Humbug!*' So when Halvard, or Scrooge, has said, '*Bah! Humbug!*' Finn will know that that is his cue to go on with his own part."

Halvard Moen read his lines carefully, but there was little of the miserly Scrooge in either the tone of his voice or his manner. Finn Eggebraaten stumbled over the words and his interpretation of Scrooge's nephew was even less convincing.

The dialogue between Scrooge and Bob Cratchit came next. Lyng looked encouragingly at Thorbjorn, but he stood stolidly mute.

"Your part comes next," Lyng said.

"I'm waiting for my cue," Thorbjorn said.

"Halvard just gave it to you. He said, '*You'll want all tomorrow, I suppose.*'"

"But you told Finn that the cue from Scrooge was, '*Bah! Humbug!*' Halvard hasn't said it yet."

Lyng bit her tongue to keep it from voicing her impatience. "That was for a different part," she said pleasantly. "Now let's start this dialogue between you and Halvard over again."

Thorbjorn evidently understood Lyng's explanation, for he managed to follow Halvard's part. But now Lyng was horrified to learn that Thorbjorn simply couldn't read aloud. That is, he managed to repeat the words so that most of them were recognizable, but when Lyng thought of the reaction of an audience to Thorbjorn's attempts, she became really frightened.

She had Thorbjorn and Halvard go over the scene once more. This time Lyng tried to imagine that she detected a slight improvement, but she knew she was merely being optimistic.

She got up from her seat and walked over to Thorbjorn. "Let's try still once more," she said. "Look at every word carefully before you read it and then see if you can't pronounce it correctly."

"I do look hard at each word first, Miss Skoglund. That's why it takes so long between them."

Lyng remained at Thorbjorn's side as he read. After he had finished, she said gently, "You will have to do better than that, or I may have to replace you with someone else."

Thorbjorn looked shocked. "I told my mother all about the show last night," he said, his voice trembling now. "She said right away that if Conrad and I did real good in it, she'd give us her egg money for a week to spend for Christmas presents."

At once Lyng regretted reproaching Thorbjorn for something he couldn't help. She wouldn't get anywhere frightening her students.

"If you put just a little more expression into Mr. Cratchit's words, you'll be all right," she said, more gently than before. "You won't be needed in the part we're going to rehearse next, so why don't you study your lines? Ingrid, perhaps you would take Thorbjorn into Professor Lokensgaard's room and coach him for a while."

"Come on, Thorbjorn," Ingrid said enthusiastically. "We'll keep on, Miss Skoglund, until you send for us."

After they had left, Lyng said, "Now for the ghost scene. Conrad, you are the first one—the Ghost of Christmas Past."

"*Are you the spirit, sir, whose coming was foretold to me?*" Halvard read.

"*I—I—I am.*" Conrad's voice shook as he stammered the words.

"*What is your business?*" Halvard read.

Conrad read '*Your*,' but '*welfare*' proved too much for him. Lyng had him repeat the word after her several times.

"*I am surprised,*" Halvard read, "*But still I think a good night's rest would have been much better for me.*"

Conrad stood shaking. Not a word came out of him.

"*Your reclamation then,*" Lyng read for Conrad, "*take heed.*"

After that she continued to read Conrad's part for him without asking him to repeat any of it after her. Halvard kept up his end of the scene and soon it was finished. Conrad looked bewildered.

"You'll be all right, Conrad," Lyng said, steadying her voice. "It takes practice to become an actor."

Halvard said quietly, "The Skriveruds live near our place. I'll have Conrad over for extra practice."

"Thank you," Lyng said softly.

The two other ghosts did not read quite so badly. Lyng helped them whenever the lines proved too much for them but did not stop for any concentrated coaching. It was already growing late, and she hoped to go through the entire play at least once.

When it came to Christmas at the Cratchits, Bergliot Aasen, who was Mrs. Cratchit, read so fast that she got completely out of breath, and the pained expression on her face made Lyng afraid that she would burst into tears any minute.

"Remember, Bergliot, that you are very happy," Lyng told her. "You have prepared a fine feast and are expecting your oldest daughter home. The rest of the Cratchits are happy too, especially the smallest children."

"But—I've—I've never been in a show before," Bergliot said. "I—I might not do right."

"Oh, yes, you will," Lyng told her. "Just be sure of your lines and then it will be easier to put the right expression into them. You, too, Peter Brandvold, remember that—and don't shout. You are Tiny Tim, who is the most lovable character in the entire play. Try to make the audience understand that. Now we'll start this scene all over again. Each of you remember how you feel on Christmas Day."

"We always drive to church at six o'clock on Christmas morning," Peter Brandvold said. "And it's so cold that it takes the rest of the day to get thawed out."

"That's no reason why you have to act like a stiff chunk of ice now," Elvera told him severely. "You listen to Miss Skoglund and say your part just the way she tells you to."

Lyng smiled in spite of herself. There was no doubt that

the members of the group were doing their best to make the play a success. But even with their cooperation and the improvement that a few of them showed in their parts, she was beginning to feel despondent about the final outcome. When it was so dark she didn't dare to keep the cast any longer, she let them go home.

The radiators in the high school room were cold, and Lyng could feel drafts from the ill-fitting windows. The gray sky through the grimy upper windowpanes grew steadily darker. She walked over to the front west window, pulled aside the limp sash curtain and looked out. The last street light on the edge of town lit up an expanse of snow-covered field that stretched toward the horizon. Not a sign of life was visible. Hastily she drew the curtain over the window to shut out the bleakness and made her way slowly down the creaking stairs. Halvard had taken care of the night lock, so she didn't have to stop for that. As the door slammed shut, she was so startled that she jumped.

On Main Street the lights in most of the store buildings were dimmed, and a metal sign in front of the Ford garage flapped to and fro in the wind. Lyng met no one and, although it was a relief not to have to speak to people, the desolation increased her nervousness. As she walked over the hard-packed, snow-covered sidewalk, it seemed to her that she heard footsteps behind her. She looked back and saw no one, but she tried to walk faster. At the end of the block, she caught sight of a feeble light in the post office. She'd stop anyway, although she was sure there'd be no mail for her.

Lyng was more than surprised to find both a letter in her post office box and a call-for-package slip. It couldn't be from home because it was so close to Christmas that neither her mother nor her aunts in St. Paul would have time to write. Her heart beat wildly. Had the school board already taken action against her? Were they sending her this letter to notify her of her dismissal and returning her contract? The reason for the call-for-package slip might be because her contract was too large to fit into her post-office box. Well, she wouldn't call for the package tonight. She had had all she could stand for one day.

Then she walked resolutely over to the window. She wouldn't be a coward and run away from things.

Miss Braa, the post mistress, held out a package through the open wicket gate. "Something inside this box smells mighty good."

There was only one thing in the world that had that sweet fragrance and Lyng would have recognized it anywhere. Grandmother Skoglund's *geburtsdags kringle*. She took up the box, carrying it carefully and lovingly and hurried home. The front part of Mrs. Swenson's house was dark, so she slipped inside unobserved and on to her own room.

She threw off her coat and cap and lit the kerosene lamp. Then she remembered the letter which she had thrust into her coat pocket. With eager fingers she reached for it and held it up to the light. It, too, was post-marked from Minneapolis and the address was written in Grandmother Skoglund's unmistakable Norwegian script.

Inside it contained one folded sheet that Grandmother Skoglund must have bought especially for the occasion.

Congratulations on your birthday. There is no one else at home, so I must write this myself. You mustn't think I forgot your present. I was up especially early to bake it so it would be cool in time to send off this afternoon. Now it is all wrapped and ready to go. Butcher Sather was most kind about giving me stout wrapping paper and cardboard. Eat and enjoy it with good health.

From your devoted grandmother,
Knudsdatter, Sina Skoglund.

The words were blurred by the tears that dropped from Lyng's eyes. She raised the letter to her lips and kissed the spot where Grandmother Skoglund had put her signature. Then she opened the box. After removing several newspaper wrappings and one of Grandmother Skoglund's snow-white dish towels, she took out the *geburtsdags kringle*.

On the top Lyng read *Lyng Skoglund, December 3*. The year must have been rubbed off in transit. Again Lyng held the *geburtsdags kringle* up and smelled it. Never—not in her entire life—had she realized how fragrant a *geburtsdags kringle* was.

Lyng thought of the many loving hours Grandmother Skoglund had put into the making of it. Weeks ahead of time she must have started to save a few pennies every day to pay for the ingredients that would go into it: citron, prunes, raisins, almonds, eggs, cardamom—not to mention butter, cane sugar, wheat flour, milk, yeast and much more. The evening before Grandmother Skoglund was to bake the *geburtsdags kringle*, she set the sponge with great ceremony and tucked it down for the night as carefully as though it might have been the birthday child. The next morning, immediately following breakfast, she put on a fresh apron and seated herself at the table from which the dishes had been cleared. Then she prepared the fruit and the nuts that were to go into the dough. No one, not even Lyng's mother was entrusted with that task. When the *geburstdags kringle* was out of the oven, a perfect figure eight, brown and dotted with fruit and nuts, Grandmother Skoglund finally put it on the blue and white platter to cool.

A feeling of warmth and peace and quiet stole over Lyng. All memories of the struggle and worry that had been with her during the day were gone. With Grandmother Skoglund loving and thinking of her and praying for her, Lyng could certainly weather any storm that lay ahead of her. She didn't even worry about the play any more. She still had two weeks for rehearsal, and nothing worthwhile was accomplished in one short try.

During supper Mrs. Swenson spoke only when absolutely necessary. She regarded Lyng with openly accusing eyes, and Lyng realized that she was in a state of high indignation. After they had finished eating, Mrs. Swenson told Lyng that she had something important to say to her. "Since you live in my house, I feel it my duty."

Lyng wondered why living in Mrs. Swenson's house should make any difference. Neither her mother nor Grandmother Skoglund ever interfered with the private affairs of the roomers at home.

"This show business of yours up at school is terrible," Mrs. Swenson said. "Reverend is quite put out about it and I don't blame him. I think you had better stop it right away."

"What is there about a school play that is wrong?" Lyng asked quietly.

"Everything."

"Have you read the play?"

"No. And I don't intend to."

"Then, Mrs. Swenson, it seems to me that you are talking about a subject of which you know nothing."

"Miss Skoglund, in my house I won't—"

"Mrs. Swenson, this play concerns my work as a teacher in the New Stavanger High School. I must ask you, therefore, not to concern yourself with it."

"I never heard anything so terrible in all my life."

"The students should have many more books to read for their English courses, and we are trying to raise money for the library by putting on this play. And we think it is a very lovely play."

"I am certainly going to tell Reverend what you have just said to me."

"From what I have been able to gather," Lyng said, "you tell Reverend Klemstad entirely too much. A man of his intelligence and high ideals doesn't want to be bothered with gossip. You will be a much more valuable helper in his congregation if you confine your efforts to your activities there."

"I never heard—" But Mrs. Swenson was too overwhelmed to say anything more.

Lyng got up from the table.

"There is another matter to which I should like to call your attention," she said. "Please lower the mirror in my room to a place where it will do some good. I'm tired of climbing on top of my bed when I use it."

"If anyone had told me that you would talk to me like this, I wouldn't have believed them," Mrs. Swenson said. But the assurance in her voice was entirely gone.

Before Lyng started the rehearsal of the play the following afternoon, she gave a speech to the cast. "Yesterday we didn't expect to accomplish much except to become acquainted with the play and to learn how each of our parts fitted into it. Today, with these preliminaries taken care of, we can go ahead in earnest. I know that every one of you will do your best to make this presentation of *A Christmas Carol* something the people in New Stavanger will always remember. Now let us begin with the first scene."

Halvard Moen recited his lines without once referring to his script, and Lyng could almost imagine him a miserly Scrooge. But Thorbjorn was not at all convincing.

"Bravo!" Lyng exclaimed at the close of the scene. "I knew you could do it."

"Did you mean me too?" Thorbjorn asked.

"Of course, I did."

Thorbjorn smiled sheepishly. "Ma helped me after we got through milking last night and Pa had gone to bed. But I told her that she didn't pronounce the words the way you did."

"It was kind of her to take such an interest in our play," Lyng said. "And with your rehearsals here and Ingrid's coaching, you will become such a fine Bob Cratchit that the audience is going to love you."

Thorbjorn positively beamed.

"Now for the ghost scene," Lyng said. "Come here, you three ghosts, and let me talk with you. In Dickens' story of *A Christmas Carol*, the appearance of the three ghosts is spectacular. For instance, the Ghost of Christmas Past—that's you, Conrad—is supposed to be barelegged, wears a costume decked with fresh flowers and a blazing light on top of his head, and he carries a sprig of holly."

"Where will we get those things?" Conrad asked.

"That's exactly the problem. Or rather, there are many," Lyng said. "In the first place, it's too cold up here now in New Stavanger for you to be without shoes and stockings. And the flowers would freeze before we got them to the schoolhouse. And I wouldn't under any circumstances, let you wear a candle on your head for fear of a fire. When Ingrid and I discussed your costumes this morning, we decided that you should wear a sheet and carry an evergreen branch instead of the holly."

"I'll take care of that," Elvera said promptly, beginning to write in a notebook she took from her pocket.

"The costumes of the other two ghosts are equally impractical. So Ingrid and I have decided that we'll have to drape sheets around all of you to make you look like ghosts, and Ingrid will also powder your faces."

The three ghosts giggled.

"But you'll have to do more than that to make yourselves ghostlike. Your actions on the stage are very important. Try to walk lightly with your heads up and your shoulders thrown back."

Lyng walked behind them, bracing their shoulders and holding their hands high above their heads to keep the boys from slouching and sprawling.

When this failed, Lyng finally said, "I know what we need here—a ghost-like atmosphere. Halvard and Thorbjorn, will you please lower the shades on the windows? Thank you. Now let us pretend we are in a cemetery on a moonlight night and are surrounded by tombstones. In the distance, three white figures approach us. Can't you imagine how they would skip and dart among the tombstones and how they would sound if they started to speak?"

The performance of the ghosts was still not impressive. But Lyng knew the boys were doing their best and she thought she detected a slight improvement.

She said, "It will take a little while for you boys to perfect your parts. But that isn't strange. After all, you have never tried being ghosts before."

Bergliot, as Mrs. Cratchit, was still nervous and her voice broke as she read her lines. Again she seemed on the verge of tears.

Lyng appeared not to notice. "I can visualize you perfectly as Mrs. Cratchit on Christmas morning," she told Bergliot. "You are waiting for your dear Bob to come home, happy in the thought of the bounteous feast you have prepared. Although the two of you have been poor throughout your married life, as money standards go, you are really rich, for you are as much in love as you were on your wedding day. Now you are surrounded by your fine family."

Bergliot blushed furiously. Thorbjorn muttered, "Aw shucks." Everyone in the cast laughed and Bergliot and Thorbjorn finally joined in.

"That's the spirit!" Lyng exclaimed. "If you are as relaxed as you are now on the night of the play, you won't have a thing to worry about."

After the practice, Peter Brandvold said suddenly, "My folks don't like me to be in a show. I teased and teased for them to let me, so they said *yes* for this once, but never again. Boy, I'm glad. I haven't had so much fun in my life."

"Our pa isn't stuck on us being in it either," Thorbjorn said. "But our ma said for him to wait and see. She said that she came from fine folks back in Norway and she had noticed that Conrad and me had begun to take after them."

"I'm glad I don't have to be a ghost," Bergliot remarked. "My mother thinks it's a sin to believe in ghosts. She thinks it might bring bad luck to act like ghosts in the play."

The disapproval of some of the parents worried Lyng. If they were not in sympathy with the play, what could she expect from outsiders? She had counted on the support of relatives and friends of the performers, and had expected them to make up most of the audience. Now she would have to take other measures to insure a good attendance. She talked the matter over with Halvard Moen.

"I think we should sell tickets ahead of time," she told him. "But I don't know how to go about having them printed here in town."

"Mr. Gorman, the editor of the *New Stavanger News*, usually makes up the handbills for auctions," Halvard suggested.

Lyng decided to speak with Mr. Gorman personally. She had no ready cash to offer him, but she would guarantee to pay him the day after the play had been given.

"You Norwegians are all alike," Mr. Gorman told Lyng. "Stick together like glue. It's only when you need something that you'll look at an outsider."

"Our play isn't a project of just Norwegians, Mr. Gorman,"

Lyng said. "It's the entire public school that is giving it. That is, the high school."

"Then why did you limit the cast to Norwegians?" he demanded.

"Why, there just aren't any students in high school but Nor—" Lyng caught her breath. Eva Gorman—his little girl! Lyng had wanted to use her as Tiny Tim but she had been afraid of criticism if a girl took a boy's part. No wonder Mr. Gorman was grumpy and uncooperative. He was hurt because his daughter had not been asked to take part in the play.

Lyng's heart went out to the frail little girl in the freshman row who scarcely ever spoke above a whisper, alone among all the children of Norwegian parents and feeling herself different. Lyng knew exactly how she must feel, thinking she had been discriminated against. It brought back to Lyng the memory of her own childhood.

"Mr. Gorman," she said, talking and trying to make her brain work at the same time, "a play is a new venture here, and it takes time to work out things. I have a part selected for your Eva, and I assure you she is perfectly suited for it. She is to be Tiny Tim's little sister Angela, the most lovable character of the entire cast. Her part occurs late in the play. Since she comes from a home where English is spoken, she has naturally a great advantage over the rest. Moreover, Eva is a very bright child, so I didn't feel she would need as much coaching as most of the others."

Mr. Gorman smiled. "Well, I guess a teacher has to be just about as careful to keep off the toes of folks as a country editor. You should have heard the calling down I got last week for overlooking the name of one of the sponsors at a baptism party out in the Elverum community east of town."

"And about the tickets?" Lyng asked.

"You'll have them in two or three days. I'll get at the job as soon as the paper is out," Mr. Gorman said. He had plenty of cardboard lying around, he told Lyng, and the ink used would be negligible, so he wouldn't accept a penny for the tickets.

Lyng went directly home and sat down at once to create the character of Angela Cratchit for the play. She had Angela wish Tiny Tim a Merry Christmas, when Bob Cratchit brought Tiny Tim home perched on his shoulder. At the Christmas feast Angela offered Tiny Tim her share of the plum pudding, which he nobly refused. And after Tiny Tim had died and Bob Cratchit returned from visiting his grave, Angela told her parents she would do her best to make up for the loss of her beloved brother. Lyng hoped the Gormans would be pleased with the part.

While Lyng was writing, it bothered her to think that she was taking liberties with this beautiful story of Charles Dickens. But if Dickens could have known how much she needed Angela at this time, she was sure the good man would have forgiven her. It troubled Lyng even more that she had told an outright falsehood to Mr. Gorman. Truthfulness was considered a cardinal virtue at home. She hoped God would forgive her because she needed the tickets for the play.

Eva Gorman brought the tickets to school on Thursday, and that same afternoon Lyng distributed them to the cast and her helpers.

"Ma says she is going for sure," Thorbjorn Skriverud said. "And I think she'll make Pa go, too. So Conrad and I can take two between us."

"The teacher in our district out in the country boards with us this year," Bergliot said. "And my mother will come."

"I'm going to ask everybody I see," Elvera said, "so I'll take twenty to begin with."

Every day after that, Lyng listened to reports on the ticket sales.

"Lots of people are waiting to hear who else is going,"

Elvera said in disgust. "That's what the waitress up at Sigvald's restaurant told me." But the next day she was beaming. "I sold twenty-two at Farmer's Club last night. I told the people, if they wouldn't buy from me, they needn't expect me to help with the exhibits this year at the County Fair."

Kaare Moen, Halvard's brother, sold ten at the bank where he worked. "Kaare talked the play up to Mr. Melhus, the president of the bank, saying that, outside of church services, it would be the only Christmas affair ever given in New Stavanger, and Kaare told him that I had one of the leading parts. Mr. Melhus is pretty strict, but he finally said that he thought that he and Mrs. Melhus would go. Right away Kaare told him that he would like to present him with two tickets. After that Kaare mentioned to the customers that the Melhuses were going and most of them bought tickets from him."

Of all the ticket-sellers, none was prouder than Einar Ilstrup when he gave his report. "I got my father to take two," he said, grinning from ear to ear. "He's never gone to anything but church before. He kind of laughed when I told him I was one of the actors."

By Wednesday night after the tickets for the play had been given out, over a hundred had been disposed of. That meant that something would have to be done to accommodate the unexpectedly large number of buyers. Lyng discussed the situation with Halvard Moen.

"We could borrow Magnus Olstad's folding chairs," Halvard told Lyng. "He keeps them in the little room behind the store for funerals, if the relatives don't want to go into any of the churches. It's mostly when bodies of people who used to live here are shipped in for burial. Magnus Olstad is our town undertaker, you know, and a good one. The folding chairs are rather small, so after the students' regular seats have been filled and the benches, we could set the folding chairs in the aisles, starting from the back. And the folding chairs could be placed around the door out in the hall too."

"The people in the hall would be seeing the play from the side," Lyng said, "But that would be better than standing through the entire performance."

Since the sales were going so well and so many people were coming, Lyng thought it would be a pity not to have the high school room looking as nice as possible. If only the place could be given a good cleaning. She decided to go in search of Professor Lokensgaard.

"Ole isn't hired to do any extra cleaning," he told her abruptly. "He does a thorough job of it once during the summer and again during the Christmas holidays."

"Couldn't he clean the high school room now instead of during the Christmas holidays?" Lyng asked.

"No, the board has made the ruling and it is my business to see that it is carried out."

"Then I'll do it myself."

"You know your place better than that, Miss Skoglund. The town doesn't hire a scrubwoman to teach high school."

Lyng decided to ignore this remark. Neither he nor the rest of the town needed to know if she was a scrubwoman.

She managed to catch Ole before he left the building, and, after considerable coaxing, he gave her the key to the back door. On Saturday morning Lyng hurried to school, being careful to put her oldest dress under one she usually wore to avoid arousing Mrs. Swenson's curiosity. Grandmother Skoglund wouldn't mind her doing this. "Always dress to suit the occasion," she used to say.

At the schoolhouse Lyng went directly to the basement for a pail of water. She had stuffed rags and a bar of soap into her bag, and as soon as she had taken off her street dress, she started her cleaning job in the high school room. She had finished washing the woodwork and the students' seats and desks and her own, when she heard someone coming upstairs. She hastily shoved the pail into her coat closet and pushed the door shut. The hall door opened and Ole came in.

"I never saw anyone so much in love with scrubbing," he said.

He left and in a few minutes he was back with two mops and another pail of water. Together they began to wash the floor. They were still at it when Professor Lokensgaard walked in. Lyng dropped her mop.

"I—I decided to clean the high school room ahead of time," Ole stammered. "It's getting too much, trying to do the whole school during the Christmas holidays."

"You should have chosen a different room to start on," Professor Lokensgaard said coldly. "This will be all tracked up after the play on Friday." But there was the slightest suggestion of a smile on his lips. "Next time you go to Reverend Tobiasen's communion table, Ole," he went on, "you might put in an extra petition for not always speaking the exact truth."

After the cleaning of the high school room, Lyng was exhausted but very gratified over its cheerful appearance.

It warmed Lyng's heart during the week which followed to see how hard her students worked. By Thursday night, after the last practice before the public performance, she was cautiously pleased over the results. To be sure, the Skriverud boys—especially Conrad—still hesitated and stammered in certain places, but Elvera, who was prompter, privately assured Lyng that she would be able to continue with any lines either of them lost. Lyng was also a little uneasy over the dinner scene at the Cratchits' for fear that Bergliot, who had only partly overcome her nervousness, might have an accident with the roast goose and the plum pudding, which Halvard's mother promised to supply in order to make the scene seem more real. And then there was always the possibility of stage fright and that the students would stand without saying anything. But Lyng could only hope and pray that all would go well.

After school had been dismissed on Friday afternoon, Lyng helped Ingrid to take the costumes and make-up equipment table and desk and other stage properties in the students' cloak from her coat closet to Professor Lokensgaard's recitation room, which he had consented to have used as a dressing room. After each item had been carefully gone over, Lyng joined Elvera who was organizing the stool and chairs and room.

"The Christmas tree of the Cratchits can go into the far corner," Lyng told Elvera. "It won't be used until the last part of the play."

In the meantime, Halvard and the other boys in the cast were busy putting up the plank benches around the high school room and arranging the folding chairs out in the hall. It was almost six o'clock when all these preparations had been completed, and the stage curtain had not yet been put up.

"Just tell me how you want it done," Halvard told Lyng, "and I'll take care of it. All of us from the country are eating our sandwiches here tonight, and I'll have plenty of time. You just go on home, or you won't be able to get back in time."

Lyng had planned to lie down for a few minutes before supper, but instead she had to rush changing her dress and combing her hair. The crucial moment was fast arriving, and there was nothing more she could do. If only Grandmother Skoglund were here! Anyway, Lyng knew she had Grandmother Skoglund's good wishes and prayers for her welfare, and they would stand her in good stead tonight.

Mrs. Swenson appeared at the supper table wearing her best black dress covered with a blue-and-white percale apron. She made no mention of her intention to go to the schoolhouse. Lyng's hand shook as she took the cup of tea Mrs. Swenson offered her, and she dropped her spoon twice before she managed to put the sugar into it. She worked hard to swallow a meat loaf sandwich and a sour cream cookie, thankful that she wasn't expected to eat a large evening meal. Before Mrs. Swenson had finished, Lyng excused herself.

In spite of the extreme cold and the deep snow, Ole stood at the front door of the schoolhouse, screening the people he allowed inside the building.

"We don't want any roughhousing up in the high school room after it's all fixed up," he told Lyng. "The kids can wait until it's time to start."

"I think you should let everyone come in," Lyng said. "Some have had a considerable distance to go and it isn't easy to arrive exactly on time."

Ole muttered that there were places downtown where people could go to warm up, but he let the long line of boys and girls sweep past him.

Elvera stood at the head of the stairs and reported to Lyng that the entire cast was already on hand. Those not in the students' cloakroom were in the process of being made up by Ingrid in Professor Lokensgaard's recitation room. Then Elvera seized Lyng's arm and pushed her toward the door leading into the high school room. "Come and see what a grand stage we have. Halvard put up the nails just like you said and strung the curtains from one end of the room to the other. There's just enough space left outside the curtain on the wall near the hall for an opening where the people can come in. I don't see how you could figure it out so exactly. After the curtains had been strung, I tried them out and then I showed the curtain-pullers how, so they'll do it all right during the play."

The costumes and the make-up of the actors had so changed them that Lyng had to look at some of them twice before she recognized them. The rumpled white hair, the drooping rope mustache, the grimy faded blue shirt and the ragged shoes had certainly made Halvard into a convincing Scrooge.

"Didn't Ingrid do a good job of powdering my hair?" he asked, turning completely around for Lyng to see him from all angles. "She followed all the instructions about my make-up that you had written."

"If you frown now," Lyng laughed, "you'll be perfect."

"My brother Kaare has promised to cover the shade of the hanging lamp with blue paper when he gets the signal from Elvera. You mentioned that, so I thought you'd like to know."

"Thank you," Lyng said.

The three ghosts, swathed in white, moved toward her. In the dim light of the cloakroom, they presented an eerie sight, and Lyng was glad she hadn't followed the details of the story, dressing one in green and one in black. On the other hand, giving each of them something to set him apart from the others—the evergreen branch of the first ghost, the braided rust-colored sash of the second one and the black silk shawl covering the head of the third—made the boys feel more important.

"Can we take off these sheets as soon as our parts are over?" Conrad Skriverud asked.

"No," Lyng said. "Remember that you are all to make a final appearance when the curtain-pullers draw the curtain at the end of the play. Take your places in line just as I assigned them to you. Elvera will give you the signal to take your bows."

"Yes, and then they are to stand there until the curtain is pulled for the last time," Elvera said.

The hum of voices could be heard from the high school room.

"Reverend Klemstad is coming," Elvera said. "He's out in

the hall. Tomine, you don't have to pull the curtain yet, so run out and take him to the seat I reserved for him."

Lyng looked in the direction of the hall. There he stood, dressed in black and white. His face was solemn, almost stern. Lyng felt the fast beating of her heart. Before turning away, she breathed a quick silent prayer.

"Every seat is full now," Elvera went on. "They're putting up the folding chairs in the aisles. Kaare said that a lot of people who hadn't bought tickets ahead of time are coming in."

Soon Elvera reported that even the folding chairs out in the hall were filled and there was only standing room left.

Ingrid Landstad, dripping with perspiration, came over to Lyng. "I dusted the actors with talcum powder," she told Lyng. "And I put it on thick on the faces of the ghosts, like you said should be done."

"All right. We'll start," Lyng said.

She took her place behind the door which swung into the cloakroom. Here, through the crack between the door and the wall, she could see the front of the high school room. Her work was over. The rest was up to the students.

"Help them to do well," she prayed.

Suddenly everything grew quiet in the cloakroom.

Tomine Flekkefjord and Ragnhild Vordal, the curtain-pullers, took their places out on the center of the stage where the two curtains met. Each girl started to pull her curtain toward her side of the room, being careful as she moved with it to keep herself behind it. As the stage came into full view of the audience, a prolonged "Oh—Oh!" broke out.

In the center of the stage burned a red tissue-paper fire in a three-sided wooden box, with an empty coal scuttle beside it. On one side of the room, Halvard, as Scrooge, sat before a dilapidated desk that had once been a kitchen table, counting green and white paper money that looked almost real. Opposite Scrooge, Thorbjorn as Bob Cratchit was perched on

a high stool borrowed from Sigvald's restaurant. He was
huddled over a desk that had been made high enough by nail-
ing wooden blocks at the ends of the legs of a small square
table. The dark corners and the long shadows on the floor
from the single oil lamp hanging from the ceiling only served
to make the stage look really like Scrooge's counting house.

As the play progressed without any prompting from Elvera,
Lyng was glad they both did well with their lines. Still,
Elvera kept her eyes fixed on the only complete copy of the
play in order to keep the conversation flowing smoothly by
putting in a word at the slightest hesitation from the actors.
A few *boo's* at Scrooge assured Lyng that the audience was
following the play.

The setting for the second act was even more realistic. The
blue paper that Kaare Moen had put over the shade of the
hanging lamp accentuated the dinginess of Scrooge's hovel
and the eeriness of the Ghost of Christmas Past. Another and
a longer "Oh—oh—oh!" from all corners of the high school
room again told Lyng that the interest of the audience was
being held.

The happy dinner at the Cratchits brought loud applause.
Lyng held her breath until Bergliot had served the goose
without a mishap. But she could see that by the time the
actors had been helped to the plum pudding (it was new to
all of them, Mrs. Moen having taken the recipe out of *The
White House Cook Book*), they were all enjoying themselves
immensely. Later in the play when Mr. Cratchit came home,
quiet and drooping, after visiting Tiny Tim's grave, sniffles
could be heard everywhere.

"The poor people," someone cried out in Norwegian. The
words ended in a sob. Lyng recognized Mrs. Klemstad's voice.

At last on Christmas morning, Halvard as a reformed
Scrooge leaned out the imaginary window marked off on the
blackboard with brown and blue chalk. He called out to

Einar Ilstrup in the cloakroom off stage and told him to take the prize turkey, hanging outside the butcher's—it was bigger than Tiny Tim himself—to the home of the Cratchits. This brought the house down, and the cheering continued until the entire cast had taken its carefully planned curtain call.

Mrs. Klemstad, her face tear-stained but smiling, pressed Lyng's hand.

Close behind her came Mrs. Swenson. "Miss Skoglund," she said, "if that Scrooge man—if he hadn't given that poor family a good big Christmas dinner, I'd—I'd have gone and done it myself."

Lyng saw Reverend Klemstad standing by the front seat near the window. After the crowd had cleared out a little, she made her way over to him.

"I want to thank you for coming tonight," Lyng said. She held out her hand and he took it.

"It was a good story," Reverend Klemstad said. "The young people did very well."

Lyng choked when she tried to speak. Reverend Klemstad, she knew, had meant what he had said. Her play had been a success, and there was no longer any doubt that she would be able to get the books for the high school library.

CHAPTER ELEVEN

As Lyng stepped outside the schoolhouse one afternoon, two little girls in white middies and blue cotton skirts came running toward her. They were rolling barrel staves and keeping them balanced with long sticks. Farther down Main Street, Lyng noticed a bright green and yellow sign that hadn't been there at noon when she returned from dinner. The sign read: "*Smooth Velvety Ice Cream and All Varieties of Soft Drinks.*" Across the tracks a man was raking his front yard. Gray smoke rose almost perpendicularly from a bonfire up into the clear spring air. Lyng took deep breaths. The smoke, the earth under the man's rake and the new leaves bursting out on the branches of the trees that lined the street, all smelled of spring.

Outside Mrs. Swenson's house the manure and the tar paper, which had covered the foundation since Lyng's arrival last fall, were gone. Screens had been put on outside the lower half of several windows of the glassed-in porch. In her own room, the storm windows had been taken off, and as Lyng hurried over to throw the sash wide open, a flood of fresh air rushed in.

What a treat it's going to be to sleep in here tonight, Lyng thought.

Before she had finished washing her hands and face, she

heard Mrs. Swenson call out, "Supper is ready." There was a pleasant, almost an excited ring in Mrs. Swenson's voice as she appeared in the doorway of the usually closed-off dining room. "We haven't eaten in here except for company since Mr. Swenson died. But this year I thought it would be nice to set the table out here during the warm weather, as long as you are with me."

It was cool and pleasant in the dining room. Potato salad and sliced summer sausage were already on Lyng's plate, and Mrs. Swenson poured iced tea out of a transparent pink pitcher.

"Mrs. Banker Knudson gave me some of her mint," she said. "Her Yankee daughter-in-law from Connecticut sent her some slips, so she raises her own mint now. She has promised me a few plants and I'm going to raise it in my garden."

"I'd like to have a garden some day," Lyng said.

"Do you mean you never planted things—vegetables and flowers?" Mrs. Swenson asked incredulously.

Lyng thought of their barren back yard in Minneapolis and the one lonely lilac bush, that after years of tending had yielded not a single blossom. "No," she said, "we didn't have any place for one at my home in the city. I always thought it would be fun to live in the country."

"That reminds me," Mrs. Swenson said. "You're going to the country tomorrow. At least you're invited. Mrs. Bjelde sent word that she's entertaining the Ladies Aid and she wants you to come out with Elvera after school tomorrow."

"That will be wonderful!" Lyng exclaimed.

"You'll enjoy going out to Bjelde's," Mrs. Swenson said. "She always serves a fine lunch. I would have gone myself except that I've promised my son's wife to help her put up pie-plant."

The next morning Elvera appeared at school in a brand-new, blue and white plaid gingham dress. Her blond hair was curled and she walked about with an air of excited importance. At noon she told Lyng that her brother Frithjof would call for them in his Ford as soon as school was out. Lyng felt more and more excited over the invitation the closer the time came for them to leave.

Her heart beat fast as she took her place beside Frithjof in the front seat. At last she was having a ride in an automobile. She tried not to show how thrilled she was. The Bjelde children would consider her naive if they knew. On the way out to Bjelde's farm, her spirits rose higher and higher. She couldn't breathe into her lungs enough of the warm spring air sweet with the smell of freshly upturned earth. She thought she had never heard such beautiful music as the singing of the birds Elvera called meadow larks. Blue violets bloomed along the road and Elvera had Frithjof stop the car so she and Lyng could get out and gather some. As they passed farm houses surrounded by groves already a bright green, Elvera volunteered bits of information about the people who lived there and related incidents that had happened to them through the years. Lyng was especially impressed with Halvard Moen's home. It was by far the most pretentious of any she had seen. The large white house was surrounded by a white picket fence. Inside a square set off by barbed wire stood a cluster of well-kept, red and white outbuildings. Except for the absence of the mountains and the river, it looked almost exactly like the painting of the Skoglund estate in Norway.

Out at Bjelde's farm, Elvera piloted Lyng into the dining room. It was crowded with women sitting on chairs arranged two-deep along the walls. Many of them had babies in their laps and beside some of the mothers stood little boys and girls. Keeping a firm hold on Lyng's arm, Elvera walked straight over to the table where a plump, rosy-cheeked woman was supervising the serving of food.

"Ma, this is Miss Skoglund," Elvera announced, loud enough to be heard above the hubbub of voices.

There was a sudden hush and Lyng felt that all the women in the room were looking at her.

Mrs. Bjelde came forward and held out her hand. "Welcome to Bjeldheim," she said. "I'm so glad that you could come. Elvera speaks of you so often."

Elvera beamed. "Miss Skoglund says it's her first visit to the country since she came to New Stavanger. Isn't it lucky for us, Ma, that we got to be the first ones to have her?"

"You must come often," Mrs. Bjelde said cordially, "now that you have found the way out here."

"Isn't that place at the table for Miss Skoglund?" Elvera asked.

"Yes, of course," Mrs. Bjelde said. "You can wait on her, Elvera, after she is seated. But I'll take her around first and introduce her to the ladies. While I'm doing that, go into the kitchen and get a fresh pot of coffee."

Then for the first time Lyng noticed the large space left clear at one end of the long table. It had been set for one person, evidently for her. Now she understood the full significance of this invitation out to Bjeldeheim today. Often Grandmother Skoglund had told how, when a distinguished guest was entertained at the manor house in Norway— whether it was the minister or some other equally important dignitary—he was always seated for meals at a table all by himself. This table at the manor house was loaded with platters stacked high with the finest cakes. And the huge cubes of butter and cheese, that were served on these occasions, towered above the head of the guest. Although there were no huge cubes of butter and cheese on Bjelde's table now, there was certainly no lack of food otherwise.

The ordeal of introductions over, Lyng was brought back

by Mrs. Bjelde to her place of honor. Elvera hovered over her, offering her the seemingly endless varieties of food being served. Lyng felt uncomfortably conspicuous with all eyes in the room still upon her.

"How do you like it up here in this part of the country?" a woman whom Lyng remembered as Mrs. Opness asked.

"I'm beginning to feel very much at home," Lyng said.

"I suppose, though, now that it's getting to be so close to the end of the school year, you're getting anxious to be back in Minneapolis?" Mrs. Opness asked.

The mention of the end of the school year startled Lyng. "Oh, I haven't even begun to think of Minneapolis," she said. "There is so much to do before school closes."

"If you're half as busy as my Bergliot," Mrs. Aasen said, "you haven't got a minute to spare. She's awfully anxious to graduate so she can take the teachers' exams over at the country courthouse this summer. Miss Fuglie, a friend of ours that's been teaching over in the Koppang School, is going to be married this spring. She's offered to help Bergliot to get this job if Bergliot graduates and passes the teachers' exams."

The idea of Bergliot Aasen taking on the duties of a teacher next year startled Lyng. But she murmured, "I hope she does."

"I do, too," Mrs. Aasen went on. "Bergliot's always been a little slow but once she gets things, they stick by her. That's why, when she was in the play last winter, I didn't have to worry about Bergliot's not knowing her part the way some of the mothers did."

"She did very well," Lyng agreed.

"Bergliot is a good girl," her mother continued. "She's already promised to pay for a set of false teeth for me out of her first month's check, if she gets the school. She wants to buy a washing machine, too, as soon as she can. There are so many heavy clothes to be washed on a farm that it would mean a lot to me to simply turn the crank of a machine instead of rubbing clothes on the board."

Lyng decided to give Bergliot extra help so she could graduate and pass the teachers' examinations—and more important, be able to teach the children in the Koppang School something if she was hired.

Several young girls came into the dining room with more sandwiches and cake and filled the cups with coffee. There was a slight lull while this was going on.

Then Mrs. Skriverud, who was close by Lyng, spoke up. "Miss Skoglund, I'm beginning to think that this education is getting to be too much of a good thing. I came from what is called better people in Norway, and I want my boys to be able to hold up their heads with the best of them. But there is a limit to everything. Both Thorbjorn and Conrad take their storybooks with them when they go out to the barn. Often we have to go and see what has happened to them because they never come back. Each time we find them sitting on the milking stool reading."

"You should be pleased," Lyng said. "If your children continue to be that much interested in school, it will help them to become successful and useful men some day."

"I know that my boys are smart," Mrs. Skriverud conceded. "They take after my side of the family—the Gubbeholmens. Especially Thorbjorn. And I'll admit he was good in that play. I was glad because I've had to fight their father to let them keep on going to school. He never understands about education. But now I'm beginning to wonder myself if the boys aren't getting a little too much learning."

Mrs. Skriverud's remark that her boys might be getting too much learning worried Lyng. She wondered if the mother was thinking of taking the boys out of school soon. If this was so, Lyng regretted that she hadn't spent more time with them, helping them to speak and write English more correctly.

Lyng's thinking was interrupted by what the woman beside Mrs. Skriverud was saying. "I think Mr. Skriverud is right." The woman was red-faced and heavy-set, and she breathed hard as she sat devouring food and drinking coffee. "What's the use of learning a lot of foolish stuff out of books? You don't need that to milk cows and feed pigs. As soon as our children get sixteen, we have them quit school. The truant officer is the one I fight with."

"No wonder. The Vasbottons are so dumb they never could learn anything," Elvera said in a low undertone.

"Elvera," her mother whispered. Aloud she said, "We're pleased that Elvera is getting a chance for a high school education. We hope to send the rest of the children into town, too."

"Wouldn't you rather have your children prepare themselves for life with a good education, Mrs. Vasbotton, than leave them to become aimless drifters?" Lyng asked, a slight tremor in her voice.

"Mine don't drift," Mrs. Vasbotton snapped. "They stay right on the farm. And there's plenty of room for them to move around. We bought our eighth quarter of land last fall."

"Quarters of land are about all they'll ever have," Elvera said, still under her breath.

Elvera's mother regarded her sternly. "Elvera," she said, "go out and look after the children. There are so many strange horses in the yard today that someone might get hurt."

A short, rather stout woman with wisps of graying hair down her neck had come in during the discussion and kept her eyes fixed on Lyng. Someone greeted her as Mrs. Baglien. "Well," Mrs. Baglien said, "I think there is entirely too much foolishness connected with the town school these days."

Lyng found it increasingly difficult to swallow the delicious food Elvera had pressed upon her. Were there many women present who were so hostile to schools? "I would like—" she began.

But Mrs. Baglien interrupted her. "When I was young, we expected to learn something at school—reading and writing and arithmetic. School was a place where you sat still and tended to business and at four o'clock you went home and helped with the chores. But nowadays, in the towns—from what I hear about New Stavanger, especially—they're doing nothing but putting on shows and reading silly love stories. No wonder they need all that time, the way they fool around. In my day the teachers tried to learn us something. And it didn't take them a lifetime to finish the job."

So that was what the people were thinking and saying of the high school in New Stavanger. At least, some people. Didn't they realize at all how hard she was working to give her students the advantages other young people all over the United States enjoyed? Lyng didn't want to become involved in an argument, yet she couldn't very well sit listening to all this unfair criticism of her work without saying something.

"I think if you visited our school in New Stavanger," Lyng said finally, "and really found out what we're trying to accomplish there, you would think more kindly of us. Young people nowadays, all over the country, are being better educated, and our boys and girls will need more education, too, than you older people had in order to compete with them. My grandmother grew up in Norway and she had a chance to get very little schooling, but she insisted that I attend the university."

Lyng had tried to speak calmly and, she hoped, with the good sense and dignity Miss Scherf might have shown had she been here.

"That's the kind of a fine speech the truant officer made to me the last time he was over," Mrs. Vasbotton said.

Lyng's throat hurt. Was she hindering rather than helping the chances of the young people to continue with their education? "I wasn't trying to make a fine speech," she said. "I only wanted you to know how important it is for your children to go to school."

"Sure," Mrs. Vasbotton said. "But just let the truth come to light and off come the silk gloves. After I let the truant officer know I wasn't fooled by him, he turned right around and said we'd be fined if we didn't send Tulla and Bulleman to school. I let him know that all he was after in the first place was to get an extra haul outside of his regular pay. And when he started to get smart, I ran him off the place. But you can't do anything with that bunch of grafters in the county seat— the truant officer got his haul all right. Before he finished the fight, Vasbotton had to fork up with the ten dollars."

Mrs. Bjelde's face grew a deep red. "The truant officer didn't get that money, Mrs. Vasbotton. There's a state law that children have to go to school until they are sixteen years of age and you know it."

"Yes, and who makes the laws?" Mrs. Vasbotton demanded. "That same bunch of grafters up in the county courthouse. I suppose that is why Miss Skoglund is so anxious to pull kids into her school. It'll mean more money in her pocket."

"Mrs. Vasbotton, how dare you say that!" Lyng asked. She regretted her outburst immediately. Giving vent to her anger wouldn't promote good will toward her cause with these people.

"Well, our taxes are going up every year," Mrs. Vasbotton said. "This time they were something awful. The money must go somewhere."

"That's because you're buying up so much land," Mrs. Bjelde told her. "Only a part of the taxes go for schools. Mr. Vasbotton was the loudest complainer at the county commissioners' meeting last week because the roads weren't better out your way. Yet he complains every time more money is voted to improve them."

"All the same," Mrs. Skriverud said, "I do think this school business all over the country is getting to be a little too much. I hope the boys don't turn out the way my cousin did down in Fillmore County. He was smart just like Thorbjorn and he always got a hundred in his studies and sometimes more. His folks sent him away to Normal School for a year. But when he got home and tried to work his father's farm, he just wasn't any good. He lost it last fall and now he and his wife have had to go to renting."

"No one gets more than a hundred in any subject he takes at school," Mrs. Bjelde told her.

"Perhaps he shouldn't have tried to be a farmer," Lyng said. "If he had continued with his education and become a teacher or entered some other profession for which he was qualified and liked, he would probably have been successful."

"That's what I've told Mr. Bjelde. We're not forcing a single one of our children to stay on the farm if they don't want to."

"Don't worry. They won't want to, if you send them into town to school the way you say you're going to," Mrs. Vasbotton told her. "Our neighbors, the Katlies, lost one of their boys that way. He stayed in town with the Florgaards one spring to study up for the exams and they've never gotten him to stay on the farm since."

"That was for the eighth-grade examinations," Mrs. Bjelde said. "You can't blame the boy for not wanting to come back the way Kjeld and Guri Katlie drive their children."

"Well, I still say," Mrs. Baglien chimed in, "there's too much monkey-business going on in our town schools. We used to have only five or six months' terms in our country district, and most of us never went longer than six years. At that I'll bet we learned more than the town scholars do in all the years the teachers are trying to make them go."

Mrs. Moen came over to the table and sat down close to Lyng and Mrs. Bjelde.

"I think it is terrible," she said, "insulting Miss Skoglund the way you women have been doing this afternoon. And the first time she has been out this way in the country. I feel ashamed for all you of you, and for myself for not speaking up before things got to this point. Halvard has never been so happy at school in his whole life. Our one regret is that Miss Skoglund didn't come to New Stavanger years ago so Halvard could have had her from the first in high school. And that Kaare didn't have the opportunity of being her student at all."

"Oh, the kids are crazy about her," Mrs. Baglien said. "And no wonder. You hear them talking about all the swell times they're having up there. But what are they learning, can you tell me that?"

"Halvard says he has learned more this year than during all his other three years combined. He says that he doesn't dread the state examinations one bit this year."

"He hasn't taken them yet," Mrs. Baglien said drily.

Lyng was so shocked at the implication of Mrs. Baglien's words that for a few seconds she thought she must have mistaken them. "He hasn't taken them yet." The sentence kept running through her mind. Halvard Moen—her prize student —whose work was so perfect that she sometimes depended on the correctness of his opinions rather than her own. If there was the slightest doubt of his passing the state examinations, there could be little hope for the others.

The purpose of the state examinations was to test how well the teacher had instructed her classes during the school year. In the fall, Lyng had had this objective clearly in mind. She had argued with Professor Lokensgaard to get him to order suitable textbooks which would prepare the students for the examinations. She had worked hard in ancient history before the arrival of the textbooks approved by the school board, so no time was wasted. And she had put on the play to raise money to buy classics. But had she allowed her enthusiasm first for making a success of the play and later getting the students to read the classics that had been purchased—had she allowed these to interfere with her regular classroom instruction? Perhaps much of the criticism being hurled at her this afternoon—or a part of it—was justified. Perhaps Mrs. Bjelde in her role as hostess was merely being polite and Mrs. Moen was supporting her.

Mrs. Aasen was talking. Her voice shook and she looked frightened. "My Bergliot thinks maybe she'll pass the examinations," she said.

"If the boys don't get their state certificates so I can stick them under the nose of Mr. Skriverud, I'm sunk," Mrs. Skriverud said. There was a note of anxiety in her voice. "I might as well give up the fight of trying to keep them in school any longer."

Lyng looked at Mrs. Aasen and Mrs. Skriverud with new interest. And all at once she felt a great respect for both of them. These two farm women were sending their children to her, both under tremendous difficulties. In fact, the hopes of their entire lives were centered on how well their children aquitted themselves at school, and especially on how well they would be able to answer questions in the state examinations. If she failed to prepare them properly—The thought was too terrible to be endured.

Lyng stood up. "I'm afraid I must be going," she told Mrs. Bjelde.

"Oh, must you? We had hoped you would spend the evening with us."

"Oh, no. I have so much to do. The state examinations and—and—"

"I know," Mrs. Bjelde said. "These must be busy times for all of you. Perhaps you will be able to come out later—after school closes."

Lyng murmured her thanks and she left hastily without making the rounds among the women to say good-by. Her one thought was to escape in order to begin at once the task of preparing her students to pass the state examinations.

All the way home she felt subdued and humble. How could she have been so sure of herself, that everything she did and said was absolutely right? Why hadn't she stopped to consider whether she was fulfilling the first duty of a teacher— to present facts to her students? "Putting on shows and reading love stories." Those women in the country probably felt about such things as she had felt down at the university when the secretary of the Placement Bureau had put so much emphasis on extra-curricular activities. She must have appeared just as ridiculous and condescending to some of the people at the Ladies Aid as the secretary had to her. They probably felt as resentful toward her.

Well, as Mrs. Moen and Mrs. Skriverud and Mrs. Aasen had intimated, the state examinations would test how well she had performed her job during the past school year. In spite of the fact that she had stressed the importance of the examinations to Professor Lokensgaard and the school board, she had given almost no serious thought to preparing her students.

As soon as she had arrived home, she took pencil and paper and sat down at her table. She would make lists of important topics to be gone over in each of her classes, and give the weak students extra time. She had better make doubly sure with the seniors. If any of them failed, it would be sheer disaster. She felt fairly sure that Halvard Moen would pass all his examinations. With plenty of coaching, Ingrid and Bergliot —especially Ingrid—ought to get through. With Einar Ilstrup it was much more doubtful. He needed help with everything and she'd simply have to manage to give it to him, even if she had to stay up all night to get her own work done.

Immediately after supper each evening she had Einar come over to the house, and she worked with him on the glassed-in porch until dark. After a drill she had given him, Mrs. Swenson said to Lyng, "You don't mean to say you're trying to make a scholar out of that poor Einar Ilstrup?"

"It isn't easy for him to learn."

"Easy for him to learn? I should think not. Why, he was ten years old before the teachers could make him understand the difference between his right and left hand. I don't believe he ever did learn to count past twenty. You're wasting your time on him."

"But he tries so hard. Now that he's this far, it would be a pity for him not to graduate with his class."

The last two weeks Lyng worked even harder to prepare the students for the state examinations. She was careful to alternate the groups as she worked with them, giving them a breathing spell between sieges of study. She saw to it that no student was kept working too long. But she did not spare herself. In ancient history she took country after country and selected important facts to be memorized about each. In American history she had the students recite the names of the presidents with the dates of their administrations from Washington through Taft, and she listed for them the principal accomplishments of each president. It got to the point that if Lyng wasn't coaching someone in something, she felt guilty.

"You'll have brain fever if you don't look out," Mrs. Swenson warned her on the Friday night before the examinations were to begin. "It's ten o'clock and you haven't been home for a bite since breakfast this morning. I'm going to heat some

milk and you're going to have to drink it, whether you like it
or not."

On the fateful Monday morning, the first examination was
in ancient history. Lyng's hand shook as she opened the sealed
envelope containing the questions. She gave a set to each student in the class and distributed the long white regulation
papers with printed forms on which the state required the
examinations to be written. Then she sank on the chair at her
desk.

Trembling from head to foot, she started to read the questions. Egypt, Babylonia, Syria, Greece, Rome. Yes, she had
touched on everything that was being asked. But would
the students remember? Would they be too nervous to set
down what they actually knew? If only they were able to
express themselves better in English!

She sat in front of the class, watching the students, and
she tried to make out how each was getting along. Thorbjorn
sat with his head almost touching the paper, scribbling furiously. She dreaded trying to decipher what he had written,
but she'd do her best. Halvard Moen wrote slowly and steadily. She could see that he felt sure of what he was putting
down. Elvera's eyes sparkled as she looked up at Lyng. Ingrid
Landstad sat staring at the questions for at least ten minutes
without writing a single word.

"She needs You, God," Lyng prayed.

Soon after Ingrid was leaning over the examination paper
and writing rapidly.

The examination in American history came that same afternoon. The students seemed more relaxed and went at their
writing more confidently. The questions certainly demanded
a thorough knowledge of the subject. While the students
wrote, Lyng caught herself offering little snatches of prayer.

As soon as the last examination paper in American history
had been handed in, and Lyng was alone, she closed both

doors. She picked up the papers, walked over to the window and sat down in the front seat in the freshman row. She'd start with the papers of the seniors.

The appearance of Halvard's paper was so perfect that it might have been engraved. It could be corrected easily and quickly. There were the answers, given briefly and accurately: the purpose of the New England Confederation of 1643; the Preamble to the Constitution—not a word nor a punctuation mark was missing; the Missouri Compromise; the Panic of 1837; Lincoln's Reconstruction Policy; the Tweed Ring; Horace Mann. Breathlessly Lyng read the answers until she reached the end of the paper. Halvard had not made a single mistake.

Ingrid's examination paper, although far from perfect, was well written and would entitle her to a good grade. It was slower going when it came to Bergliot's, but she, too, finished well above passing. Lyng sat holding Einar's paper for a moment before she began reading it. There wasn't one question in the examination that she and Einar hadn't discussed thoroughly together. But—well—she'd read the paper and find out how much of the answers he had retained. The New England Confederation had evidently faded into oblivion with him, for there was only a blank space where the answer should have been. But he had only a few mistakes in the Preamble to the Constitution, and he had put down the essentials of the Panic of 1837. The last question which was to be in essay form on *The Advantages of Being an American*, Lyng choked over. "Every boy and girl, high or low, smart or dumb, rich or poor, has a chance for an education in America." When Lyng added the credits she had given on each question, she found that Einar had a passing grade. He passed in all the other subjects he took from her and so did the other three seniors.

The papers of the students in the lower classes were, in

general, good, too. Those who failed would have other years in which to repeat the subjects before graduation. The important thing was that all of the students had done their best.

They were such fine young people, willing to meet a person who worked with them more than halfway. Lyng was very proud of them and thankful to have been their teacher.

CHAPTER TWELVE

ON THURSDAY Lyng brought the examination papers and the list of final grades into Professor Lokensgaard's office for him to see.

"They're not bad," he admitted. "And there couldn't have been any cheating going on. I saw to it that every textbook was locked in my office, and, as you know, I inspected every desk to make sure that no student was hiding a single paper."

"No," Lyng told him, "the students didn't cheat."

"I suppose we are safe in having graduation now," Professor Lokensgaard said. "But with only a week before school closes, we won't have time to prepare anything elaborate."

"We ought to make this a great event in the lives of our seniors," Lyng said. "One to which they can look back with much pleasure."

"All right. You take care of it. Only don't make it run into money. And let me know your plans before you carry them out."

Lyng decided that it would be no fault of hers if this first commencement of the New Stavanger High School was not a memorable occasion. She would start work immediately.

The four seniors had their first class meeting that same afternoon. Halvard Moen was elected president; Bergliot

Aasen, vice-president; Ingrid Landstad, secretary, and Einar Ilstrup, treasurer.

"What's the use of having a treasurer when there isn't any money?" Einar Ilstrup asked.

"We may decide to buy something and then you will collect what each of us is to pay," Ingrid teased. "Maybe you'll be asked to go and pick it out, too."

Einar looked scared. "Why can't I be vice-president?" he asked. "He doesn't have anything to do."

So it was arranged that Bergliot and Einar were to exchange offices.

"You should have elected a class adviser," Lyng reminded them.

"You're that," Bergliot Aasen said.

"Would you like to select your class colors, now that you have that matter settled?" Lyng asked.

The choice turned out to be purple and gold, and the class flower, the American Beauty.

"We've never had any American Beauties up here," Ingrid said. "But they sound wonderful. Some day we may and then we can say it was our class flower."

On Monday morning the seniors had their pictures taken in a group. Lyng was very anxious to have them photographed, since the pictures would be seen by relatives and friends of the graduates and would be tangible evidence of what they had achieved. She went down beforehand to make the arrangements with Mr. Thune, the photographer; and when he told her the total price of the four pictures would be three dollars, she said she would be in at the end of the week to settle with him. From the students, she collected a quarter apiece, since Bergliot and probably Einar would not be able to pay more. After the picture had been taken, Mr. Thune said he intended to display it in the show window of his studio for the entire town to see and Lyng felt more than repaid for her own outlay of money.

On Tuesday evening the seniors had their picnic. Lyng suggested that it would be nice to invite the rest of the high school students and, of course, Professor and Mrs. Lokensgaard. The more people participating in the affair, the more important it would seem and the more quickly news of it would spread around.

It was agreed that everyone who came to the picnic should contribute an item of food. Einar said that he could bring sugar lumps because they bought them by the hundred-pound sack at home. Bergliot Aasen asked if it would be all right for her to furnish a quart of beet pickles. Her folks raised them on the farm and put up a lot every fall. Professor Lokensgaard said his wife wanted to be responsible for the coffee and the cream.

When Lyng told Mrs. Swenson about the picnic and the arrangements, Mrs. Swenson insisted on making doughnuts and her favorite cookies—oatmeal rocks. Later she told Lyng she was sticking in the picnic basket a bag of coffee, ground just right, and a quart of coffee cream. "Just to be on the safe side," she said. "I've attended Ladies Aids where Mrs. Lokensgaard has served and I've never once had a good lunch. I don't suppose they have anything but skimmed milk in the coffee at that house."

Mrs. Swenson seemed to take it for granted that she was to accompany the doughnuts and the oatmeal rocks to the picnic and Lyng made no objection. Mrs. Swenson was an expert where food was concerned, and good coffee was important at a picnic. Besides, Mrs. Swenson seemed to take such pride in being with the young people that Lyng didn't have the heart to disappoint her. Then too, Mrs. Swenson, of all people in town, would let the world know if the picnic was a success.

The crowd met at the schoolhouse. Professor Lokensgaard and his wife were the last ones to arrive. Mrs. Lokensgaard was a large-boned woman who seemed ill at ease, almost frightened. And, except for a few low, hurried words while being introduced to Lyng and as many more during the serving of the coffee, Lyng heard nothing from her all evening.

Einar Ilsturp took them all in his father's dray wagon to the picnic spot on the river. After supper the young people sat around a huge fire toasting marshmallows. Then they played games: Skip-Come-a-Lou, Four-in-a-Boat, the Needle's-Eye, Last-Couple-Out, and Farmer-in-the-Dell. Even Mrs. Swenson joined in the fun. As for Lyng, all the high school students wanted her for a partner, and finally out of breath, she begged to be allowed to rest during just one game. From a rock on the high bank, she watched the moon come up and cast a wide, corrugated streak over the running water below so that the woods became a network of lights and shadows.

On the way home, Lyng was surprised at the number of American songs the students knew: *Swanee River, My Old Kentucky Home, Columbia the Gem of the Ocean, Tenting on the Old Camp Ground, America.* Some grade teacher must have done a good job of Americanization in singing class at least. Back in her own room, she went immediately to bed, and at once she was sound asleep.

On Wednesday afternoon the Class Day exercises were held out on the school grounds. Ole and his son Marius had done their best to cut away the weeds on the spot where an elm tree, the memorial gift from the senior class, was to be planted. The elm tree had been dug up and brought in from Moen's farm by Halvard and Einar, and Halvard, as the president of the class, made the presentation speech.

After the tree planting, Lyng went directly to the *New Stavanger News* office, to see Mr. Gorman. Of all the ways of publicizing the graduation, none would be as effective as some good write-ups in the local paper.

"But such a mass of material," Mr. Gorman objected. "I don't think I should give up so much space in my paper to the local school. With haying coming on, the farmers will want news of what their neighbors are doing about it. And I ought to have a good-sized article on hog cholera."

"But the first class to graduate from the New Stavanger High School is a milestone in the town's history," Lyng argued. "In years to come, people will be using these issues for gathering historical data."

Mr. Gorman shrugged his shoulders. "Oh, all right. But you should know that a newspaper man is much more interested in giving news to the present generation than collecting items for dusty files to be opened by generations yet unborn."

In spite of herself, Lyng had to laugh. "I have given you at least sixty names in these stories," she told him. "See if that isn't going to appeal to the generation now alive and reading."

Lyng had scarcely reached home on Thursday afternoon when Mrs. Swenson rapped at her door. In her hand she held the latest copy of the *New Stavanger News*.

"Well, Norway County is sure to know we've got a graduation class this year," Mrs. Swenson said, handing the paper to Lyng.

Across the top of the front page in heavy black print was the banner headline: "NEW STAVANGER GRADUATES ITS FIRST HIGH SCHOOL CLASS." Underneath smaller headlines proclaimed: *"Halvard Moen, President; Einar Ilstrup, Vice-President.* Over another column Lyng read: *"Halvard Moen. Valedictorian; Ingrid Landstad, Salutatorian."* Still farther down on the front page were stories about the senior class photograph, the picnic, the Class Day exercises and the Junior-Senior Banquet to be held that same evening.

So Lyng's experience of helping put out the *Lincoln High School News* had, after all, proved useful, even though the secretary of the Placement Bureau hadn't considered it worthy to be included as an extra-curricular activity. It had also been worthwhile for Lyng to sit up several nights the past week to write these stories herself which were being printed in the *New Stavanger News* today.

At the Junior-Senior Banquet that evening, everyone arrived carrying a copy of the *New Stavanger News,* and everyone found his name mentioned in it at least once.

"Mine is printed five times," Einar Ilstrup counted. "Gee, I'm going to buy a copy to send to each of my brothers and sisters and to all the rest of our relations."

As it turned out, Mr. Gorman had to print five hundred extra copies to supply the demand. He telephoned to Lyng and urged her to bring in the follow-up stories with full details, including excerpts from speeches to be made by town dignitaries and the graduates.

The actual graduation exercises were, of course, to be the climax of the commencement activities. Lyng went to Professor Lokensgaard's office after the banquet to discuss with him where the exercises were to be held.

"I don't see why we can't just meet in the high school room," he suggested. "Except for the kerosene that would be burned in the lamps, there should be no expense. And the days are so long now that there wouldn't be much spent for that."

"No," Lyng said firmly. "The seniors have been sitting in that room four long years. Their graduation night must be something special. Besides, that shabby room is no place for any festive occasion."

"Where then would you like to have the exercises held?" Professor Lokensgaard asked.

"Reverend Klemstad's church is the loveliest place in town for anything like that."

Deep lines appeared on Professor Lokensgaard's forehead. "That's asking a good deal," he said. "As far as I know, our churches have only been used for regular religious services, weddings, funerals and baptisms."

"That doesn't mean they couldn't be used for other occasions."

"I wouldn't want to ask Reverend Klemstad," Professor Lokensgaard said. "If you feel so strongly about it, you might try. But don't be disappointed if you meet with a pretty stern rebuff."

Before going to bed that night, Lyng made an appointment with Reverend Klemstad for ten o'clock the following morning in his study. As soon as she arrived there, she came to the point at once.

"The community built a schoolhouse for such occasions," Reverend Klemstad told her coldly. "The church is God's house."

Lyng's eyes flashed. "Do you mean to tell me that there is anything ungodly about our high school commencement?"

"I didn't say that. But—"

"But what? Reverend Klemstad, our high school commencement is an important event in the lives of our young people, and it must be conducted in a dignified manner. You know there is no dignity about that shabby, ill-kept high school room."

Lyng held her breath. She had challenged Reverend Klemstad openly now, but she was past worrying about the consequences.

"Must a high school commencement call for such a very fine place?" Reverend Klemstad asked.

"Reverend Klemstad, you are interested in our young people. Otherwise, you wouldn't spend the time and effort required to serve as the president of the school board. Wouldn't you like to be instrumental in making commencement night a beautiful memory for our seniors and their relatives and friends? If you will allow us to have the exercises in your church, you will be doing that."

Reverend Klemstad's face relaxed a little. "It is true that I am the president of the board," he conceded. "Since this is our first commencement, we naturally have no precedent to go by. And it is also true that my church is the finest meeting place in town."

"That's wonderful!" Lyng exclaimed, beaming at him. "And now may I count on your presenting the diplomas in English?"

Reverend Klemstad laughed outright. "You certainly do not waste any time or opportunity to attain what you want, do you?" Then he became serious again. "There is a ruling in our church that all functions shall be conducted in the Norwegian language."

"The presentation of the diplomas from an American public school would have to be in English. And I did want to quote parts of your speech in the account of the exercises which will be printed in the *New Stavanger News*."

"Oh, all right," he agreed. "But you might as well come over to my study after I have written my speech and go over it with me. I should like to make sure that what I shall have to say will be quoted exactly."

When on Monday morning, Lyng reported the result of this interview to Professor Lokensgaard, he asked a little sarcastically, "Is there anything else you can think of, Miss Skoglund?"

"Yes," she said promptly.

Professor Lokensgaard regarded her with real concern.

"We must have an invocation and a benediction at the exercises. Since our seniors come from all three churches, I think all three should be represented on the program. I would suggest that we invite Reverend Tobiasen and Reverend Johnsrud to open and close the exercises."

"Miss Skoglund, you do not know what you are asking."

"What is there so unusual about asking a minister to give the invocation or to pronounce the benediction at a high school commencement?"

"That isn't what I have reference to. Reverend Klemstad wouldn't approve of having the other two ministers in his church. And I doubt very much that they would come if they were invited."

"I don't see why. All three have members of their church in the graduating class. Surely they would approve of sending these young people out into the world with God's blessing? I'd be glad to ask Reverend Klemstad and the other ministers, too."

"No," Professor Lokensgaard said sharply. "That will have to be a matter for the board to decide."

"Do you want me to go to them?"

"Miss Skoglund, how many times do I have to remind you that any matter to be brought up to the board must be presented by me, and me only!"

"Will you let me know by tonight? I am preparing the story for the paper."

"I'll try."

It was late that night when Professor Lokensgaard called Lyng to his office.

"Is it all right for me to go ahead with my story?" she asked.

"Not quite so fast, Miss Skoglund. I met with the board at Melhus' bank. All the members were present, including Reverend Klemstad. At first Reverend Klemstad insisted that in his church he, alone, must conduct all the religious rites. But the members of the other two churches objected to the point of threatening to take the entire ceremony into one of their own churches. Finally, a compromise was reached. The exercises will be held in Reverend Klemstad's church, and as president of the school board he will present the diplomas. But Reverend Johnsrud will give the invocation and Reverend Tobiasen will close the exercises with the benediction."

"And the invocation and benediction will be in English?" Lyng asked.

"Strangely enough, Reverend Klemstad brought up that matter. He said that, as president of the board of education of a public school in the United States, he would have to insist on both being given in the language of the land."

Lyng made no comment.

"Well, it was left that way. The school board members of the other two churches promised to get in touch with their ministers and to explain the situation to them. I expect to hear from them both soon."

The following noon Professor Lokensgaard reported that the entire program of the high school commencement was to be given in the English language.

Lyng was up early on the day the graduation was to take place. When she came out into the kitchen, Mrs. Swenson was preparing breakfast.

"I thought, since there was no regular school, you would sleep a little later," she told Lyng.

"The seniors and I are going to decorate the church."

"You think of everything, don't you? Well, the world doesn't have to be set upside down for that, does it?"

"No, but I want it to be especially nice—the church, I mean."

Mrs. Swenson's face brightened. "I'll tell you what," she said. "I'll call Mrs. Blacksmith Sydfjord. She's taken over the job of looking after the decorations. I'm sure that when I explain to her that Reverend Klemstad is to be the main speaker on the program, she won't object to letting you borrow them. Only you'll be careful about not breaking the branches of those big palms, won't you? And the wax lilies are awfully delicate. We've used them only in daylight so far—on confirmation day and at old Gustav Glomsrud's funeral and when the Druggist Johnson baby was christened. I'd kind of like to see the effect when the electric lights shine on them in the evening."

Lyng's first impulse was to decline Mrs. Swenson's offer. The very thought of using wax lilies that had lain on old Gustav Glomsrud's coffin made her shiver. But she was beginning to learn how important it was to have the good will of everyone, and there was no question that Mrs. Swenson meant to be helpful. After all, the lilies and palms could be set where they would scarcely be noticed. So Lyng said, "Thank you, Mrs. Swenson. They'll look nice with the flowers and greens we're going to get out in the woods, Elvera Bjelde and Peter Brandvold and I."

"You always think up the hard things," Mrs. Swenson said. "But at that, no one can accuse you of being lazy. You'll be needing vases and jars for the flowers and greens. I'll see that there'll be plenty of both when you get back to the church."

That evening when Lyng stood in the vestibule of Reverend Klemstad's church and looked in, the beauty of what she saw was breathtaking. The altar rail was completely hidden by ferns and other greens. There were bouquets of lilacs and yellow honeysuckles at the altar, on the organ, on several small tables and at the ends of the first five pews on both sides of the center aisle. Everywhere there was a sweet fragrance of ferns and flowers.

Mrs. Klemstad struck the first chords of "War March of the Priests" from *Athalie*. The procession started forward, headed by Reverend Klemstad and followed by Reverend Tobiasen and Reverend Johnsrud. Lyng was more moved than she had been by the splendor of the academic procession at the University of Minnesota on her own graduation day. The crowd rose to its feet and turned around to greet those who were marching down the aisle. Lyng and Professor Lokensgaard followed the ministers, and after them came the graduates, single file.

Ingrid Landstad was shy and nervous as she delivered the salutatory, and she had to be prompted twice by Elvera who was following the lines, word for word, on the paper she held in her lap. But Halvard Moen stood upon the platform, erect and unafraid, and Lyng felt sure that he would have done credit to the largest high school in the entire State of Minnesota.

Then Reverend Klemstad rose from his chair and turned toward the four young people on the platform.

"Members of the graduating class," he began. "As the president of the Board of Education of New Stavanger, it is my duty and privilege to present these diplomas to you upon the completion of—"

Lyng sighed with relief. Reverend Klemstad was repeating the speech exactly as she had taken it down for the *New Stavanger News*.

When he handed the four rolls of parchment to the graduates, she could sense the excitement of the audience, even though they did not feel free to applaud.

As soon as Reverend Klemstad sat down, Reverend Tobiasen came forward. He raised his arm, and as he stood there slightly bent he held the palm of his hand open toward the audience. "The Lord bless thee and keep thee," he said in his halting English. "The Lord make His face to shine upon thee and give thee peace."

No one stirred as he walked slowly back to his seat.

Then Mrs. Klemstad began to play *The End of a Perfect Day*, which she had learned especially for the occasion. The audience pressed forward to congratulate the graduates.

An elderly man with a long, narrow, gray-streaked beard approached Lyng and held out a gnarled and work-hardened hand.

"So you are Miss Skoglund," he said. "I have been hearing much about you. Especially lately. I am Einar Ilstrup's father. I want to thank you for all you have done for my boy. You have made a new person of him."

As he left, a woman shook hands with Lyng. "I am Maren Peterson's mother," she said. "I had intended keeping Maren home next winter. There is so much to do on a farm and I need her help. But after tonight—well—I just haven't got the heart to do it."

Bergliot Aasen's mother pressed Lyng's arm. Tears were streaming down her cheeks. "You don't know what this evening means to me," she said.

It was late when finally Lyng was in her room and alone. But she sat down on the chair at the table and made no effort to undress.

It had been an evening she would never forget. She could still see the eagerly upturned faces of the crowd as they followed every movement of those sitting on the platform in the front of the church: the three ministers, side by side; Ingrid and Bergliot in their white dresses between Halvard and Einar Ilstrup, and herself on a chair beside Professor Lokensgaard. She could still hear Reverend Klemstad's carefully weighed words in English, telling the graduates how fortunate they were to have grown up in a community like New Stavanger, which offered opportunities for the development of their minds as well as guidance for the salvation of their souls. Best of all, his brief *Thank you* to her as he shook her hand at the close of the program.

How wise Lyng's mother had been when she had insisted that Lyng go to the university. And how unselfish of Grandmother Skoglund to ask Lyng to go as a favor to herself. Lyng would let them know how she felt about this when she got home. She'd also make a point of telling Miss Scherf how much she appreciated her guidance at the university, and especially the influence that had made Lyng decide to become a teacher. There was no doubt in her mind now that teaching was the most wonderful profession in the world.

Finally Lyng undressed and went to bed. Still she couldn't sleep. The first streak of dawn had begun to show through her window when at last she lost consciousness.

She was awakened by a knock at her door. Her room was bright with sunshine. Mrs. Swenson, carrying a tray, came in.

"I let you sleep," Mrs. Swenson said. "There is a limit to what a body can stand. Here's some coffee to help open your eyes. I heard you stirring in bed, so I knew you were awake."

"Oh, thank you," Lyng said. "You shouldn't have bothered."

"It wasn't any bother. I had saved out some oatmeal rocks and doughnuts from the picnic, and the coffee kept hot at the back of the stove. Anyway, there are going to be plenty of mornings soon when I won't have to bother about anything except the four empty walls around me."

When Lyng went for the mail, she found a long, narrow, white envelope in her post-office box. The printed return address told her that it was from the Placement Bureau of the University of Minnesota. She tore the envelope open and took out a single sheet with a few typewritten lines written on it.

Dear Miss Skoglund,
We have recently been in touch with the state inspector of high schools, and he has given a most excellent report of your work in New Stavanger. In view of this, we are advising you of a vacancy for next year. It is in the high school at Moorhead, Minnesota, which is located in the same part of the state. Your

salary will be twenty-five dollars more a month than we were able to secure for you last spring, and you would teach English only, with no assembly room duty. Please advise us at once if you are interested.

ALICIA SMITH
Secretary to the Placement Bureau.

Lyng stood still. She had heard a lot about Moorhead, its fine schools and beautiful homes.

Then she thought of how hard her students had tried. She thought of Maren Peterson's mother who needed Maren at home on the farm but who didn't have the heart to keep her there. And of Conrad and Thorbjorn Skriverud sneaking out to the barn with their books and sitting on their milking stools to read them.

No matter where she went, she would never find a janitor as kind as Ole. The other day he told her that by hook or crook, he was going to wangle paint out of the school board. And this summer, when his son Bennie had his vacation, the two of them would do the job on her high school room together, so it would be shining and bright for her to come back to in the fall. As for Professor Lokensgaard, now that she could look back over the past year, she realized how unselfish he had been. He had fought her battles for her with the school board, even when he had only half believed in her causes.

Reverend Klemstad, after you learned to know him and understand him better, was actually a great man. No wonder the people in his congregation were so loyal to him. Once he believed something should be done, nothing could prevent him from its accomplishment. He reminded Lyng of a minister Grandmother Skoglund once told about. This minister, back in Norway, headed a group of four men who carried the coffin of one of his parishioners seven miles up and down a mountain, through deep snow and in terrific cold, so that the dead woman could be buried in a consecrated churchyard. Maybe, next year, now that Reverend Klemstad had let down the bars about English in his church for the commencement exercises, he would let her teach the Sunday School class in English.

She might as well admit it. She didn't want to go to Moorhead, for all it had to offer. She had started too many things here which she was anxious to continue with. Grandmother Skoglund said that a roaming hen never hatched a fine brood of chickens out of her nest. Well, she would stay around and see what happened to hers in New Stavanger. She had learned a lot herself since last September, so she ought to be able to do a better job next year than she had this past one. She knew now how silly she had been in thinking it necessary to rid her students of everything Norwegian. The lessons in industry and thrift and honesty and the careful training in religion would only make better Americans out of them. It was her job as a teacher in the public school to add to their own heritage the best America had to offer.

Lyng went back to her room. From the drawer of the table she took out the contract Professor Lokensgaard had given her the day she had turned in the results of the state examinations. How much more this one meant to her now than the contract she had signed just a year ago! Yet the only difference between the two was a slight salary increase in the later one. With great care, she signed her name to the contract before her.

Her students would be pleased to learn she was returning in the fall. They had begged her to come back and to let them know the exact day of her arrival so they could be on hand at the railway station to welcome her.

Lyng smiled and stretched her arms. It was pleasant to be able to sit back and catch her breath now that the closing-of-school rush was over. This room of hers was cozy, even though it was small. In Minneapolis this summer she'd go down to Dorge, their photographer, and find out how much he wanted to make a print of the painting of the Skoglund estate in Norway and frame it. The picture would look well on the wall here beside the mirror. She'd bring back with her some photographs of Grandmother Skoglund and her mother and the boys and her two aunts. Her friends in New Stavanger would like to see her family.

Lyng closed her eyes and laid her hand lightly over them. "God, you've been good to me," she whispered. "Thank You."